THE BLACK AMULET

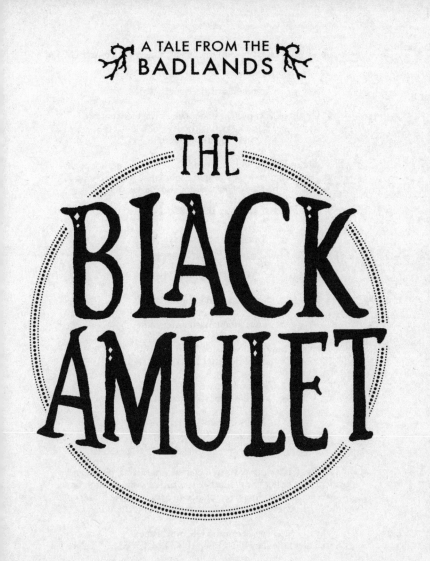

A TALE FROM THE
BADLANDS

THE
BLACK
AMULET

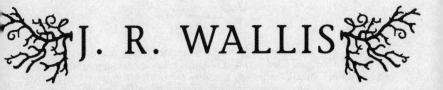

J. R. WALLIS

SIMON & SCHUSTER

First published in Great Britain in 2018 by Simon & Schuster UK Ltd
A CBS COMPANY

1 3 5 7 9 10 8 6 4 2

Simon & Schuster UK Ltd
1st Floor
222 Gray's Inn Road
London WC1X 8HB

www.simonandschuster.co.uk
www.simonandschuster.com.au
www.simonandschuster.co.in

Simon & Schuster Australia, Sydney
Simon & Schuster India, New Delhi

A CIP catalogue record for this book
is available from the British Library.

PB ISBN: 978-1-4711-5794-3
eBook ISBN: 978-1-4711-5795-0
eAudio ISBSN: 978-1-4711-7666-1

Typeset in the UK by M Rules
Printed and bound by CPI Group (UK) Ltd, Croydon, CR0 4YY

For everyone who loved the first book.
Thank you!

'An apprentice must never approach a Vampire without his Master because magic is the most effective means of despatching them. But even a Badlander who has Commenced must be confident of creating a *fengnett*.'

'While 'Vampire' is the most commonly used name, apprentices should be aware that more traditionally minded Badlanders, and indeed older publications, may refer to these creatures by their Anglo-Saxon names, *hreremus* (bat) and *blódgeótend* (shedder of blood).'

EXTRACTS FROM

The Badlander Bestiary

Pocket Book Version

'Scrying is the preserve of great Badlanders, and those who use scrying as a means of transportation are greater still. How then to define the very few who have ever scryed through time itself?'

EXTRACT FROM

Scrying, Just Spying?

by Thomas Merricoates

# ONE

It was easy enough to spot the Vampire at the far end of the alleyway. As she peered round the corner of the last building in the street, Ruby spied the creature standing inside a yellow cone of light thrown down by the single street lamp, staring into a shop window.

She tiptoed round the corner, keeping close to the wall, and slid into a deep dark doorway to hide. As she moved closer to the Vampire, the old-fashioned revolver Ruby was holding tutted, then swore quietly for good measure. To be fair, the gun had been grumbling for the last ten minutes, making sure Ruby knew exactly how it felt about her hunting such a dangerous creature, urging her to turn back. A speaking gun, let alone one that could curse so well, would have scrambled the brains of most people – as would seeing a Vampire in a small market town in the middle of the night – but to Ruby none of it seemed exceptional now.

Up until a few months ago, she'd been living a regular life. But she lived in the Badlands now, a place on the fringes of the everyday world that most ordinary people knew nothing about. Not only was magic possible there, but the Badlands was also inhabited by strange and vicious monsters, making it very dangerous. But, in spite of all the extraordinary creatures that could be found there, Ruby was by far the strangest living thing of all because she was the only girl.

As far as she knew, the Badlands had only ever been a place where men and their boy apprentices had worked, tackling monsters and other nasties to keep ordinary people safe. Ruby always glowed with pride whenever she remembered she was the first girl Badlander. Even if it was still a secret for now.

'Keep it down, will you?' she hissed as the gun tutted again, before stringing together another collection of rather fruity-sounding words that would have embarrassed anyone who knew what they meant.

'Ruby, for the last time, go home,' it whispered. 'You might be brave, but you're too stubborn for your own good. You're out of your depth with this one.'

'I know what I'm doing.'

'Tackling a Vampire is almost impossible without magic. Why you've insisted on hunting it down is beyond me.'

'Why do you think?' hissed Ruby. 'All Victor Brynn makes me do is read books. It's like being back at school. We never go hunting like proper Badlanders.'

'That's because you've got a lot to learn under the circumstances.'

'You mean because I'm a girl.'

'I *mean* because you can't do magic given how your Commencement went so wrong.'

This time it was Ruby's turn to tut before peering out of the doorway and checking down the alleyway.

The Vampire was still there, under the street lamp, staring into the shop window. The white wooden sign hanging above the door had 'Hewitt's Butcher's Shop' painted on it in crisp black letters. Ruby guessed the smell of old blood must have drawn the creature there. The Vampire looked pale and gaunt in the gloomy orange light. A dark tangle of hair rested on the narrow shoulders of its black suit jacket. Ruby could see the glint of long, sharp fingernails. Despite being old, perhaps even centuries, there was an obvious strength in its lean frame, like the unseen energy trapped in a coiled spring. It was a powerful creature.

Ruby hadn't known she was hunting a Vampire at first. She'd discovered the telltale signs of something living in the cellar of a disused warehouse in the closest town to where she lived, and had spent the past few nights tracking it when she was supposed to be asleep. Victor Brynn, her mentor, hadn't suspected a thing. When she'd realized she had a Vampire in her sights, Ruby couldn't contain her excitement. This was exactly the type of dangerous creature she'd been looking for to convince Victor Brynn she should be allowed out hunting like a normal Badlander, not studying with her nose in a book all the time.

So here she was, ready and prepared like any Badlander should be to kill this monster.

3

Ruby ducked back into the doorway and took a deep breath. She felt around in one of the pockets of her old army camouflage jacket for what she needed. The problem with having limitless pockets, charmed to hold any number of useful objects, was that it required concentration to find what you wanted. But her mind was suddenly skittish and wouldn't focus clearly on what she needed. She wished she hadn't brought the gun along now. It had succeeded in putting the tiniest doubt in her mind that she could pull this off.

She took another breath and refocused, and her fingers closed round the object she was after. When she pulled out a small glass vial from her pocket, the golden liquid inside it was sparkling enough to light up her face.

'Jump 'em Juice!' groaned the gun. 'So that's your plan? Surprise the creature? Then what?' Ruby pointed to a small gold pin on her lapel.

'You'll need Vamp Venom for that.'

Ruby reached into her pocket again and brought out a small vial full of clear liquid.

'*And* you'll have to stake the creature right through the heart to kill it. Give it up, girl, while you've still got t—'

Ruby stuffed the gun in her waistband to shut it up.

She peered round the doorway. The Vampire was sniffing the air now, its head tipped back. When it swivelled and started walking in her direction, Ruby pulled back. The creature finally had her scent. All she had to do was get ready.

She unscrewed the cap from the vial and glugged the

Jump 'em Juice, wincing at the unexpected tartness, so citrusy and dry it made her gums tingle. Ruby expected to disappear instantly so when she didn't she started to panic, especially as there was no more juice left in the vial. She studied the instructions on the back. In black lettering was the promise:

Works Instantly
— Guaranteed —
Courtesy of Deschamps & Sons

When she heard a polite cough, she looked up into the bright green eyes of the Vampire, the pupils slit vertically like a cat's. There was nowhere for Ruby to go but further back into the deep dark doorway.

'Hullo thuu-rr, litt-ul guurl,' it said in a twangy American accent. 'Thought I smelt ya.'

Ruby plucked the gold pin from her lapel and it sprouted instantly into a golden spear. She jabbed at the creature, forcing it backwards. When the point nicked its hand, all the creature did was watch the cut heal.

'What can ah say? One of the puu-rks of beee-longing to the Undead.' It smiled and showed two white fangs. Then it cocked its head to one side and frowned. 'Ah guess you know what ah am. But what exactly uurr you? Yuur definitely not a yew-shual gu-rrl.'

Ruby was too busy trying to undo the vial of Vamp Venom. Her hands shook. She couldn't prise the top off.

'Allow me, ma'am.' The Vampire plucked it from her hands and dropped the vial onto the hard cobbles below.

When Ruby heard it smash, something inside her broke too.

'Oops. Ape-ologies.' The Vampire shook its head. 'I am just so-oo clum—'

It stopped when Ruby, and the spear she was holding, vanished with a small **POP!**

The Vampire stared into the apparently empty doorway and hissed, then reached out both arms. A deep cut appeared along one of its palms and it pulled back its arm with a yelp as it felt a body pushing past, knocking it off balance. It recovered in time to hear the sound of boots clattering down the alley.

# TWO

R uby could see herself and the spear she was holding, but, judging by the Vampire's reaction back in the alley, she guessed she was invisible to the rest of the world. This was confirmed by every shop window and mirrored surface she ran past, in particular car wing mirrors; none of them showed her reflection.

But Ruby knew the smell of a frightened girl, the blood pumping hard round her body, would lay a trail for the Vampire to follow whether she was invisible or not.

She pulled the gun from her waistband as she ran.

'Jump 'em Juice and Slap Dust?' she asked it breathlessly.

'What about them?' the gun replied.

'I can't use them together, can I?'

'No. Well, not unless you want a nasty reaction. You'll have to wait for the Juice to wear off before using Slap Dust to get yourself home.'

'How long will that take?'

'No idea. You're the Badlander. I thought you'd have known that when you were planning all this,' it said, sounding more than a little smug. Ruby huffed and puffed as she kept running. 'So I'm guessing things aren't going to plan then?' the gun continued.

Ruby stuffed it back in her waistband and gritted her teeth as she clumped on down the street in her black boots, hoping for the Juice to wear off as quickly as possible so she could use her bottle of Slap Dust. The Dust was something Badlanders used all the time to vanish from one location and reappear in another at will and was therefore very useful in most situations that required a quick exit, especially life-threatening ones like the one Ruby found herself in now.

Carrying the golden spear made running slower and Ruby's arm was starting to ache so she paused, tapped the point three times and the weapon quickly shrank back into the gold brooch it had been before. The spear was useless without the Vamp Venom, which was fatal to a Vampire if plunged into its heart, so there was no way of killing the creature now. Ruby's plan had been ruined because of the slow effects of the Jump 'em Juice, but she couldn't understand what had gone wrong.

Maybe the vial of Juice had passed its sell-by date?

Perhaps it was a low-strength version?

There was no obvious answer that she could think of.

As she hooked the golden brooch onto the lapel of her jacket, Ruby looked back up the street. There was no sign of the Vampire. But she did see something else: a trail of black bootprints glistening under the street lamps on the pavement she'd just run down, leading right to where she was standing.

Ruby lifted up one leg and saw the zigzag pattern of the sole of her boot on the ground. Little gears clicked and ticked in her head, and then she remembered something Victor Brynn had told her a few weeks before, when a Door Wurm she had tried to use to unlock a door had shrivelled up in her hand before she'd had time to insert it in the lock.

Clearly, some things that work for men and boys in the Badlands don't work as well for girls, Victor Brynn had said, inspecting the dead Wurm in her hand. *We need to be aware of this – record everything we learn.*

Ruby felt a small chill in the marrow of her bones. Maybe the Jump 'em Juice was something that didn't work properly for girls either, given its delayed reaction and now the strange side effect of the bootprints too. She kicked off her boots and then her socks for good measure: she couldn't risk leaving any more of a trail. The boots landed on the pavement with a loud *clump* and Ruby saw their vague reflection in the nearest shopfront, an antiques shop, as well as in a large, full-length mirror given pride of place in the window display.

It was then that the Vampire came walking briskly round the corner at the top of the street. As Ruby had feared, it was following the line of bootprints while sniffing the air. Ruby started running again in her bare feet. But it didn't take her long to notice she was now inking footprints on the pavement. She swallowed hard, and something heavy seemed to hit the pit of her stomach. Being a girl in the Badlands was full of surprises and, right now, they were not good ones. She made a mental note that Jump 'em Juice was yet another thing not for girls.

For a moment, as the Vampire strode towards her, Ruby began to doubt herself, unable to see any way to escape. But, as the creature walked inexorably towards her, a glimmer of a plan came to Ruby.

Carefully, she began retracing her steps, planting her feet back into the marks they'd already made. She wobbled as she stepped backwards, and tried not to think of the Vampire coming closer. And closer.

When it passed by her, it sniffed the air hard and looked at the boots and socks discarded on the pavement, frowning as it tried to work out what had happened. It gave another sniff, looked around and then kept walking, following the footsteps down the lit street.

Ruby stood watching the creature, her heart beating so hard she was worried the Vampire might hear it. She knew there wasn't much time until it reached the end of the trail of footprints and realized it had been fooled. It was now or never.

She pulled out the gun and, before it could say anything sarcastic, she shot the glass of the shopfront, pulling the trigger again and again, careful not to hit the mirror behind it. The glass window fell in large triangles and then shattered into smaller ones. Ruby picked up her boots and smashed out the fangs of glass in her way.

She was already thinking about home as she clambered through. The soles of her feet prickled as the glass cut her, despite her best efforts to tread lightly, and spots of blood appeared on the broken shards. Ruby kept focused on home, trusting in her scrying talent enough to know what would happen next. And then it was there in the large mirror that was part of the shop's display: her bedroom, dark and calm, as clear as a photograph. Reaching into her pocket, Ruby pulled out a tin of polish and popped off the lid. Taking a scoop of the polish, she smeared it over the glass and felt it start to give as she pressed on it, feeling her way through the mirror.

Suddenly, the Vampire was there at her shoulder, its breath hot in the whorl of her ear. It reached out wildly, floundering to grab hold of Ruby even though it couldn't see her, and, as she stepped through the mirror, it caught hold of her arm and yanked her back. The creature was strong. Ruby tottered back and the image of the bedroom in the mirror flickered and started to fade as she stopped thinking about it. The Vampire had found a pocket of her jacket now and was tugging hard, its fingernails hooked into the fabric. Its other hand flashed through the air as it tried to get hold of more of her.

And then, suddenly, everything stopped. Ruby heard voices in the street and looked round to see a police car skidding to a halt in the road; one police officer was already out of the car and running towards the shop.

The Vampire was nowhere to be seen. It had vanished.

Ruby didn't need to think twice. She refocused on the mirror again and when her bedroom reappeared she stepped through it, the glass wobbling for a moment and then pinging back to its normal rigid state and reflecting just the street again.

The only evidence that Ruby had been there at all was a whirl of black footprints on the pavement that led up to the mirror, some discarded socks, a pair of boots and a smashed shopfront. All the police officers could do was scratch their heads as they stared and tried to make sense of it all.

As for Ruby, she stood in her bedroom, waiting for her heart to calm down. The gun was muttering something, but she just threw it onto the bed.

She waited some time for the Jump 'em Juice to wear off, wary of leaving any black footprints for Victor Brynn to quiz her about in the morning. Then, after watching herself reappear in the bedroom mirror, she pulled a rug over the two footprints she'd made, picked the glass out of her feet and went downstairs, padding quietly past Victor Brynn's room so as not to wake him.

She hung up her jacket on the peg in the hallway and then went to the kitchen. She drank down two glasses of cool water filled from the tap and ate two slices of bread sprinkled with sugar to calm her nerves and cure the shock still tingling in her body. She sat slumped in a chair, inspecting the cuts on her feet again, thanking her lucky stars that the Vampire had decided to leave when the police arrived.

But if she had been in the hall, watching, then Ruby might not have been so relieved . . .

The flap of one of her pockets flipped up and over as a small bat emerged, clawing its way out until it was blinking, working out where it was with its tiny green eyes. It fluttered up into the air and found a vantage point on another jacket.

When Ruby walked past and crept back up the stairs, the bat followed her, careful to stay high enough so as not to be seen.

A door opened along the landing as Ruby reached the top of the stairs, and the bat fluttered higher, looking for a hiding place, and found the ledge of a small dusty window so high up it would have needed a stepladder to clean it. It peered over the edge, watching the two people below. A man and the girl.

Victor Brynn stood on the landing in his nightshirt, looking at Ruby through weary eyes. He cleared his throat.

'I couldn't sleep either, too used to working at night, I suppose, or maybe it's just my age. Anyway, I thought I'd wake you up to do some fieldwork, which I know you've been dying to do. Imagine my surprise when I found your bed empty.'

Victor Brynn raised the small piece of polished scrying glass hanging on the leather string around his neck. 'I couldn't see everything given it was so dark but it was interesting observing what I could.' Ruby turned red at the edges when she realized he'd been watching her.

'Perhaps it was no bad thing. Maybe you learnt more on your own than you ever would have done with me around.'

To Ruby it seemed as if he was waiting for an answer so she just nodded.

'Good.'

Ruby breathed a silent sigh of relief as Victor Brynn turned back to his bedroom door, happy the lecture was over. But then something else occurred to him and he paused and looked round at her again.

'I'm indebted to you, Ruby, for killing the Witch in Hampstead and saving my life. And that is why I agreed to take you on as my pupil to try and help you learn about being a Badlander, despite your obvious limitations with magic. I'm happy to accept that the *wyrd* has created this opportunity for both of us, that fate has worked in our favour to give us *both* a second chance at life. But I won't continue with our arrangement if you don't respect me or my wishes, even if you are brave and resourceful.

'What we are doing is too dangerous for you to be reckless like this. I dread to think what the Order might do to you if they find out, or to me if they discover I'm teaching a girl. For that is what you are, Ruby, a girl in a world run by men. There's no getting away from it, however much you want to be accepted as a Badlander. One day, I hope we might show them they're wrong, but you're going to have to do it according to my rules. You can't change how the Order is run overnight. It's been controlled the same way, by men, for centuries.'

Victor Brynn shut the door sharply behind him, to make a point. Ruby listened to him climbing into bed, the mattress springs creaking.

She heard something shuffling above her and, thinking it must be a bird or a mouse, ignored it. There was always some little creature moving about in the walls of the house.

Two green eyes watched as Ruby opened her bedroom door and clicked it shut behind her. Fluttering about, the bat eventually found a place to sleep, hanging from the latch of the little window, like a tiny black fruit, its wings folded round its body to keep warm.

THREE

At the same time, elsewhere in the Badlands, on a deserted part of Hampstead Heath, a boy wearing a herringbone coat and a red silk scarf, with his brown hair combed up into an elaborate quiff, was watching a small, hunched figure as it scurried towards the dark shape of a large wood ahead.

Standing beside the boy was a man with thick black hair parted so neatly that, in the moonlight, his head looked like it had a white scar across it. He was dressed in a smart brown leather trench coat and wore expensive-looking slip-on boots with thick soles and pointed silver toes. He seemed to own the very air around him.

'So, Thomas Gabriel,' said the man, 'this seems a good opportunity to show me what you've been learning. As your new mentor, I need to report back to the Order on your progress with magic, and how you're taking to it, after the unfortunate demise of your Master.'

'I'd be happy to, sir. And may I say how honoured I am to have Randall Givens, head of the High Council of

16

Badlanders, as my new mentor. I hope to be as famous as you one day, sir.'

'That's kind of you, boy, and, although I applaud your ambition, it's a little early to be thinking so far ahead, don't you think? For now, show me what you can do.'

Thomas Gabriel nodded and started walking, and then something occurred to him and he looked back.

'Aren't you coming with me to watch?'

Givens produced a small piece of scrying glass and breathed on it, wiping it down with a white handkerchief. 'I'll observe from a distance; it'll give me a better view of things. Unless you'd like me to come with you because you think you might need help?'

'Oh, no, that shouldn't be necessary, sir.'

As Thomas Gabriel turned back, he saw the hunched figure ahead of them disappear between the trees. He drew out a bottle of black dust from a coat pocket, popping out the small cork. After tipping a single grain of the dust into his hand, Thomas Gabriel put the bottle away.

'Don't you think it might be a little reckless to use Slap Dust where trees are involved?' asked Givens.

'I should be fine, sir. I've mastered the art of short travel.'

Thomas Gabriel muttered an instruction before slapping his hands together. He shot forward like a stone from a catapult, skimming over the ground, the ends of his red silk scarf flying behind him.

In a matter of seconds, the boy caught up with the small figure and passed it, guiding his body past the oncoming

17

trees as they sped towards him. He slowed suddenly as the fizz of the Slap Dust faded from his hands and he landed lightly on the ground, barely rustling the leaf litter. Knowing Givens would be watching, using his scrying mirror, Thomas Gabriel smiled, but not too smugly, wary of giving the man any reason to find fault with his display so far. Composing himself, he turned to face the small creature, a Gobbling. It was a particularly ugly one with knobbly elbows and kneecaps and a spine so hunched its head looked as though it would roll off without a chest to rest its chin against.

Its grey, hairy body was heaving as it tried to catch its breath. Two black eyes looked ready to pop out of their sockets as they tried to take in how the boy had seemingly whizzed ahead out of nowhere.

Thomas Gabriel folded his arms and shook his head. 'It's not your night.' He pointed at the gold signet ring around one of its thumbs. 'Gobblings like you shouldn't go grave robbing on my *æhteland.*'

In response, the Gobbling gave three sharp calls into the night sky. Thomas Gabriel heard a rustling among the trees, and saw more grey bodies moving between the trunks. A ring of Gobblings emerged to surround him, yellow teeth bared, their ears pricked towards him. Their cold black eyes gave nothing away. A foul stench wafted off their hot bodies like the dirty smell of dung.

Thomas Gabriel raised an arm, forcing worried grunts from the ring of creatures.

'*Grist*—' Thomas Gabriel paused as he tried to remember

18

the exact word he needed. He was determined not to refer to *The Black Book of Magical Instruction* in his pocket because he wanted to show Givens he had the measure of magic. The word shimmered in his head when he finally remembered it.

'*Gristbátian!*' he said clearly, with as much authority as he could muster.

A fine spray of white sparks rose from his fingertips, surrounding him in a ring of prickly energy that sent the Gobblings tottering backwards, scared by the power this boy seemed to have. Mouths full of sharp teeth appeared at intervals around the edges of the ring, hovering in the air and snapping viciously at the Gobblings, forcing them further back.

'Magic, you see?' grinned Thomas Gabriel. 'And, being a Badlander, there's plenty more where that came from. Now, give me the ring,' he said, addressing the Gobbling he'd been chasing. But the creature just hissed, then spat at the boy, who dodged the slimy, shiny missile.

'Get it for me, will you?' said Thomas Gabriel and a tiny creature with a single eye in the centre of its forehead shot up out of his coat pocket like a firework and landed on the Gobbling's hand and began tugging at the ring. It struggled because it was so small and delicate with a tiny, fairy-like body and lacy wings. The Gobbling lashed out and sent the little creature fluttering up like a butterfly.

'You don't want to mess with my pet. A One Eye might be useful for sniffing out magical things, but it's got big teeth too!' The One Eye gave a little cry and darted back to the Gobbling's hand. This time it opened its tiny mouth to reveal a set of very large teeth that sprang forward. They were sharp too. When it bit down, the teeth went straight through the Gobbling's thumb, slicing it clean off. The Gobbling screamed horribly as the winged creature flew back to the boy's shoulder and perched there, removing the ring and giving it to Thomas Gabriel before tossing the thumb to the ground.

'No creature steals on my patch!' boomed Thomas Gabriel as the shrieking Gobbling dropped to its knees and scrabbled in the dirt for its severed thumb.

'Now—' But he stopped as, quite suddenly, the ring of sharp teeth snapping at the Gobblings and protecting him, disappeared. Thomas Gabriel's triumphant smile dropped away as he realized the spell he had cast wasn't working any more.

'*Gristbátian!*'

White sparks flickered up round his fingers again, but this time they died away without having any effect.

For a moment, no one seemed to know what to do.

Excited growls started up around Thomas Gabriel. Some of the Gobblings were brave enough to take a step forward, and then all of them started closing in on the now defenceless boy. The One Eye flew at the nearest Gobbling with a scream, but there were too many. Thomas Gabriel stared in horror at a Gobbling mouth, open wide, the jagged bottom teeth frosty with spit, and then he felt something sharp nick the side of his face. He dodged away, tripping as he did so, and fell to the ground.

The next thing he felt was a sharp blast of air and, when he opened his eyes again, Thomas Gabriel saw Givens standing beside him, conjuring white sparks of magic out of his fingers at the Gobblings. The boy did not recognize the spell that Givens was using, but it caused the creatures to vanish swiftly, one after the other, with a popping sound, until they were all gone.

Givens had barely broken sweat. He smoothed back a loose strand of black hair before bending down to pick up the ring Thomas Gabriel had dropped.

'A spell fading from the fingers like that can be a sign of an improper Commencement,' said Givens. 'Are you sure you Commenced correctly, boy, followed all the rules? No problems with the ceremony, were there?'

Thomas Gabriel shook his head as he stood up and brushed himself down.

'Hmm, must be down to your skill with magic then. The spell you chose is hard to master and use effectively, needing great concentration not only to cast it but to hold it too. Clearly, you've still got a lot to learn, and there's not much time either.'

'What do you mean, sir?'

Givens produced a white envelope from a pocket and handed it to Thomas Gabriel. The boy's name was written on the front in neat black ink.

Inside was a white card with a clock face on it, the second hand ticking round. Below it was written:

The High Council formally invites
Thomas Gabriel
to its annual meeting on
15th May

'You've been summoned to show the High Council your skill with magic,' said Givens.

Thomas Gabriel stared at him, his mouth open. For a moment, there was nothing but the ticking of the clock on the invitation.

'It's highly irregular, I agree,' continued Givens, 'but there are rumours that your Master, Simeon, didn't want you to Commence and receive magic. Certain colleagues say he confided that very fact to them only days before he died.' Givens coughed. 'The High Council has to be sure you're meant to become a Badlander, given your Master's unfortunate demise. They therefore want to assess your magical skills with a test.'

He leant forward and lowered his voice. 'Some Council members are looking for any reason to prevent you carrying on being a Badlander. Certain people want your *æhteland*. It's a prime location in London. Simeon was a crafty old fox to keep it as long as he did.' Givens smiled and straightened up. 'But I have every confidence you'll show them you're meant to be a Badlander. It's only March. You've still got a few weeks until the meeting. That should give you plenty of time to practise your magic. I can help advise you too, of course.'

Givens peered at Thomas Gabriel's face without waiting for the boy to reply.

'That Gobbling gave you a nasty bite. You need to return home and see to it. I must get back to my apprentice anyway. We've been surveying a Ley Line over the last few weeks and, however able he thinks he is, he's young and I can't leave him for more than a few hours. There's always so much for us Badlanders to learn, isn't there?'

Givens managed a rather overripe smile before reaching into his pocket for a bottle of Slap Dust. He looked intently at Thomas Gabriel. 'The Ley Line we're assessing runs fairly close to the cottage you inherited from your Master. Perhaps I could meet you there for some magical tuition? You're clearly in need of it before the Council meeting.'

Thomas Gabriel shuffled his feet. 'I don't really go there. Too much to do on my *æhteland* here in London.'

'Oh, that seems such a waste. I'd be there as often as I could if I was lucky enough to have inherited a country retreat from *my* Master. I'll be in touch then about when we'll meet again. In the meantime, do study hard, won't you? The Council's test will be an extremely thorough examination of your current magical skills and potential. They'll be looking for any excuse to fail you.'

Givens gave another broad, insincere smile before slapping his hands together and vanishing to leave Thomas Gabriel alone among the trees. The bite on his face was starting to throb. But something else far more uncomfortable was troubling him. It wasn't the shame he felt at having to be rescued by Givens, it was fear, lodged like a spear deep between his ribs, that made his heart tight and his breath short.

Thomas Gabriel already suspected why the magic had failed him, but hadn't dared tell Givens. The man had been right to ask about Thomas Gabriel's Commencement because the boy should never have Commenced at all. His Master, Simeon Rowell, had forbidden it with his dying breath yet Thomas Gabriel had disobeyed him, stealing the silver key required for Commencing and receiving magic. Thomas Gabriel hadn't wanted to believe magic might leave him because of what he'd done. But now he couldn't think of anything else.

When Thomas Gabriel arrived home, he waved away the One Eye as it fluttered around him, advising him to clean his face as Givens had suggested. He walked on quickly, rubbing away the blood with his sleeve. He didn't stop until he was standing in the library, a large, round room with bookshelves lining the walls all the way from the floor up to the domed ceiling which had at its centre a large, circular skylight full of night sky.

The book he was looking for, *To Commence or Not?*, which dealt with anomalies occurring after the Commencement of apprentice Badlanders, was catalogued in the library on one of the topmost shelves. He used magic to levitate and, as he rose, his chest swelled with pride as he looked down at the floor. He was already about ten metres up, close to the top of the book stacks, and he wondered if perhaps he was worrying too much about his problems with the Gobblings earlier.

'Maybe Givens was right,' he said to his One Eye as it fluttered up beside him. 'Perhaps I just did the spell wrong. I'm still learning. Maybe it wasn't anything to do with my Commencement—'

Thomas Gabriel dropped like a stone, the levitation spell vanishing as if all the power had been cut.

His arms flashed out as he tried to grab hold of the bookshelves. When the toes of his shoes landed on a shelf, he started to fall back and threw out a hand, the fingers clamping down like a beak. He juddered and, with all his strength, pulled himself close to the stacks of books, using both arms, and clung on like a limpet.

He was about five metres up. Not high enough to make jumping down impossible, but that wasn't the point. His magic had failed. Again. Just like it had among the trees with the Gobblings. He stared at the book title in front of him: *Great Badlanders Vol. 5*. He looked down the row and guessed there must be at least fifty volumes. It had been his dream to be listed in one of those books for as long as he could remember.

When he let go and dropped to the floor, it seemed to him he fell more quickly due to the heaviness in his heart.

He used the ladder the second time to find the book and *To Commence or Not?* told him everything he knew deep down already, but hadn't wanted to admit to himself.

*

25

If an apprentice is not invited to Commence by their Master then the bond between them is broken forever, according to the Ordnung. This can lead to disappointment and anger in an apprentice. Remember, however hard it might be to say 'no' to an apprentice, it is doubly hard for them to hear it. In some cases, boys may try and take the key by force and there have been instances of injury and even death when Masters have been ill-prepared for the reaction of their apprentices to a refusal.

The protective charm around the key will keep its magic safe from any unintended use, so if an apprentice, deemed unfit to Commence, does steal the key then their Commencement will fail. In most cases, the ceremony never happens at all, but, on the rare occasion that the Commencement ceremony occurs, the magic will degrade eventually. The apprentice will feel the magic starting to slip away from them over time. Having tasted its power, this can be a most difficult truth to accept. The apprentice will be left bereft of magic eventually. Ultimately, this may well lead to madness, despair and death.

Thomas Gabriel stepped away from the book as though it was an object laced with an infectious disease. He looked at the One Eye perched on his shoulder.

'You're good with magical things. How do I fix this?' Sensing an unwelcome change in the boy's mood, the tiny creature fluttered into the air as if to escape.

'Well?' Thomas Gabriel sounded impatient. When he reached out to grab it, it flew higher, out of reach. 'Tell me how to sort out the problem.'

'I can't,' it squeaked.

'You have to!' shouted Thomas Gabriel. 'I've got to fix it before the High Council meeting. If the Order finds out my magic's not working because I took that key from Simeon and Commenced without his permission, I'll be kicked out. I'll be no one.'

The One Eye shot up higher and crouched on the topmost bookshelf, keeping out of sight. It only reappeared when the fuse inside the boy seemed to be spent and he was sitting quietly on the floor with books strewn around him, muttering to himself.

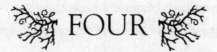# FOUR

Ed walked out of the main school building, bending down when he noticed a shoelace was undone. Other kids were leaving too, streaming out around him and scurrying down the steps, eager to make the most of what was left of the sunny afternoon now classes were over.

A sudden, sharp slap to the back of his head sent stars fizzing across Ed's eyes. By the time he had blinked them away, there was only laughter disappearing among the bobbing heads and clicking of shoes. It could have been one of any number of his classmates, until a boy with brown, shoulder-length hair glanced round and gave himself away.

Ed wanted to shout or run after him. But he didn't. Creating a scene would only make things worse and he was doing his utmost to fit in at St Joseph's. So he stayed where he was, trying to let the anger drain out of him, as the other boy dared him down the steps, waggling a crooked finger. In another life, Ed might have reached into his pocket for his catapult and whizzed a silver ball bearing close enough to the boy's ear to graze it as a warning and melt the grin off his face.

But Ed wasn't a Badlander any more. He was an ordinary boy now, wearing a blazer, not an overcoat with limitless pockets. When the other boy gave up and walked off, laughing, with his friends, Ed's fists uncurled, and his sweaty palms started to cool.

Ed was still taking time to adapt to school, even though he was bright and quick-witted. Lessons weren't the problem. It was adjusting to how life at St Joseph's worked that made him stick out as being different. And standing out was not a good thing if you wanted to get on quietly with making friends and trying to be ordinary.

Occasionally, Ed would stop and stare in the mirror at the new version of himself, without his overcoat, wondering if he should go back to live in the Badlands, even though it was a dangerous place. It was a world he knew so well, better than the new one he found himself in now. Ruby and Thomas Gabriel were in the Badlands too and he knew he could count on them, especially Ruby, who'd been so brave, helping him and taking on creatures and showing she could be as good as any boy. But she'd also proved that the things a person really wanted the most never came easily and that's what made them so precious. So Ed would always walk away from the mirror, convinced he didn't want to return to his old life because being an ordinary boy had always been his dream and he couldn't give up on it now.

But there was something Ed couldn't ignore as easily about

his past as a Badlander. There was still magic inside him after his Commencement in the Badlands. The ceremony had gone wrong after Ruby had Commenced with him by accident, leaving them with half the amount of magic a Badlander would normally have received. It meant they could only perform spells together.

Ed heard the magic whispering to him in quiet moments, addressing him as Jones, the Badlander name his Master, Maitland, had given him as a baby. The magic kept telling him to give up trying to be an ordinary boy called Ed because he'd been so good at taking on monsters and protecting people.

Ed did his best to ignore the magic, but it never seemed to give up. It was in pain. Ed knew it wasn't meant to be in the ordinary world where he wanted to be. It wanted to be back in the Badlands where it could be used, so it kept urging him to return there.

Some weeks earlier, in class, he'd lashed out without thinking because the constant whispering had made it seem like a person had been there, right beside him. All the other kids had burst out laughing. Even the teacher told him 'to pay attention' before droning on again. At lunchtime, he'd had to wade through looks and sniggers. Kids had tapped him on the shoulder, tempting him to turn round and take a swipe at them. He'd stared at them through tired eyes, the bags beneath them so dark they were almost purple because the magic was whispering to him at night too, keeping him awake, and disrupting his dreams.

School was an unforgiving place. No one forgot things. Ed had learnt that once you were seen as a certain person you could never be anyone else. Everyone had looked at him differently after that day in class.

Today all the other kids seemed to be hurrying somewhere important as he walked down the steps. He had nowhere to go except home. He loved his parents, but he missed having friends his own age he could talk to. He missed Ruby and Thomas Gabriel.

He'd tried inviting kids from his classes to his house, but nobody came, not even the ones who seemed to have no one else either. Once, a group from school had turned up at his door to see if he wanted to play football in the park and, for a brief moment, his face had lit up. But that was before he'd noticed a sly look between two of them, something his clever eyes had spotted because, in the Badlands, he'd always been on the lookout for anything suspicious, however subtle, in case it was a clue about a monster or something that might save his life. Standing on the doorstep, Ed had known the only thing being kicked in the park would be him, not a football. So he'd shut the door quickly.

Usually, his walk home took about twenty minutes, but he chose a longer route that afternoon, wending his way through the streets, wanting time to think. There seemed to be no prospect of fitting in at school, however hard he tried, and the magic inside him seemed to take heart from it, addressing him more and more, and urging him to give in to it.

Ed took his frustration out on a white pebble, kicking it so hard across the pavement he almost lost his balance. He wondered whether going to see Ruby or Thomas Gabriel to talk to them about how he was feeling might help, even though it meant returning to the Badlands.

The white pebble had pinged off the wall beside him and landed further on and he kicked it again, even harder this time. Going back to the Badlands, if only for a moment, would feel like a failure.

Maybe you are a failure, Jones? taunted the magic inside him.

Ed stopped, his foot raised, ready to kick the pebble again, and then the anger inside disappeared like a burst balloon, and he put his leg down.

'I'm not a failure,' he whispered. 'My parents wouldn't love me otherwise.' The magic didn't say anything back and Ed felt a little fizz in his veins at silencing the voice.

Ed's parents were the bright spot in his new life. They'd welcomed him back into their lives with open arms. He had been stolen from them as a baby by his Master, Maitland, and replaced with a *fæcce* that had died. Not only were his mother and father kind, they were loving too. Ed had known it when he'd listened to them lying about his adoption in the headmaster's office at St Joseph's, the story they'd come up with to avoid any difficult questions about where Ed had come from. Their *'new-found joy'* was how they'd described him and Ed felt the same.

It hadn't been so easy at first, though. Ed's parents had

32

been under a curse for years, until Ruby killed the Witch that had enslaved them. Like Ed, they were readjusting to normal life. He'd heard them at night, crying out in their sleep, shouting for Mrs Easton the Witch, whom they'd worshipped.

Thomas Gabriel had told Ed that other people in Hampstead, who'd been under the curse of the Witch, were creeping out at night, looking for her, still under her spell somehow. On hearing this, Ed had worried for his parents, fearing they would never fully recover. But they had settled quickly as he'd spent more time with them and the connection between them had strengthened. Victor Brynn had mixed potions for them too, helping their minds become calmer and clearer. And, now his mother and father had improved so much, Ed worried about them very little.

A noise made him come round from his thoughts. He'd been walking automatically, and it took him a second to get his bearings. The street was lined with houses on either side that looked sleepy in the afternoon sunshine. At first glance, there was no one about. And then Ed caught sight of them. Kids from his school, peering round the corner back down the road. He recognized one of them immediately, the brown-haired boy who had tried picking a fight on the school steps. All their heads jerked back out of sight when they saw him looking. There was laughter followed by sounds of them shushing each other.

Ed was already on the move. He took a left down a cobbled alley between two houses and heard distant shouts and the clatter of shoes. He knew the alley, having taken it occasionally on his route home from school. It connected to a main road beyond. Ed knew if he got to the busy street he'd be safe enough with other people about.

But as he walked briskly down the alley, his shoes ringing on the cobbles, he saw a section of metal grille fencing, rooted in two concrete blocks, blocking his way. Clipped to it was a sign saying 'Urgent Works in Progress'. Ed rattled the fencing and tried to get a grip, but the wire was stitched too tightly to poke his fingers through and get a hold. He took a running jump to grab hold of the top and haul himself up, but it was too high to reach.

The voices grew louder.

But then a sharp gust blew down the alley and a body materialized beside him. It was Ruby. She gave him a big grin.

Ed's mouth managed exactly the opposite shape as the faint smell of Slap Dust faded.

'I thought you'd be pleased,' said Ruby. 'According to my scrying mirror, you're in a spot of bother.'

'You shouldn't be spying on me. You're not supposed to be here.'

'Victor Brynn sent me. I'll tell you why if you come with me.' She waggled the bottle of Slap Dust she was holding. Ed looked at her and shook his head.

'I ain't a Badlander no more.'

Ruby put her hand to her ear as the voices neared the alley. 'Okay, well, I can scare them off if you like.' She pulled the gun out of her waistband.

'Jones!' it shouted. 'How the devil are you?'

'I'm called Ed now, remember?' groaned the boy. 'And put it away,' he hissed at Ruby. 'It'll only make things worse.'

'Worse?' Ruby's face melted into a grin. 'Oh, yeah. I remember how school works now. So what do you want to do then? We could try magic of course.'

'Give me a boost up so I can climb over the fence.'

'Only if I get to call you Jones.'

'Ruby!'

'It's weird calling you Ed.'

The boy muttered something dark and not very cheerful under his breath. When he nodded curtly, Ruby clasped her hands together and he stepped up on them and reached up for the top of the fence and scrambled over.

Ruby tipped a speck of Slap Dust into her hand and popped the cork back in the bottle before announcing where she wanted to go and slapped her hands together. She vanished and reappeared at the end of the passageway just in time to see the boy she knew as Jones run past her.

When she looked back, she saw a group of boys sprinting towards the other end of the alley. They piled into the fencing with a great clatter and then started to hoist each other up after realizing it was the only way over.

Ruby turned and started running. 'Hey, Jones! They're still coming.'

'Yeah, well, run faster then!' he shouted without looking back.

She caught up with him. 'I know school isn't supposed to

35

be fun. But it really shouldn't be as bad as this. What have you done?' The boy just gritted his teeth and kept running. 'I mean, do you really want this life? Are you sure you—'

He ran even harder so what she said next was lost in the air behind him.

The main road wasn't that busy and they found a place to hide after ducking into someone's back garden through a hole in the fence. The group of boys came running past soon after. It took another five minutes for the two of them to be sure the coast was clear.

When all they could hear were the normal sounds of the city, and the beating of their hearts, Ruby reached into her pocket and pulled out a small glass vial full of red liquid.

'Victor Brynn made this potion for you. Said it might help with the "you know what?"' She waved her hands as if she was casting a spell.

'Thanks.'

'Apparently, you told him the magic's getting louder.'

'A bit,' shrugged the boy as if it was no big deal.

'Really?' Ruby's forehead wrinkled as if she was trying to see right inside him. 'I know you're not sleeping. You wake yourself up.'

'You shouldn't be scrying on me.'

'Victor Brynn asked me to. He wanted to know how bad it was, so he could judge the strength of the potion.'

Ed held up the vial. The red liquid looked like blood. But he popped out the cork and glugged down the mixture, handing the empty vial back to Ruby. She rolled it between her fingers and Ed knew she wanted to say something else. He looked at the ground, wishing she would just get on with it, and sighed to hurry her up.

'I don't get the magic speaking to me like you do because I'm in the Badlands, but I'm finding it hard too. Last night I tried taking on a Vampire without magic and I was lucky to get away.'

'I'm not coming back to the Badlands, Ruby.'

'I know,' she said, trying not to sound too disappointed. 'It's just, well . . . it's just a shame how things have ended up, isn't it? We're not exactly living the way we imagined, are we? Victor Brynn hasn't got a potion I can take to help me with magic.'

'It would have been all right if we hadn't Commenced together,' said Ed, raising his voice.

'And what if we hadn't? Do you really think you'd have got your parents back if I hadn't taken that key? Without magic, or me, you'd never have got what you wanted.'

Ed thought about that.

'The only reason you saved me from that Ogre the first night we met was so I could help you become an ordinary boy. Well, I'd say it all worked out better than you expected. What's that thing called again? The wee . . . ?' Ruby clicked her fingers. 'You know? To do with fate.'

'The *wyrd*.'

'Yep, well, I'd say fate's worked out pretty well for you, right?'

Ed looked down at his school shoes and decided Ruby was just letting off steam. It was like that in the Badlands with no one to talk to about how you felt.

'If you're finding it too hard being a Badlander who can't do magic, maybe you should give up,' he said.

'And go back to being an ordinary girl?' Ruby shook her head. 'No chance. My life was horrible, being shipped from one foster home to another.'

'My parents could adopt you.'

Ruby sighed. 'But I've got my own home now and Victor Brynn to look out for me. And don't forget I'm a runaway. I bet social services and the police are still looking for me.' And she folded her arms as if daring Ed to say something else just as stupid.

The boy looked at her and then just gave up thinking and laughed.

'What's so funny?' asked Ruby.

'We're exactly the same.'

Ruby thought about that. 'Stubborn, you mean?'

Ed nodded. He turned and walked away. 'Thanks for the potion,' he said without looking back.

'It's been nice hanging out,' said Ruby, raising her voice, and rising up onto her tiptoes as though taking the strain on some invisible rope tied between them. 'Maybe we could spend more time together?' But the boy didn't look back. 'From what I've seen, you're not exactly building up much of a birthday card list. Friends *are* important.'

'We've swapped places, Ruby,' said the boy as he kept on

walking. 'I don't think it's a good idea we see each other. Thank Victor Brynn for the potion. And stop scrying on me.' He walked on, scuffing his feet, when he heard a whisper in his head.

She's right. Friends are important. Why don't you go back to the Badlands and be with her?

Ed strode on, taking bigger strides as if trying to leave the magic inside him behind. Eventually, he glanced back, but Ruby was gone and his heart wobbled for a moment.

It was the middle of the night when the magic woke him up. The voice spoke to him clearly, louder than ever before, telling him it would never go away, potion or no potion, and, for the first time, Ed was afraid. In the dark on his own, it was hard not to believe it was telling the truth.

You know you've made the wrong choice, Jones.

He put his head under his pillow. But the voice kept on and on, like a finger picking at a scab. As Ed tried to ignore it, his mind drifted back to what Ruby had said.

Friends are important.

Spooked by the magic knowing what he was thinking, Ed got out of bed and went downstairs to fetch a glass of water. But the magic inside him came too, like a moth trapped in a jar.

When his mother shuffled in, slip-sliding in her slippers, she took him in her arms and Ed remembered how glad he was not to be in the Badlands any more.

'I thought I heard you. What's keeping you awake, darling?'

He looked up at her and, when she realized he'd been crying, she hugged him closer. 'What's the matter?'

'You and Dad like having me around, don't you?'

'Like?' His mother shook him. 'Ed, we *love* it.' She looked deep into his eyes. 'Aren't you happy?'

'Most of me is.'

'You mean the magic isn't?'

'It keeps telling me to go back to the Badlands. Calls me Jones.'

His mother leant in. 'Leave my son alone,' she whispered into his ear. 'He doesn't need you. Just like his father and I don't need that Witch any more.' She grabbed Ed's shoulders and beamed at him. 'Know what I've learnt? Love's much more powerful than magic.'

No, it's not.

At the whisper, Ed heard his heart shatter into pieces, but he still kept smiling at his mother because he didn't want hers to break too.

After he'd gone back to bed, he lay awake, thinking hard about what to do. The magic was his problem so it was up to him to solve it.

There's no one who can help you, especially here. And I won't stop speaking until you go back. Or go mad.

Ed's jaw ticked hard as his brain thrummed. Then he wrote down a name in the journal he kept beside his bed for writing in when his mind was so full of thoughts he couldn't sleep.

The old Lich *at St Crosse College? He can't help you!*

'Maybe he can,' whispered Ed. 'He did before. Told us about Dark Bottles and whispering gravestones last time. He knows more about the Badlands than anyone else.'

But Ed knew going to speak to Du Clement meant going back to the Badlands and he wasn't sure how he felt about that. He decided to sleep on it.

When he woke up a few hours later, with the morning light creeping its fingers round the edges of the curtains, he panicked for a moment, before realizing it was a Saturday. No school, for two whole days.

He remembered the name on the pad. It seemed even more obvious what to do now. Going to see Du Clement was the best option. What else could he do? No ordinary person could help with such an extraordinary problem. It was worth it, decided Ed, even if it meant returning to the Badlands.

Yes, and it'll be good to see Ruby, won't it?

'Don't get your hopes up,' whispered Ed. 'I ain't gonna be casting no spells with her. I just need some answers to be able to get rid of you.'

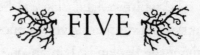

Victor Brynn had propped open the back door before starting to mix the brown paste for a special tonic he was preparing. He wanted to make sure he could hear Ruby digging in the herb garden after instructing her to plant a new crop of rosemary bushes. Planting at dusk, he'd told her, when she'd complained about doing such a chore, imbued the herb with extra energy, meaning the vials of salt and rosemary they were going to make would be extra strong and a useful weapon against a lot of creatures.

As Ruby's complaining had turned to exasperated grumbling, Victor Brynn had merely pointed a finger in the direction of the garden, making it clear she had no option. He knew he was strict, but that was because he wanted her to learn as much as she could about being a Badlander. Secretly, he hoped Ruby might gain enough knowledge to shake up the High Council of the Order and show them the *Ordnung* needed to change and allow girl apprentices. But he hadn't told her that yet. There was still a long way to go before she was ready to face the Council.

He paused to listen to the distant *clang* of Ruby's spade, then waved his hand at the lights in the kitchen, asking them to brighten a little more, before returning to his wooden bowl. The tonic was to help him with the after-effects of being a No-Thing, a Badlander turned so rotten inside that using magic depended on drinking the blood of living things.

Despite being rescued from such a pitiful existence, Victor Brynn hadn't recovered fully. He still suffered ferocious episodes when his body would crease up with pain and glisten with cold sweats as the dark hunger for blood rose up. Such longings came without warning. So much so, in fact, that Victor Brynn believed a bubble of poison from the Witch's bite that had turned him into a No-Thing was travelling up and down his body, trying to force him back into the foul creature he'd once been.

He stirred the paste harder to make it as smooth and shiny as possible and then he stopped as he heard another noise besides the distant chime of Ruby's spade in the garden. Someone was in the cottage, walking down the hallway. Striding down, it seemed. Victor Brynn put down his mixing bowl, his fingers flexing out of sight behind his back, conjuring up little white sparks of magic. Nobody was expected. No one ever was.

When he saw Thomas Gabriel peer round the door, Victor Brynn tutted and picked up the mixing bowl again. 'I thought we agreed you'd let us know in advance if you were coming by. You gave this cottage to Ruby, but the Order still believes it's yours and I'm doing my utmost to keep her a secret from them, remember?'

'Sorry.' Thomas Gabriel shrugged and shuffled his feet. 'How's her training going?'

Victor Brynn mixed a little harder as he thought about that. 'You know what she's like. I've got her digging in the garden to instill some discipline.' He raised his head and smiled as they both heard the distant sound of the spade hitting the dirt.

'I meant how's she managing without being able to do magic?'

'She's learning, slowly. What about you? Who's been appointed to replace Simeon as your Master?'

'Randall Givens.'

'I see,' said Victor Brynn, raising his eyebrows. 'I imagine not the most patient of men. Those who've made it as high up the Order as he has rarely are. But I daresay you're learning a lot from him, especially when it comes to using magic. He's very skilled as far as I recall.'

'That's why I'm here.'

'Oh?'

Thomas Gabriel listened to the distant chime of Ruby's spade as he wondered how to say what he wanted. It seemed his courage was being dug out of him too.

Victor Brynn raised an eyebrow again.

'Well, I'm … I'm having a bit of trouble with magic,' said Thomas Gabriel.

'And you're too embarrassed to ask Givens? Well, ask away,

if that's why you're here. Magic's a tricky beast. Is it your control? The Anglo-Saxon? I don't get a chance to discuss magic with Ruby for obvious reasons so I'd be delighted to help. Why don't you tell me about the last time you used it?'

'I don't . . .' Thomas Gabriel looked at the floor.

'I won't bite your head off. What do you want to know?' Victor Brynn smiled and waited for the boy to say something.

Thomas Gabriel licked his lips. Victor Brynn's kind, smiling face made the words harder to find. 'What . . . what was it like being a No-Thing?'

The man's smile flickered and then vanished. He set his mixing bowl down and wiped his hands on his apron and then looked warily at the boy. 'Have you been bitten by a creature? Is the magic inside you infected?'

Thomas Gabriel shook his head. 'No. But just tell me,' he asked again. 'What's it like? Is it as bad as they say in the books?'

Victor Brynn observed the boy in silence, weighing him up like a difficult word he wasn't sure how to pronounce.

'Being a No-Thing is the worst thing in the world,' he said finally. 'Not just the thirst for blood but the magic gone rotten inside you, telling you to do horrible things. You can't say no to it because it's in control of you. But you're a Badlander, Thomas Gabriel, and that makes you magic's master. If it's not doing the things you want it to, you need to be strong. Hasn't Givens taught you that? Wear an *undersync* if you must. Meditate. Without a clear mind, the magic will twist you in knots. You're in charge. Remember that. You

Commenced and allowed it into your very being and the magic must always be grateful for your sacrifice.'

Victor Brynn conjured some white sparks round his fingers. 'Magic is yours to command now you've Commenced.' He made a little fist and hurled a few white sparks and made the spoon in the mixing bowl start stirring on its own. 'Go on, tell the magic in you to stop the spoon. Tell it to do what you want. That it must obey you.'

Thomas Gabriel raised a shaky hand and conjured some sparks, but they died away before he could cast the spell.

'It's nothing to do with controlling the magic,' he whimpered. 'It's me. I wasn't meant to Commence. I took my Master's key without his blessing before he died and now the magic in me's fading and there's nothing I can do to stop it.' He reached into his pocket and took out the invitation that Givens had handed him. 'I've got to pass a test in front of the High Council and they're bound to find out what I've done and punish me.'

There was nothing but the ticking of the clock on the white invitation for a moment as Thomas Gabriel looked at Victor Brynn. 'So tell me how to become a No-Thing. At least I'll still be able to do magic then.'

Victor Brynn opened his mouth, but, before he could say anything, a small bat glided down from a window ledge high up and landed on the floor. It flickered and flapped on the ground and then changed into a pale, gaunt-looking man with dark hair and long, pointed fingernails.

'Greetings y'all,' it said in an American accent. 'I couldn't help bu-rrt overhear yuu-rr convuurr-sation. Now, luckily f-uur you, boy, I am at liberty to help yuu-h. I just gotta deal with the old man fu-rst. I've had maa-h eye on him f-uur a day or so now.' The Vampire grinned. 'Been saving him up till I was real hungr-ee.'

It strode across the room towards Victor Brynn who managed to gather his thoughts fast enough to fire a white shot of magic from his hands. But the Vampire morphed back into a bat that dodged the bolt easily and flew towards the man's neck, its claws clamping down onto the white skin.

It hissed and bared its teeth as Victor Brynn staggered back, hitting the table hard and stumbling to the floor. Before the bat could take a bite, Thomas Gabriel's One Eye shot out of his coat pocket like a missile and barrelled into it, knocking it from Victor Brynn's throat.

There was a terrible screeching and flapping as the two small creatures fought on the floor. When the One Eye lunged and missed, chomping on air with a huge **SNAP!** of its teeth, the bat fluttered up to safety on the window ledge and looked down with beady green eyes.

The One Eye gave a little scream and followed. Yet, by the time it arrived, it met a man perched on the ledge. The Vampire plucked the One Eye out of the air and squeezed so hard something cracked. The hand opened and the One Eye dropped to the floor, landing with a small, ugly noise, and lay motionless.

Before Thomas Gabriel could rush to the poor dead creature, Victor Brynn caught hold of him and dragged him out of the room. The boy found himself pinned to the wall, the man's fists gripping the lapels of his herringbone coat so hard he was lifted up onto his toes.

'Listen to me! I have no idea how this Vampire got here, but that's for another day. We need to work together now if we're going to stay alive. You have to focus. Forget about your meeting with the High Council,' he said, glancing down at the ticking invitation Thomas Gabriel was still holding. The boy nodded and put the piece of white card back in his pocket and readjusted his coat.

'Well, ain't this ah pri-tty pick-el!' shouted the Vampire. 'We all ga-hn dun and got off on the wrong foot, sirs. So why don't we try start-ing urgaain? My name is Thaddeus Squire and I ah-m pleased to make the acquaintance of you gentlemen.' The creature sniggered. 'I s'pose you already guessed what I am? But I ain't one of y-uur regulation Vampires. On account of being old, I picked up a few extra tricks along the way. You boys wanna find out wh-ut they are?'

'Quiet!' shouted Victor Brynn. 'Whoever you are, you made a mistake coming here.'

'Is that so? Seems like I'm in exactly the right place for what a-hh need. Ain't that right, Thomas Gabriel?'

Victor Brynn turned and looked at the boy. 'Don't listen to it,' he whispered. 'It's focusing on you because you're young and impressionable. It thinks it can trick you. It'll use *léasspellunge*, empty talk, to try and fool you.' Victor Brynn shook Thomas Gabriel. 'Are you listening, boy!'

'Don't be so-h hard on that th-uur kid. Being young ain't

a crime.' The Vampire laughed. 'Sorry fer interrup-ting, but I got the sort of ears that pick up all kinds ah things. I can even hear y-uur hearts pumping round all that bl-uurd. I want me some of that by the way when we're done talking. Jabbering makes me thuurr-sty.'

Thomas Gabriel watched Victor Brynn peering round the door frame, weighing up the situation. He was dimly aware of the Vampire rabbiting on, talking about the different centuries it had lived through and how Badlanders were the same in America and Great Britain, too stuck up for their own good. But the boy could also hear something else as well. It was a voice inside him, crisp and clear. The Vampire was in his head, talking to him beneath all the chatter just as Victor Brynn had warned him, but it was difficult not to listen to it.

I can give y-uh what y-uh want, Thomas Gabriel. All I gotta do is bite y-uh and turn that magic in y-uh bad. That way y-uh'll end up a No-Thing like y-uh want. I've turned a few Badlanders bad back where ah-m from and boy, I reckon they l-uurved being a No-Thing much more than being a Badlander. So just give up the old man and I'll see y-uh right with one little bite. One nibble to the ne—

'Thomas Gabriel!' Victor Brynn was shaking him. 'Did you hear what I said? Are you ready?'

The boy blinked.

Reel the old man in for me. I'll make sure the magic'll never leave y-uh.

Thomas Gabriel nodded and stood up tall.

'Very well,' said Victor Brynn. 'Even after making the *fengnett* with *seolfor*, I'll still need your help.'

Victor Brynn muttered some words under his breath and then flashed a hand open and shut four times, firing out a little silver spark each time that shot into the air to make four corners of a square. '*Cnyte*,' muttered the man and a net made from silver began to weave itself into existence.

A net to catch a Vampire or wh-uun to catch y-uur dreams in, Thomas Gabriel? It's him or me. Y-uh know what I mean? Tick . . . tick . . . tick, that invitation of y-uurs is countin' down, remember? So what're y-uh gonna do, Thomas Gabriel?

Victor Brynn grabbed hold of one side of the net. 'Get the other corners, boy!' He lowered his voice. 'The net will draw the creature in once we reveal it and stretch it out. It won't be able to resist its song. Ready?'

'Ready,' said Thomas Gabriel.

Ready then?

When Victor Brynn moved towards the doorway, Thomas Gabriel didn't, and held on tight. The net pulled taut, but the fine weave was too strong to tear. Instead, Victor Brynn was jolted off balance and pinged backwards before Thomas Gabriel let go, causing the man to tumble to the floor. The boy threw his half of the net over him, catching Victor Brynn like a fish in the fine mesh. The man screamed as the Vampire shot down from its perch and landed beside him. It took Victor Brynn's head in its powerful hands and opened its mouth, revealing two white fangs.

Before the creature fed from the body, it asked Thomas

Gabriel to remove the silver net from around the dead man because it was an encumbrance, exerting a force on the creature it didn't like, which was putting it off its food. So Thomas Gabriel unwrapped Victor Brynn.

Balling up the net, he opened the wood-fired oven and shoved it in. As he stared at the flames through the glass, a little part of his brain unlocked and he started to remember who he was and what he was. He heard the sucking sounds of the Vampire feeding behind him and it felt like he'd woken from a dream as his mind became his own again. How could he have done such a thing? He took a small step towards the back door through which he could see the garden, all in the dark now the sun had gone. He couldn't hear the sound of Ruby digging in the garden and wondered where she was and why she hadn't heard anything and come running.

He took another step.

Behind him, the sucking noises stopped.

'Y-uh okay, boy? I forgot about y-uh for a while th-uur, what with eatin' and all. Multeye-tasking ain't never been mah strong point.'

Thomas Gabriel heard the Vampire standing up.

'Boy, I gotta th-urst on. So why don't we just fu-rrget about y-uh being a No-Thing so y-uh can come and be mah dee-ssert instead?'

As the Vampire advanced towards him with shiny red lips, Thomas Gabriel racked his brains for a spell, anything that might be useful. Now was the time he needed the magic in him the most.

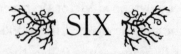 SIX

Once the sun had gone down, the air had grown chilly surprisingly quickly, and Ruby had jammed the spade into the earth and left it there. She'd planted about half of the rosemary bushes, which, she decided, was enough. So she'd snuck round the cottage out of sight of the kitchen and fetched a jar of imps from the VW camper van in the outhouse. The vehicle had belonged to Maitland and was never used by Ruby or Victor Brynn, but was useful for storing items.

After letting the creatures out of the jar, she'd instructed them to finish planting the rosemary. Once they'd trooped off to do as she asked, Ruby had let herself into the cottage through another door and gone upstairs. She needed a pee and wanted to warm up. But most of all she wanted a sit-down. Her legs and arms were sore from digging and she'd grown two ripe blisters on her right hand.

So she'd lain on her bed and shut her eyes. She hadn't meant to doze, but she'd slipped into a nightmare in which she'd encountered the Vampire from the night before.

Waking up in a panic, sweat prickling on her brow, Ruby heard screaming coming from downstairs and pinched herself to check if she was still dreaming. But she was very much awake.

As she'd crept out of the room and tiptoed down the stairs, she'd heard an American voice, which she recognized instantly, and shivered as she wondered what had happened to Victor Brynn. Going closer to the kitchen doorway, she got her answer.

The man's body was lying in the doorway to the kitchen. His face was white, a look of fear frozen on it. His eyes had been sucked deep into their sockets. There were two puncture wounds in his neck, red and raw. Ruby felt the world wobble around her, but she couldn't afford to let Victor Brynn's death get in the way of what she needed to do now.

It was hard, though, and her knees shook. She heard the Vampire talking to someone, but she didn't care who it was. Instead, she turned and ran to the study.

Quickly, she searched the desk drawers for the golden brooch and a vial of Vamp Venom she'd made up following her run-in with the Vampire, hoping for the chance to prove she could take on such a creature again one day and win. And now here was that chance. But Victor Brynn was dead. Dead!

She opened the walnut case that sat on the desk with a shaky hand and took out the gun, stuffing it into her waistband, telling it to be quiet as it complained about being woken up.

As she crept towards the kitchen, Ruby heard the cries of Thomas Gabriel alongside her own jumbled thoughts . . . *How had the Vampire got here? Had it followed her?*

She drew out the gun and it tensed in her hand when it saw Victor Brynn's body in the doorway and heard the Vampire in the kitchen.

'I'm with you, Ruby,' it whispered. 'Think hard about what you need to do.' Ruby gripped the gun so tightly it seemed to be holding her up and she was glad it was her friend.

'Y-urr gonna give me that neck of y-urrs, boy!' shouted an angry American voice.

Ruby peered ever so carefully round the door and saw Thomas Gabriel sitting inside a rather misshapen transparent sphere. His arms were clasped round his knees and his head was buried deep in them.

'That bubble ain't gonna last!' shouted the Vampire. 'Y-uur magic's fla-hhky – I heard y-uh tell the old guy. So why make it hard on yuhr-self?' The Vampire poked at the sphere with a crooked forefinger, creating a hollow sound. Little sparks ran over its surface and the whole thing juddered and creaked as if ready to collapse.

'Might as well let me in now, li-ddle piggy.'

'Shut up!' shouted Thomas Gabriel, who looked up for a brief instant before burying his head in his knees again.

Ruby could see a broken bottle of Slap Dust on the floor, the dark powdery contents spilt, and realized there must have been a struggle that had left Thomas Gabriel with no option but to protect himself with magic. Ruby had no idea why the boy was here. And she had no idea how the Vampire had found the cottage, but she knew it had to be her fault somehow. She looked at Victor Brynn on the floor because she knew what else that meant.

'Focus, Ruby,' whispered the gun.

Ruby nodded and took a deep breath.

The Vampire gave an excited yelp and Ruby peered round the door frame again. The bubble around Thomas Gabriel was failing now, and a small, raggedy hole was growing across the transparent skin.

'I told y-uh!' said the Vampire, clapping its hands like an excited child.

Thomas Gabriel was desperately trying to summon more magic, but the white sparks kept slip-sliding round his fingers like soap suds, dropping to the floor around him, then vanishing.

Ruby stuffed the gun into her waistband and tapped the golden brooch three times so it became a spear. She uncorked the glass vial and poured the Vamp Venom into a groove that ran down the shaft of the weapon, filling it up. One clean shot was all she needed. But her aim had to be true for the spear to go right through the creature's heart.

As the last of Thomas Gabriel's bubble vanished, Ruby picked out a spot on the Vampire's back as the creature looked down at the boy. But, as she drew back her arm, ready to hurl the weapon, she heard the *whoosh* of Slap Dust as someone else arrived in the hallway.

Ed looked around, remembering what it had been like to live here. Then he saw Ruby, spear raised in her hand.

'Vampire!' she screamed.

But when Ruby looked again the Vampire was gone. In its place was a small furry bat fluttering towards her. Ruby hurled the spear anyway, aiming for the body. It flashed through the air and pierced one of the bat's leathery wings, its momentum carrying the creature with it. The head of the spear embedded itself in the door of the larder, the shaft quivering.

The horrid black creature flapped and chattered, squeaking terribly. It hissed as Ruby ran towards it. She grabbed the end of the spear to pull it out, but the bat flapped its one good wing and slid down the shaft, landing on her hand and biting down, making her yell. She staggered back, two small puncture wounds visible in the fleshy part between her thumb and forefinger.

When the bat's skewered wing started melting, Ruby knew the Vamp Venom must be having some effect. The bat dropped to the floor with a raggedy, burnt wing no good for flying any more, and scuttled like a clockwork toy towards the open door into the garden.

The wounds in Ruby's hand were starting to hum and she wobbled again, feeling like she was about to fall. An arm curled round her and then somebody was wrapping a tea towel round her hand.

'What are you doing here?' was all her brain could manage to ask as she looked at the boy who was helping her.

'To talk about Du Clement, but I'll tell you why later,' said Ed. 'We've got more important things to do now.'

Ruby blinked. And then she looked at the body of Victor Brynn and found she couldn't swallow. She knew she was about to cry. 'We've got to send him off the right way, haven't we? According to the *Ordnung*.'

'That'll have to wait too.'

'But I thought—'

'Ruby, you need to finish the job or else that bite will infect you. Kill the Vampire and the infection will die too. It's the only way.' He started dragging her towards the door, waving at Thomas Gabriel to come with them, but stopped as something occurred to him. 'Now I'm here in the Badlands again, you should call me Jones, not Ed.' The other two looked at him and then at each other. 'I don't want the new me getting mixed up in all this. So, while I'm here, it's Jones.'

Ruby managed a weak smile. 'Welcome back, Jones.'

The three of them stood outside the house at the edge of the garden, their breath frosting the air. It was dark. Quiet. Jones found his brain reaching back to everything Maitland had taught him when he'd been an apprentice, that hidden part of him coming alive again. It was like a computer downloading a file. There was no time to think. He just had to act.

He began to follow a thin trail of blood slicked across the grass. But soon the blood died out and instead there were shoeprints in the dewy grass.

'He's changed from a bat to a man to move quicker and get as far away as he can,' said Jones, striding on.

The footprints led to a fence that bordered the garden and beyond it, across a field, was the edge of a forest. 'He'll go to ground in there.'

'Hide and regenerate,' agreed Thomas Gabriel.

'Come on,' said Jones. 'We need to find him. Finish him off.'

Jones climbed over the fence and helped Ruby over. When he offered a hand to Thomas Gabriel, he looked him in the eye. 'You'll have to do magic,' he told him. 'Make a *fengnett*. Can you do that?'

Jones felt the other boy's hand wilt in his as Thomas Gabriel took a breath.

'Can't you do the spell?' said Jones.

'It's not that.'

'What then?'

Thomas Gabriel stared down at his feet because he couldn't bear to look at Jones and Ruby across the fence. 'The magic inside me's going rotten. I should never have taken the key from Simeon.' He looked up at them as something in his shoulders lifted. He felt better for telling them his secret.

'I told you,' piped up the gun in Ruby's hand. 'I said taking the key would affect your Commencement if you went through with it! You need to tell the Order what's happened.'

'Is that why you were here?' asked Ruby. 'To ask Victor Brynn about it?'

'Yes,' nodded Thomas Gabriel. 'I thought he might know what to do.'

58

'What about the Vampire? Where did it come from?' asked Jones.

'I don't know how. We were talking and then . . .' Thomas Gabriel's voice tailed away and he looked towards the forest.

Ruby coughed. Shuffled her feet in the dirt. 'I think it was our fault,' she said quietly.

'Your fault, you mean!' complained the gun.

'It must have followed us somehow,' continued Ruby, 'after we went hunting for it.'

'If you hadn't been so desperate to go after that Vampire in the first place,' said the gun, 'Victor Brynn would still be alive.'

'It doesn't matter whose fault it is now, does it?' said Thomas Gabriel curtly as he climbed over the fence. The gun grumbled on, but he ignored it and looked at Jones and Ruby. 'You'll have to make the *fengnett* if we're going to deal with this Vampire.'

'But I'm not a Badlander any more.' Jones's heart dropped into his stomach. This wasn't how he'd been expecting the evening to go. He heard little whispers: the magic inside him was excited. He muttered something under his breath and then cleared his throat.

'Have you got *The Black Book of Magical Instruction*, Ruby?'

She shook her head. 'Why would I? I can't do magic on my own, remember?'

Thomas Gabriel produced his own copy of the black leather book from a pocket and held it out.

'Go on, take it,' he said. 'It's not much use to me,' and he thrust it into Jones's hands.

59

As the gold lettering on the cover caught the moonlight, Jones heard a clunk inside him. It was as if his heart had shrivelled up and dropped into his stomach. He closed his eyes, then opened them again.

The others were still there.

And so was the book in his hands.

'Let's get this over with then,' said the boy,

The trees were densely packed. Thomas Gabriel, Ruby and Jones picked their way slowly between them, watching out for the Vampire.

'Just like old times, eh, Jones?' whispered the gun as noises rustled in the dark around them and the odd mysterious shape flitted among the trees. But Jones just grumbled something and strode on. Ruby walked faster too, to keep up with him, even though she felt woozy from the bite, a headache throbbing in her temples.

'Did you come in here a lot with Maitland then?'

'Yeah, when I was little, so I could learn about being a Badlander. That's why Maitland lived in the cottage, so the forest was close enough for training up apprentices. Didn't Victor Brynn bring you here?'

'He said I wasn't ready to come in at night.'

'It's a dangerous place after dark all right,' said Jones. 'Just stay close.'

Ruby aimed the gun into the dark spaces between the trees, ready to take on anything that might be lurking nearby, but her arm wobbled and she felt a little dizzy. Her hand was hurting too. Secretly, she was glad Jones was with her, although she was never going to admit it.

They kept moving, picking their way carefully. There was barely any moonlight or starlight poking through the canopy of trees, making it hard to see very far ahead.

'He'll go to ground like all injured animals do,' said Jones. 'All we gotta do is follow the trail he's left.' He pointed to the spatters of blood on the fronds of waist-high bracken. There was the odd spot on the ground too. They carried on a few more minutes in silence and came to a clearing. As far as Ruby could tell, the path divided into two.

Thomas Gabriel and Jones stood at the head of one path each and peered into the gloom.

The puncture wounds on Ruby's hand were really stinging now and her legs wobbled once more, forcing her to sit down suddenly as the world began to spin.

Jones noticed and came running, followed quickly by Thomas Gabriel.

'Take deep breaths,' said Jones. 'We'll do the magic here as soon as you feel ready. It's as good a place as any.'

Ruby nodded. The world started to slow down and soon she was feeling less dizzy and managed to stand up.

A tingle started up in her chest as Jones handed her *The Black Book of Magical Instruction.*

'I might be using magic, but I'm not saying the spell,' he said. 'You're the Badlander, remember, not me.'

'What am I looking for?' she asked.

'The spell for a *fengnett.*'

But, as Ruby flicked through the pages, she could barely focus with her hand stinging so much and she handed the book back before plopping down on the ground again.

'You'll have to do it, Jones. I'm sorry.'

Jones muttered and grumbled as he flicked through the pages, tutting from time to time. When he found the right one, he held out a hand and Ruby grabbed it.

He spoke the spell quickly and closed the book, making Ruby a little jealous but sad too, remembering how Victor Brynn had always been on at her about learning to pronounce Anglo-Saxon words properly.

Her thoughts vanished as something released inside her chest, allowing the magic to flood out of her. She saw Jones react to it too. A look of revulsion twinned with wonder crossed his face as he opened and closed his free hand four times and sent silver sparks rushing out of his fingers, creating four corners of a square suspended in mid-air.

'*Cnyte*,' he said.

Silver threads began stitching themselves together and, as Ruby watched the magic working, she felt Jones pull his hand out of hers now that everything was done. He wiped it on his sweater as if it was dirty.

'No, I ain't doing no more,' he hissed and Ruby realized he must be talking to the magic inside him again.

It didn't take long for the *fengnett* to form but it was a bit droopy and Jones realized he hadn't cast a very good spell, so he plucked it from the air. With Thomas Gabriel helping, he hooked it up between two trees to stretch it out properly. It was so finely wrought, it was as delicate as gossamer. Strung out, it looked like a very large, square-shaped spider's web.

'Will it work?' asked Ruby.

'Course. Now it's stretched out, it'll draw the creature in with its song as long as it's not too far away.' Ruby heard the threads of the net start to vibrate, as if an invisible rain was falling on them. She could hear musical notes too. Delicate. Faint. Like an orchestra was playing far off in the trees. She tilted her head to try and hear more, but it didn't help. The harder she tried, the further away the notes seemed.

All three of them crouched in the undergrowth, peering over the wobbly tops of the bracken.

Just a few moments later, the Vampire appeared through the trees, coming down one of the paths that led into the clearing. One of his arms was hanging limp against his body, bloody and useless. The Vampire's face was pale and shone with sweat. He was shuddering as he walked, trying to stop himself moving. But it was no good. His legs kept picking themselves up. He looked like a puppet being manoeuvred down the path.

He let out a cry as he saw the *fengnett* strung between the trees and raised his one good arm to shield his eyes as if the net was shining too brightly at him.

'Puuuhlease!' he cried out. 'Ahh-ll do anything. Ahh-ll help y-uh with anything y-uh want. I was never gonna eat y-uh, boy!' He strained to look at Thomas Gabriel. 'Ah w-uhz never gonna drain yuu-r bl-uurd. Ain't y-uh gonna have su-hm mercy?'

'You're getting what you deserve for killing Victor Brynn!' shouted Thomas Gabriel.

The creature started to scream as it drew closer to the net, a hideous shrieking sound that sent drowsy birds fluttering up from the trees. Ruby, Jones and Thomas Gabriel were silent as the Vampire was finally dragged into the net. The creature let out another scream, so loud this time that Ruby covered her ears. It flailed about, like a fly caught in a spider's web, and then started to smoke and melt.

When Ruby looked again, the Vampire was gone. The throbbing pain in her hand had disappeared too and the puncture wounds had healed. Suddenly, she felt much better, as if something bad had been sucked out of her, and gave the boys the thumbs up before they all rose from behind the bracken and walked towards the net, which was still playing its delicate song.

Jones and Thomas Gabriel stood at either end of it, ready to unhook it. Before they did so, Jones removed something caught in the weave and held out his hand for the others to see. In his palm was one of the Vampire's fangs, sharp and white with a long root.

'Ruby, you should have this. So everyone knows what you've done,' he said. 'It's rare to have a Vampire tooth.' He looked at her. 'I don't want it.'

'Thanks,' said Ruby. Before she put the tooth in her pocket, she noticed how sharp it was as it caught the moonlight. 'Does that mean I get to make the *mearcunge* too?'

'Jones should mark the kill,' said Thomas Gabriel. 'He did the spell.'

'But—' Ruby paused when she heard a noise above the trees.

And then all three of them heard it – a flapping sound above them, drowning out the delicate song still being played by the *fengnett*. A dark shape broke through the canopy, dropping down towards Ruby. There was no time to run. She cowered and twisted and turned as two large feet opened their talons and reached out. They hooked her shoulders and the pain made her gasp. And then her feet peeled up off the ground and her stomach lurched into her throat as she was lifted into the air.

Ruby rose fast, the forest floor disappearing beneath her. She fumbled for the gun in her waistband, but dropped it and heard it cursing as it plummeted to the ground. Jones's shouts and Thomas Gabriel's cries were lost as she rose through the canopy and soon all she could hear was the beating of leathery wings and the rush of wind in her face as she tried to look down at the treetops below.

SEVEN

Ruby dangled like a piece of meat on a hook. The creature's talons dug into her as the dark canopy of the forest slid by beneath her and the wind roared in her ears.

She'd worked out what the creature was now. A Snarl. A flying lizard roughly the size of a cow. She'd read about them in one of the many books Victor Brynn had made her read. Snarls were vicious, with an appetite for people. Having dropped the gun, her first thought was to use the Vampire's tooth and stab at the creature's leg. But forcing it to let go of her meant she would almost certainly fall to her death.

Trying to ignore the cold and her fear, Ruby dropped the tooth into a jacket pocket and reached for something else. The points of the Snarl's talons dug deeper into her shoulders as she moved. But Ruby told herself that being eaten by the creature would be far worse. Snarls had long beaks lined with sharp, hooked teeth that tore the flesh from their prey. Death would be awful and it would not be quick. The book had said that Snarls picked at their food over days rather than gobbling it down, keeping it alive as long as possible to guarantee it was fresh. Ruby gritted her teeth at the pain in her shoulders as she rummaged around in her pocket, imagining the bottle of Slap Dust she wanted in her mind's eye. And then felt it between her fingers.

It was difficult prising it out of her pocket. The Snarl see-sawed gently as it flew, meaning Ruby's body rolled from side to side as she dangled and she kicked out her legs to keep as straight as she could. It was difficult to remove the cork stopper too, and she was scared of dropping the bottle, her only means of escape. With the stopper finally popped out, Ruby tried to pour some of the dust into her hand, but the wind blew it away in a black powdery cloud such was the Snarl's speed through the air.

The creature dived into a sharp left turn, taking Ruby by surprise, and she almost dropped the bottle, most of the dust spilling out into the sky.

Just a few grains left now.

Ruby licked her lips, ignored the pain in her shoulders and tried again. But, as she went to pour out the last grains of dust, she realized they were flying lower and lower, descending quickly into a section of forest. She had no idea how long they'd been in the air. Ten minutes? Twenty? How far had they flown?

The answers to these questions had no time to materialize as Ruby was dropped from a height of nearly two metres into a very large nest that sat on the ground. It was made from sticks and lined with leaves and the woolly hides of sheep that had clearly been ripped from the bodies of their former owners.

The bottle of Slap Dust slipped from her hand as she landed hard and it clattered into the dark. There was no time to look for it because she was instantly up on her feet and worrying about what else was in the nest. Three Snarl chicks were all eager for a piece of her, their beaks snapping open and clicking shut, tails swishing behind them.

Ruby pulled a stick from the wall of the nest and thrashed it about. She hit the most hungry and fearless chick full in the face as it came at her, sending it tumbling backwards into its siblings and knocking them over. They pecked and screamed at each other for a moment before refocusing on Ruby with bright red eyes, their tongues darting out from their beaks.

Ruby could see the chicks well enough, despite the dark, and realized it was because a white light was filtering up through the bottom of the nest as if someone had placed small floodlights in the ground beneath it. When a white spark shot up through the base of the nest, fizzing up into the air, the stick in her hand drooped as her mouth opened. It had looked like a white spark of magic.

Ruby raised the stick as the chicks inched closer, their small talons tapping. The creatures were warier of her this time, their eyes watching the stick she was holding. She kept glancing around for the bottle of Slap Dust, but she couldn't see it.

When Ruby heard voices behind her, she wanted to turn round and look, but she was scared of the chicks rushing at her if she gave them the chance. As far as she could tell, there were two people shouting, a man and a boy, and then the adult Snarl came crashing through the trees and landed beside the nest, roaring its disapproval. Ruby heard a man speaking in Anglo-Saxon and knew then that the voices must belong to Badlanders, a Master and his apprentice. A dull sonic thud boomed through the air, making Ruby's teeth rattle. Something struck the Snarl on the side of the body, knocking the animal to the ground. It lay panting, its wings flapping weakly, its talons flexing, and then was still.

A boy, rather smaller than her, appeared in her line of vision and threw out a golden rope that snaked through the air and lassoed one of the chicks round the neck. He tugged hard and yanked the chick out of the nest onto the ground. As it struggled to stand up, a tall man strode into view with white sparks whizzing round the ends of his fingers. A few words later, a flash of white from his fingers, and the chick was no longer moving.

The boy was already twirling the rope above his head again and let it loose, snaring another of the chicks and dragging it out of the nest. Ruby decided not to hang around any longer. She dropped the stick and started to clamber out of the nest on the other side. But the sticks were rickety. They moved under her weight. And, even worse, some were covered in something slippery. At first, she thought it might be dew. But she soon realized it was blood. Her hands glistened with it.

Looking down, she saw a cow's head between her feet and swallowed down the urge to be sick. Her hands were slipping on the sticks as she tried to climb up and out. She reached the top and then, looking for a way down, saw her bottle of Slap Dust lodged between two sticks. She reached across and grabbed it, and just had time to see there were a few precious grains in the bottom before her feet gave way and she tumbled out of the nest. The hand of her outstretched arm hit the ground first. She heard a nasty click deep in her wrist and the air inside her lungs shot out with a grunt.

She closed her eyes to stop herself feeling sick and, as she lay there on the forest floor for a few slow seconds, she heard the squawking of the last chick cut out suddenly. She thought her wrist might be sprained or, even worse, broken, because it was so painful.

Ruby became aware of two voices talking and decided the safest thing to do was to lie there and pretend to be unconscious for now. She kept her eyes firmly shut, with one hand tight round the bottle of Slap Dust to conceal it as she lay in the dirt.

Randall Givens smoothed down his black hair as he observed the unconscious girl on the ground, resisting the urge to prod her with the silver toe of his boot, to see if she was alive. His brown leather trench coat flared around him as he bent down instead to feel for a pulse in her neck.

'She's alive,' he said to the boy standing beside him. 'Though it looks like she's taken a painful bang to the head,' continued Givens, studying the large, egg-shaped lump on the girl's forehead. 'And that left wrist looks nasty too,' he said, peering at the swelling. 'Let's see what state the rest of her is in.'

He fired a few sparks out of his fingers and they rushed round her body. Some of them clustered round the wrist, the lump on her forehead and a graze to her face, and more gathered on the tips of her shoulders where the Snarl's talons had pierced her old army camouflage jacket through to the skin.

'No other damage apart from the obvious. Do you see where the Snarl must have grabbed her by the shoulders, Wilfried?' said Givens, standing up and brushing his knees down. The boy nodded. Although Wilfried was young, at the most eight or nine years old (although he didn't know for sure since he was an orphan), he had an inquisitive and serious air about him. His eyes ran up and down the girl on the ground, looking for any clues.

'Now then, Wilfried, what do we do in a situation like this?'

'We need to find out who she is and where she's from, sir.'

'And the best way of doing that?'

'We could go back to the van and mix a potion, something she can drink to tell us who she is.'

'We could, but what if she wakes up before the potion's ready? And, even if she doesn't, she's bound to panic when

71

she comes round because she'll be scared and certainly in pain judging by the state of her wrist. How would you get an ordinary girl like this to drink a potion then? Force it down her throat?'

Wilfried looked down at the toes of his brown lace-up shoes for an answer. He was a diminutive boy and looked even smaller in his grey woollen coat that was too big and hung off his narrow shoulders, his hands only half visible at the ends of the sleeves.

'Magic is the only solution to our predicament here,' said Givens. 'First, to heal her injuries, and then to find out what we need to know. We'll also need it to wipe her mind of all the horrors that have befallen her. Our duty isn't only to protect ordinary people, but, in the case of this girl, it's to treat her gently and put her back safely wherever she came from. Only then will our job as Badlanders be done. So you can see how important Commencement is, how magic is the very key to being a success in the Badlands, whatever situation arises. Not just in the heat of battle with whatever foul creature you might encounter.'

'Yes, sir.'

Givens looked down at the girl again and whispered some words. The white sparks round her wrist and the injuries on her head, face and shoulders started to change colour before vanishing. The lump on her forehead began to shrink. Her swollen wrist started to reduce in size.

'Make a note of what you've seen, Wilfried,' said Givens.

The boy took out a small ring-bound notebook from

his pocket which had *Wilfried's Learning Book – Keep out!* scrawled on it in spiky writing. He prised out a pencil lodged in the metal ring binding down the side of the notebook.

'Now there's no way of finding out more about her until she's awake and ready to speak so let us attend to the matter at hand in the few minutes it'll take for everything to heal.' Givens shot out a hand and more white sparks thundered from his fingers. They hooked round the Snarl's nest and lifted it off the ground, placing it down some metres further on beside the dead adult and its chicks.

The nest had been covering a small rupture in the ground that was full of bright light and out of which sparks of magic fluttered up occasionally and then vanished.

'So, Wilfried, what of this vent in the Ley Line?'

'It's dangerous to leave it open. It could grow larger.'

'And how would you suggest closing it?'

Wilfried crouched down to have a look. 'We could probably use a *nædle* like we did with the other opening we found a few days ago.'

'Yes, I would say so,' said Givens, peering into the hole too. He caught a magical spark as it fizzed up towards him and watched it fade between his fingers and then dissolve to nothing.

'It's a shame the girl meant we had to intervene. We were gathering such useful information about the effect of magic on the Snarl chicks. The book I'm writing about magic and monsters will be a bestseller, Wilfried.' Given smiled at the thought. And then he sighed. 'Remind me, how many anomalies have we found along this Ley Line we've been surveying for the last few weeks?'

'Two vents, sir, three smaller ruptures and four cracks.'

Givens pursed his lips. 'Then we'll take a short break from our survey and return home. I could do with a night in my own bed anyway.'

'Why are we going home, sir?'

'Where does magic come from, Wilfried?'

'The land, sir.'

'Precisely. Hidden deep in the ground until the first Badlanders learnt to use it. So if a Ley Line is becoming unstable, allowing magic to escape, it means our absolute control over it is being threatened. We need the right advice on a problem like this to stop it getting worse. As head of the High Council of the Order, I'm able to speak to "the Cutter" on such a matter.'

'Who's that, sir?'

Givens glanced at the girl who was still lying there with her eyes shut before proceeding.

'I'm going to tell you something very few Badlanders know, Wilfried. The Cutter is a man who has such a kinship with magic that he understands its very essence. He has such a gift for magic that not only can this man cast the greatest of spells, but it's said he used to be able to cut the magic out of Badlanders or alter their magic if a Commencement had gone wrong. Imagine that, Wilfried. Someone who has the power to take away the greatest gift a Badlander can ever have.'

Wilfred shuddered at such a thing.

'Now you won't tell anyone this secret, will you, Wilfried? I can trust you, can't I?'

'Of course, sir. I won't tell anyone.'

Givens stared at the boy down his long nose and smiled. 'Good. An apprentice should always keep his Master's secrets. Why?'

'Because trust helps keep us safe and sound, sir.'

Ruby may have looked unconscious to Givens, but she was very much awake, her mind fizzing with thoughts about 'the Cutter' and whether this person could possibly help her and Jones and Thomas Gabriel with their magical problems.

Over the last few minutes, she'd started to feel much better as the magic healed her, and she had kept quite still, biding her time. Victor Brynn had told her that Masters often showed off in front of their apprentices. It was meant to be inspiring, to make the point that an apprentice was lucky to be with their Master, so they wanted to work even harder. But it was also a test, to see if a boy could keep a secret. Victor Brynn had made it very clear to Ruby that he wanted a different type of relationship with her, one that was honest and open, befitting of the respect he owed her for saving his life. She had always loved him for that. Secretly, she'd thought of him as the father she'd never had.

But now he was dead.

Ruby shuddered as she felt a tinge of sadness curdle the insides of her tummy. Once more, she tried to focus back on the two Badlanders, waiting for the opportunity to use the last remaining Slap Dust to get away.

But, when she felt a warm sensation inside the hand holding on tight to the vial of Slap Dust, she started to panic. The dust was reacting to the air because the stopper had been off for so long. Even with her thumb over the top, it was only a matter of time before the last few grains fizzled to nothing and Ruby would have no way of getting home. She had another problem too: the dust would start to smell the more it reacted. If either the boy or the man smelt it and realized she had Slap Dust, they'd search her and find her limitless pockets full of things only a Badlander would own. That could only lead to trouble.

She had to get away. Fast.

She sat up so quickly, the blood rushed to her head.

'Sir! The girl's waking up,' she heard the boy cry out to his Master.

Givens walked over to the girl who was clutching her arms around herself as she got to her feet. He stopped and raised his hands to show her they meant no harm.

'How are you feeling?' asked Givens gently.

'A bit sick,' said the girl.

'That's only to be expected after what's happened. You took quite a tumble and hit your head. What exactly do you remember?'

The girl opened her mouth to speak and then started to shake as she noticed the dead Snarl and its chicks.

'There, there,' said Givens. 'We can help.'

'Stay away!' shouted the girl and started backing towards the treeline. 'Who are you?'

'We are Badlanders, the noble protectors of ordinary people from creatures that live secretly in the dark around you, which makes us very special indeed. Only minutes ago, my apprentice and I saved you from certain death.' Givens conjured some white sparks round the ends of his fingers. 'But we're going to help you forget any of this ever happened. It won't hurt at all.'

He observed the girl's reaction and hoped Wilfried was watching it too, understanding how magic was something so special that ordinary people were dumbfounded by it. 'Why don't you tell us who you are? And where you're from? We want to help you. That's what we Badlanders do.'

'I'm gonna wet myself if I don't get to pee right now!' she blurted out.

This time it was Givens's turn to open his mouth at such a strange outburst.

'I need to pee!' repeated the girl as she started hopping from one foot to another. Her face scrunched up as if she was about to cry.

'Well, I . . . well . . .' Givens had not expected such a reaction from the girl. But then he didn't know the first thing about such creatures. He was acutely aware that Wilfried was watching and the Badlander's mind ticked over as the girl in front of him started to hop even faster from one foot to another.

She pointed to the treeline, providing Givens with an answer.

'Yes, of course. Wilfried here will keep an eye out for you. Make sure you don't come to any harm. The forest isn't a safe place to be at night.' The girl nodded and set off quickly towards the trees.

Givens raised his eyes at Wilfried, urging him to follow. The boy obeyed without a moment's hesitation and Givens gave a silent moment of thanks for having such an obedient apprentice.

Ruby walked as fast as she could out of the clearing and didn't stop when she passed the first trees. The bottle was growing hotter in her hand and the grains of dust were starting to smell too. Soon they would be gone.

The boy was trying to keep up, tramping through the undergrowth.

'Don't go too far!' he shouted. 'It's not safe.'

But Ruby strode on faster, breaking out into a run.

'Wait!'

Ruby wove between the trees and then stopped behind a particularly large oak with a wide trunk. She peered round it to see the boy looking about him, wringing his hands.

'Where are you?' he hissed. 'This isn't a place for playing games.'

Ruby looked up into the tree when she heard something and saw a pair of red eyes staring down at her. A wide grin of teeth glinted. Something sticky and foamy dripped to the ground and Ruby smiled as she thanked her lucky stars. It was a Slobbering, a vicious, toothy creature with a big enough appetite for a girl her size. More slobber dripped. Some splattered onto her jacket. It fell onto her hair. A smell like stagnant water rose up around her.

'Come on, what are you waiting for?' she whispered at it, emptying the last grains of Slap Dust into her hand.

The creature launched itself at her and Ruby announced where she wanted to go and slapped her hands together.

Nothing happened.

The Slobbering landed on her and knocked her to the ground. It ripped a mouthful of material from her jacket, leaving a raggedy hole as she pushed it away.

With the Slap Dust struggling to work properly, Ruby began disappearing limb by limb as the Slobbering came at her again, the material from her jacket flapping between its teeth.

The last thing she saw was the Slobbering launching itself at her, threatening to swallow her whole, its jaw unhinging so it could take her in one gulp. Ruby gave a loud scream for good measure so the boy might hear, and even the man in the clearing too . . .

. . . and then she was standing in the driveway in front of the cottage she now called home. Through a window, she saw Jones and Thomas Gabriel deep in conversation. They appeared to be arguing. Various weapons lay on the table, the gun among them. Ruby ran as fast as she could across the drive and in through the front door.

When the two boys saw her, they stopped speaking and just stared as though they were unsure it was really her.

'Jones, I've found out something that might be useful,' Ruby said before the boy flung his arms round her, almost knocking her over. He held on tight for a moment.

'I thought you'd gone,' he gasped.

# EIGHT

R uby tried not to cry as she looked down at Victor
Brynn's corpse. But something inside her broke
and the tears streamed from her eyes against
her wishes. Even though it was very late at night, and
she was tired and sore, she knew the man's body needed
to be honoured. So she tried her best to recite the *wyrd*
rhyme as Jones and Thomas Gabriel stood in silence in
the garden, their heads bowed and their hands clasped
respectfully.

> 'Do not be afear'd
> It is only the *wyrd*
> That says you must go
> From this world that you know.'

Ruby took a breath and held the gun tighter.

'You're doing well, Ruby,' it said. 'It's always a hard thing
to say the *wyrd* rhyme. Isn't that right, boys?' Jones nodded
and so did Thomas Gabriel. 'No one knows when it's their

time. You just have to accept it not only in your own life but in other people's too.'

'The gun's right, Ruby,' said Jones. 'The *wyrd* knows when it's time.'

'But it was all my fault. If I hadn't gone after that Vampire—'

'It's no one's fault,' interrupted Thomas Gabriel. 'It's just the *wyrd*. That's why we say the rhyme. The more we say it, the more ready we are to accept our own end. Whenever it may be.'

Ruby sighed and took a breath before carrying on, the two boys and the gun all joining in to help her.

> 'Do not be afear'd
> It is only the *wyrd*
> That wants you to leave
> Which means I won't grieve.
>
> Do not be afear'd
> It is only the *wyrd*
> That rules all our lives
> And always decides
>
> The length of one's life
> All its joy, all its strife,
> So do not be afear'd
> It is only the *wyrd*.'

In the silence, Ruby scattered a pinch of brown dust over the body and it began to melt. As they all stood in the moonlight, listening to the hiss of the corpse, Ruby felt a little part of her heart melting too.

When it was over and the last white bubbles were popping on the grass, Ruby wiped her nose on her sleeve and gave a great wobbly sigh before taking a small white packet out of her pocket.

'What have you got there?' asked Jones.

'Seeds.' Ruby waggled the little packet.

'What sort of seeds?'

'Special ones. Victor Brynn gave them to me, in case.'

'In case of what?'

'In case he died.' Ruby opened the packet and scattered the little brown seeds onto the grass where Victor Brynn's body had lain. They burrowed into the ground like little grubs and vanished.

'Are they dreaming seeds?'

'Yes. Victor Brynn said they'd let him speak to me in my dreams if he ever had to leave me. I want to see him again. He wasn't like either of your Masters. He was kind.'

'Dreaming seeds never grow, Ruby,' said Thomas Gabriel. 'Victor Brynn's dead. There's no way of speaking to him now.'

'He told me they might do if I watered them and treated them well. *And* I read a book about them. *Into the Beyond* by D. P. Thompson.'

'There is no "beyond". Everyone knows that book's a load of old rubbish,' Thomas Gabriel muttered under his breath.

'Well, I suppose I'll find out, won't I?'

'Is that your plan for carrying on learning about being

a Badlander?' asked Jones. 'Hoping for glimpses of Victor Brynn in your dreams *if* the seeds grow?'

'Part of it.' Ruby folded up the white packet and put it in her pocket. 'I thought I'd go and see the Cutter too.'

'I've never heard of anybody called that,' said Thomas Gabriel.

'Well, I told you, that's the name I heard,' said Ruby, sticking out her chin.

'That Badlander was probably making it up,' said Jones. 'Masters do all sorts of tricks to test apprentices. He was probably telling that boy something just to see if he could keep a secret.'

'I can scry on him and find out for sure. Jones, if there's someone in the Badlands who can alter our Commencement, it'll mean I can do magic on my own. Then the Order will have to let me be a proper Badlander.'

'The Order would never allow a girl in,' said Jones. 'They're stuck in their ways.'

'Victor Brynn didn't think so. He told me the other night he hoped we might prove them wrong one day. And it wasn't only me he said it to.' She pointed the gun at Jones. 'Go on, tell Jones what you told me.'

The gun cleared its throat. 'Victor Brynn kept saying that, one day, he wanted to convince the Order that Ruby was good enough to be a Badlander. As long as she carried on studying and learning what he taught her, he thought it might be possible. He said the Order was so rotten it needed a big shock to show it the error of its ways.'

Ruby smiled. 'I could do that, Jones, if I can do magic.'

Jones frowned because he couldn't imagine the order ever admitting a girl.

'I'm not going back to my old life,' said Ruby. 'I couldn't bear it.' She shuffled her feet. 'I thought you'd be excited. If we can find someone to fix our Commencement, you won't have the magic inside you. So what's the problem?'

Jones folded his arms. 'This Badlander you met: if he's high up in the Order, like you said, I bet he's wary of other Badlanders trying to find out things about him. You get caught scrying on him and that'll be the end of everything for you and me.' Jones shook his head. 'My idea's better. Instead of scrying on this person, we go and see the *Lich*, Du Clement, about our Commencement. We can ask him about this person called "the Cutter" and see if he really exists.'

'But I'm a good scryer, Jones. I won't get caught.'

Jones kicked at a tuft of grass in frustration.

Thomas Gabriel cleared his throat and the other two looked at him.

'Ruby's right,' he said. 'Scrying on someone's easier than going to see the *Lich*. We almost got caught last time. And Du Clement's as mad as a bag of frogs.' Thomas Gabriel sighed as he shuffled his feet and rubbed his nose. 'There's something you need to know.' He took out the invitation from his pocket. The clock was still ticking.

'What's that?' asked Jones, peering at the white piece of card.

'I've got to perform a magical test in front of the High Council in a few weeks' time.'

'Good luck with that,' said the gun.

'It's not just my problem. Once they find out my magic's failing and why, they'll cast me out of the Order and take everything back from me.'

'You mean they'll take this cottage?' gasped Ruby.

'Yes, *and* my *æhteland*.' He looked at Jones. 'And when another Badlander takes it on the first thing they'll do is assess it for magical anomalies. They'll find out about you, Jones, and who you are and what you've done. And when they do they'll punish you for Commencing with a girl, just like they'll punish me for Commencing when I shouldn't have.'

There was no sound except for the ticking of the clock as everyone thought about that.

'I want to know more about this Cutter,' said Thomas Gabriel. 'If he's as powerful as Ruby thinks, he might be able to help you two, but he might be able to help me too so Ruby keeps this place and you aren't found out, Jones. I know I did wrong, Commencing when I shouldn't, but I'm not a bad person. I didn't do it to ruin your lives too.'

Jones chewed a spot inside his cheek as he thought it all through.

'Look and see what you can then,' he said to Ruby. 'But don't do anything without asking first.'

'You can stay here and help if you like?' shouted Ruby as Jones started walking back to the house. 'You could take one of those special Badlander tonics like I'm going to do, so I can do some scrying now. Don't you remember, you made me drink some tonic once to stop feeling tired before we took on the Witch and freed your parents?'

'I'm going home,' he said. 'Back to where I belong. I should be asleep like a normal kid in the middle of the night.'

Thomas Gabriel left too, returning home to see if he could find out anything about the Cutter from his extensive library of books.

The full-length scrying mirror stood in a room of its own. Jones had given it to Ruby some months ago. It had been a present, his way of saying thank you to her for rescuing his parents from Mrs Easton, the Witch.

The casing surrounding the mirror was made from oak, which had been stained a deep red colour. Jones had told Ruby he'd immediately thought of her when he'd seen the mirror in Deschamps & Sons, the department store that sold all sorts of things that Badlanders used.

Ruby loved it. Not only was it a generous present, but, whenever she was in its presence, she felt a tingle in her hands and wanted to use it. After arriving in the Badlands, Ruby had discovered her gift for scrying very early on. Victor Brynn had told her that her talent for it was better than some Badlanders who'd spent years learning the art. Sometimes she wondered if her ability was to do with being a girl.

Ruby rubbed the glass with a special cloth to remove dust and dirt, allowing 'the best possible scrying experience' according to the brochure that had come with the mirror.

There was a premium polish too, a limited edition made with exotic oils and plants with long names given in both Latin and Anglo-Saxon that Ruby could not pronounce.

Having sipped some rather nasty-tasting tonic, her mind was much brighter and more awake, and Ruby had no trouble thinking about the man and the boy, Wilfried. Suddenly, there they were in the mirror as if she had flicked a switch to turn on a television.

They were sitting in what looked like a luxurious van, with black leather seats and wooden panelling lining the dashboard and the doors. The man was driving with the boy in the passenger seat. They were silent as the headlights pierced the dark road ahead. Sometimes a vehicle came the other way, lighting them up, making them seem to grow suddenly in their seats.

Wilfried was hunched over, writing in a leather-bound notebook. The pages of the book glowed, giving off just enough light to write by. Ruby asked the mirror to focus in on what he was writing and she saw a crude drawing of the Snarl with a brief description next to it, detailing how the creature had been overcome. There was a stick figure too in one corner, with the words 'girl' and a small diary entry below. As Ruby read the short paragraph, she realized it was about her and felt reassured to know her plan had worked – they believed she had been eaten by the Slobbering, meaning she'd got away without raising suspicion.

She spent the next hour or so watching the two Badlanders. It was pretty boring, with little conversation, although there seemed to be a cool tension between them that surfaced occasionally. Ruby noticed it first when the man snapped at the boy for dropping a bag of pear drops, even though it was his fault for turning a corner too fast. There were other times too, such as when the boy dropped his pen or when he moved his feet clumsily and accidentally kicked the inside of the passenger door. Eventually, the man told Wilfried to close his notebook because he found the light from the pages annoying.

Ruby had almost dozed off when the crunch of gravel, followed by the zip of a handbrake, made her sit up. The van's engine cut out and there was a moment's silence. The interior light clicked on as the doors opened.

Wilfried and his Master were clearly very disciplined. Instead of going straight to bed, even though it was early morning, they brought in everything they needed from the van first. It was a different type of vehicle to the camper van that Jones and Maitland had used. It was much bigger and roomier with a bathroom and a kitchen. There was even a kind of living room with a soft leather sofa in the shape of a 'U'.

The man and the boy still didn't speak much, being too busy unloading, but eventually, when they were finished, they sat down in the kitchen and drank a cup of tea.

The man cleared his throat and seemed ready to get something off his mind. 'Losing the girl was a black mark against you, Wilfried.'

'But sir—'

The man raised his hand and the boy stopped speaking.

The two of them sat silently for a while. And then the boy spoke again.

'Do I still have a chance of Commencement, sir?'

The man took a sip of tea and then set down his cup in its saucer.

'For the moment, yes. You're young. It's human nature to fail. Everyone does. But it's the mark of a Badlander to learn from their mistakes. I'll be watching out for that.

'You're to be up early in just a few hours and attend to your chores as usual. I will go to see the Cutter after breakfast, which you will make for me in the usual way. Shall we say nine o'clock?'

Ruby stood up and stretched. The image in the mirror vanished. It was time for bed. The tonic she'd taken was wearing off and she was now desperately tired after everything that had happened over the course of the night. She was feeling sad and very emotional about Victor Brynn too and she knew her exhaustion wasn't helping her mood at all.

After returning home, Ed had lain in his bed for some time, unable to sleep. The magic had kept him awake to begin with, telling him how good he'd been at conjuring up the *fengnett* with Ruby. The voice had sounded stronger, as if his visit back to the Badlands had energized it.

You're a natural, Jones.

You should go back and live in the Badlands with Ruby.

You could mentor her now Victor Brynn's gone.

Ed had put his pillow over his head at first. Then burrowed down deep under his sheets. But he couldn't get away from the voice until, finally, it stopped of its own accord, like a candle that had been blown out.

But, even so, he couldn't sleep after that. In the silence, he became aware of something waking up in him, like a cat stretching after a long sleep. He wasn't sure what it was at first. But it didn't take long to work out what it was. It was a sense of pride. He had done something good tonight, by taking out the Vampire, because he had made the world a little safer.

Ed felt a glow inside that warmed him. He hadn't felt so proud of himself for a long time. Not, in fact, since he'd been an apprentice to Maitland, working to make the world less dangerous for people. Ordinary boys in their ordinary lives could never do something that mattered so much. And Ed thought about that. His head became so full of thinking, it felt like someone was turning a handle, churning out thought ... after ... thought ... after ... thought.

In the end, Ed got up, dressed and left the house. He slipped into the dark street and his senses came alive because he was back in the Badlands now, creeping through the dark where anything dangerous could be lurking. Ed crossed over the road to the row of derelict houses and wrenched open an old, warped door.

He walked around the house for some time, inspecting each room, looking for signs of any creature living there. The longer he stayed, the more he remembered the telltale signs to watch out for, like strange patches of cold air floating in a room that could suggest the presence of a *gliderunge*. Or glistening marks that might appear on damp walls if you breathed on them, indicating an infestation of hammer beetles. Or how to listen for Clampet Trolls living under the floorboards.

A part of him felt ashamed for returning so readily to his old ways, but another part of him secretly enjoyed it too because, after living for some months as an ordinary boy, he had remembered how important being a Badlander was. He wasn't sure when he'd forgotten that.

It was almost morning by the time he crept back into his house and climbed into bed. He fell asleep as soon as his head touched the pillow.

He dreamt about meeting the Cutter, a tall man with knives for hands, who sliced him into two boys. One, called Jones, returned to the Badlands, happily hunting creatures there because he was good at it. The other, Ed, lived with his parents, slowly making friends and going to school, no different to anyone else. The Cutter told him that it was the only way for him to live now that he was a boy with two names who wanted to be two different people.

In the end, Ed woke up breathless and wrapped in his sheets, frightened and confused.

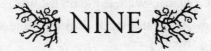

NINE

R uby felt sorry for Wilfried as she sat watching him in the scrying mirror the next morning. The scrambled eggs he'd made were just how his Master liked them and the coffee was to his taste as well, judging by the way the man wolfed his breakfast down. But he was still hard on the boy, scolding him by finding fault in things where there was none. Ruby watched him point at dirt on the floor where there wasn't any, and tap the rim of a china cup that was most likely chipped decades before. The man even complained about the spray of wild flowers on the kitchen table that had drooped in the vase.

Ruby watched Wilfried absorb these comments like they were arrows and Ruby shouted at the man once or twice. He couldn't hear, of course. But it made her feel better.

'Ruby, Masters are supposed to be hard on their apprentices. It toughens them up,' said the gun, lying on the floor beside the scrying mirror.

'Victor Brynn wasn't. He was right about the Order needing to change. It's full of ambitious men being horrible to kids. No wonder Jones wanted to be an ordinary boy.'

'Why are you so keen on being a Badlander then?'

Ruby picked at a thread that had come loose in the seam of her old black jeans. 'Well, using magic was pretty high on the list at first. And using cool stuff too, like weapons and things that are charmed.'

'Like me, you mean?'

'I suppose so, yes. But it's not just about that anymore or even wanting to be the first girl Badlander. It's about making the Order understand it needs to change. That would be a good thing to do, right? In memory of Victor Brynn?' Ruby swallowed down something that seemed to have got stuck in her throat and said nothing else.

The gun was quiet for a while as it thought about what she'd said.

'If Victor Brynn thought you could do it then perhaps you will. You just need to believe in yourself, Ruby, the way he did.'

Ruby nodded. 'I was hoping you'd say something like that.'

When the two Badlanders had finished breakfast, Wilfried was banished to the garden to weed and pick various herbs. His Master went to his study, and plucked a black leather book from the shelves and sat down at his desk, pulling a black pencil out of a pot.

Ruby leant forward, cross-legged on the floor like a frog about to spring, keen to see what he might do next.

But the man didn't write anything. Instead, he drew the

picture of a key. The drawing was simple, the only details a series of curly runes that ran along the stem. He tipped the book upside down, shaking it hard until a real key fell from the page and clattered onto the table.

'It's an Imagining Book,' said the gun, sounding excited. 'Anything you draw becomes real. It's very rare. He must be high-ranking, like you said. What do you think the key's for?'

Ruby shook her head as the man in the mirror inspected the key carefully. When he seemed satisfied, he ripped out the page with the drawing still on it and balled it up and then walked over to the open fireplace opposite his desk. After dropping it into the empty hearth, he raised a hand and flashed a white spark out of a finger that hit the ball of paper causing it to burst into flames.

Returning to the desk, he picked up the key and approached a large painting on the wall that reached from the floor to the ceiling. The background of the picture featured a rolling landscape of green hills under a bright blue sky. There were houses of varying sizes dotted about, with the smaller ones painted a long way into the background. The smallest ones were barely more than tiny squares with twirls of smoke drifting out of chimneys on a hill. In the foreground of the painting stood two large Trolls, one on either side, painted almost life-size given how large the picture was. Their grey, scaly hands were raised as if ready to reach out of the picture and grab hold of whoever might be close by.

The man stood quite still as the creatures in the image

started to move and lean forward, their noses popping out through the canvas. They sniffed the air and then, seemingly satisfied, shrank back into the picture. As soon as they had stopped moving, the man held up the key and presented it to the front door of a small house on the left of the picture. There was nothing to distinguish it from any of the other buildings, but, as he held up the key to the canvas, the picture seemed to scroll forward, bringing the background closer and closer until the frame was filled with the life-size front door of the house. The man pushed the key into the lock and turned it. There was a click and the door opened inwards as the man turned the handle and pushed.

Ruby couldn't see clearly what was beyond the door, but there seemed to be a corridor with stone walls and candlelight flickering across them. The man stepped through the doorway and disappeared inside. But the scrying mirror did not move forward with him.

'Follow him, Ruby!' said the gun.

'I can't. Something's stopping me.'

'A charm, you think?'

Ruby nodded. All she could do was sit back and wait. When the picture returned to normal, she leant forward and saw that the door of the house through which the man had disappeared was still open.

She stood up and went closer to the mirror and studied the Trolls in the picture, going nose to nose with them.

'Careful,' whispered the gun. 'They're Brute Trolls.'

'They can't see or hear us,' said Ruby. But, as she looked

past their wrinkled snouts into their murky green eyes, she thought she saw something looking back and took a few paces back. The creatures looked big enough to snap her in two.

After a couple of minutes, the picture rushed forward again and the man reappeared, stepping through the door and back into the study. He shut the door behind him and locked it. The house shrank back into the background of the picture again until it was indistinguishable from all the others. He glanced at the picture to check all was as it should be before tossing the key into the hearth and setting fire to it with some conjured white sparks. He watched it flare up and melt away. Before he left the study, the man picked up the black Imagining Book from the desk and put it back on the shelf from where he had taken it and then closed the door behind him.

Nothing stirred. And then the room disappeared from the mirror, leaving Ruby staring at her reflection because she had decided not to follow the man. One of the rules of scrying, she had learnt early on, was that she could only scry on someone she had met before or on a place she had actually visited. Without the man in the room, the mirror could no longer connect to the study.

Ruby sat silently.

'Well?' asked the gun.

'I'm thinking.'

'Hard work, is it?'

Ruby sighed. 'With you in the same room, yes.'

'We could brainstorm.'

'You're a gun.'

'A gun with ideas.'

Ruby sighed again.

'We're clearly meant to be a team.'

'Is that so?'

'The way the *wyrd*'s gone with Maitland and now Victor Brynn, the universe obviously wants us to work together.'

'Does it?'

'Of course. So what do you think about taking a closer look at that picture? Although I don't know what we can do about that strange key. We're stumped with that.'

'You might be.'

'Ah, so we've got a plan then.'

Ruby paused and took a deep breath. She smiled. 'Yes, we have. Ready?'

'I suppose so, but about this key—'

'*We've* got a plan, remember?'

Ruby tucked the gun into her waistband and picked up a bottle of Slap Dust and emptied some dust into her hand. She asked to go to the room she had just seen, then banged her hands together and vanished.

*

The room smelt of pine and polish and in the distance she could hear the sound of Wilfried and his Master working in the garden together. Ruby hoped that they would stay outside long enough for her to do what she needed to.

She looked over at the picture on the wall, studying the

two Trolls carefully. Although nothing about them seemed unusual, she took the gun out of her waistband before plucking up the courage to take a step closer when . . .

'Stop!' hissed the gun.

Ruby wobbled on one leg. 'What's the matter?'

'A charmed picture only comes alive when you get close enough to it.'

'How do you know?'

'Because I've seen them before. If a picture like that came alive every time someone came into the room those Trolls would be hopping out constantly. They'd have been onto you as soon as you arrived.'

Ruby stood still, watching the Trolls for any flicker of movement. Still there was nothing. Heeding the gun's advice, she turned round and walked to the bookshelves, and ran her fingers down the various spines until she found the black Imagining Book. She took it to the desk and sat down, opening it to the first page just as the man had done. It was blank. Nothing but the finest, crisp white paper. Ruby took a black pencil from the pot on the desk and held it above the page. But instead of trying to draw anything she started to shade the paper lightly, colouring it in. As the page filled with a grey sheen, the outline of a key began to emerge, exact in every detail where the man had pressed down on the previous sheet of paper.

With the shape of the key revealed, Ruby began to trace it, her hand as steady as she could make it. She found it was easy enough following the groove of the lines with the tip of the pencil. Even the runes on the stem could be copied. Finally satisfied with what she'd done, Ruby inspected her work. But, as she admired it, she looked up suddenly, as she realized she could no longer hear the *snip* of shears or the *ping* of stones coming from outside.

She gave a little gasp when she heard voices in the house.

Ruby picked up the book and turned it upside down. She shook it as the man had done. But nothing happened. No key fell out. She shook harder. Something started to emerge, like it was popping out of a mould. One end of the key, the toothy end, dropped down. But the rest of it didn't appear. Ruby kept shaking the book as she heard footsteps. Short and clipped.

Ruby took the end of the key, which felt lukewarm like a freshly baked loaf, and pulled it from the page. It was even at first, but gnarled further down, with the bow end of the key misshapen and ugly. The smell of hot metal prickled her nose and she tried not to sneeze.

Ruby tore out the page and closed the Imagining Book. Then she was up as quickly as possible. She placed the black book back on the shelf and turned to the painting.

Closer and closer came the footsteps.

There was nowhere for Ruby to go except home. So she clamped the key between her teeth and quickly found some Slap Dust in her pocket. She vanished just as the door to the study opened.

Ruby arrived breathless back in her room and stood for a moment, waiting for her blood to cool down. She was biting so hard on the key, the muscles in her face were vibrating. Only when she'd relaxed and taken the key out of her mouth and gathered her breath, did she dare conjure up the study, using her mirror, which was easy to do now she'd been there. The two Trolls in the picture on the wall were still standing guard on either side. Spokes of sunlight poked through the window behind the desk, lighting spots on the red carpet.

The man was leafing through a large book he'd plucked from the shelves. As he did so, Wilfried walked slowly into the doorway and stood with his head bowed. When his Master found what he wanted, he thrust the book at the boy.

'That's the way to pick marjoram,' he said, stabbing at the page. 'Go and give it some more practice.'

Wilfried nodded and walked out.

'Lunch in an hour!' his Master shouted after him. 'And I'd like you to make sure the van's packed with enough supplies for at least a few days' travel. We're going back to look at that Ley Line again, but before that we're off to an abbey tonight. St Anselm's. We've got some business there for the Order. I want the van stocked with lots of rosemary and salt, as well as jars of Silver Fire before we leave this afternoon. The abbey has a reputation for *Wihta* so we need to be prepared.'

TEN

Ed hadn't heard the magic speaking to him all day. At first, it had felt wonderful not to have the voice distracting him, especially because it was a Sunday meaning he had time to himself to play on his computer and watch television. But, as the hours wore on, he realized the magic wasn't saying anything because it didn't need to. His own thoughts were bubbling inside him after spending a bit of time the night before on his own in the Badlands. The magic knew, like he did, that ordinary life seemed a little different now. Further away somehow. As if someone had put a friendly arm round his shoulder and walked him backwards a few metres to give him a different view.

'Okay, love?' asked his mum when he came downstairs.

'Sure.'

But his glass of milk tasted a little sour and the cookies he munched didn't seem as crunchy as usual.

'Guess what?' said his mum as she put on her coat to go out. Ed smiled and shook his head. 'Your father and I are planning a big summer holiday. All three of us. Somewhere hot with lots of fun things to do.' She opened a brochure and tapped the page. 'See. There's waterskiing, sailing, snorkelling . . .'

Ed looked at the glossy pages full of smiling people having fun.

'Looks amazing,' he said.

'You don't sound so sure. We can go always somewhere else.'

Ed blinked. 'No, it seems great. I'm . . . it's all just a bit new, that's all.'

'Course it is.' She kissed him hard on the head. 'I've got to pop out. Marie's got "man" problems again,' she said, rolling her eyes. 'Wants a chat, as usual. You okay on your own for a bit? Dad's out too.' Ed nodded.

'Don't forget, it's family movie night. You're choosing the film, remember, so get cracking.'

'I know.'

He sat on his own at the table, thinking about school and holidays and his mum's friend Marie, who he'd met a few times and was all lipstick and bouncy blonde hair and big teeth. His mum's perfume lingered in the air like an afterthought and Ed reminded himself just how terrible it would be to lose her and his father if Thomas Gabriel was found out by the High Council. But there was a nagging feeling he'd lost something irreplaceable in return for his new life. Leaving the Badlands had left a small hole in him he couldn't fill.

Ed was thinking so hard that when a jar suddenly appeared on the kitchen table, containing a handwritten message, he almost bit his tongue in two. He knew it was from Ruby because he recognized the handwriting.

I only scryed on you for a moment!
  We're going to see what we can find out about the Cutter.
  Wanna come? In the sitting room if you do.

Ed drummed his fingers on the table, taking a minute to think about what to do. In the end, he went to fetch his emergency bottle of Slap Dust from the drawer in his bedroom.

After arriving at the cottage, he found Ruby and Thomas Gabriel in the sitting room as the note had said.

'Jones!' said Ruby, beckoning him over to the large ring of Slap Dust sprinkled on the floor. But the boy said nothing as he stood looking around, wondering if he'd done the right thing. Suddenly, he wasn't sure.

'Jones?' He looked at Ruby like a startled bird. 'Are you okay?'

'I think so.'

'You look . . .'

'Confused,' said Jones, nodding.

'About what?'

Jones bit his lip. He felt too embarrassed to tell them how special he knew being a Badlander was, given how much he had always gone on about wanting to be an ordinary boy.

'Being here brings back too many memories,' was all he said and pointed at the mantelpiece. 'Maitland used to check that with his finger every day to see if I'd cleaned it.'

'If it's so difficult being back, why did you come then?' asked the gun.

Jones scowled. 'Cos it sounded important. We need to find out about this person the Cutter, don't we? What have you found out so far? I've got to get back home for movie night later, you know.'

The problem was, Ruby couldn't tell him much. Nothing about the secret room beyond the picture. Not even the name of the Badlander she'd been scrying on or where his house was located. Which meant all three of them had to travel there together, guided by Ruby.

'Ready?' she asked when they were standing inside the ring of Slap Dust. The boys nodded. Ruby closed her eyes and thought of where she wanted to go and there was the sound of the Slap Dust fizzing.

Thomas Gabriel looked around the study. In the late afternoon sunlight coming in through the window, he recognized where he was immediately and he didn't like it. Not one bit.

'This is Randall Givens's house,' he hissed. The other two looked blankly at him.

'You've been here before?' asked Jones.

'Yes! Givens is my mentor. I came to visit him when he took me on. He's the one assessing my magical ability. And he's the one who gave me this.' Thomas Gabriel took out the ticking invitation from his pocket and waggled it in the air. 'We have to leave. Now!'

'Calm down,' said Ruby. 'Givens isn't here. He left with his apprentice at least an hour ago.'

'Calm down?' Thomas Gabriel managed to say. 'This man is the head of the High Council. If he knows I'm in his house without his permission, he'll throw me out of the Order straightaway. He'll say I'm not fit to be a Badlander.'

Ruby patted Thomas Gabriel reassuringly on the shoulder. 'He won't find out we were ever here.'

'Do you really think someone like Givens is going to leave his house unguarded when he's away?' replied Thomas Gabriel.

A sudden **BANG!** from upstairs made him flinch. 'See! We need to go!'

'We need to stay! We have to get into the secret room that's behind the picture,' hissed Ruby, pointing at it.

Ruby glared at Thomas Gabriel and he glared back. And then they heard the sound of laughter and the patter of feet. Jones put his ear to the study door and listened and then he opened it, peering carefully into the hallway. The laughter grew louder.

Jones turned and grinned at the others. 'Imps,' he said. 'It's just naughty imps.'

Thomas Gabriel put his head round the door and saw a large group of imps at the bottom of the wide staircase. They were eating and drinking, watching as two brave imps came surfing down the stairs on tea trays, arms out, knees bobbling with the bumps and trying to keep upright. Half the crowd cheered and the other half groaned as one imp came crashing down, the empty tea tray squirting up into the air and landing on top of it.

Thomas Gabriel took a breath. Adjusted his collar.

'What on earth is going on?' he bellowed, striding out into the hallway. He was greeted with nothing but silence. Pairs of red eyes looked up at him and then all the imps looked down at the floor in unison. Thomas Gabriel felt emboldened by that so he crossed his arms and turned up his voice another notch.

'As some of you may know, I'm under the mentorship of Mr Givens.' Thomas Gabriel twirled some white sparks round his fingers to make the point, hoping they wouldn't go droopy and fade away.

Whispers travelled round the imps in front of him.

'So!' said Thomas Gabriel. 'Who's going to tell me what's going on here?'

It didn't take long to get to the bottom of what was happening. A group of imps had discovered the charm on their jar had come loose a few months ago and, whenever Givens was away, the imps had let themselves out. It had only been a matter of time before they'd started letting the others out too. Having the run of the house meant they'd disabled all the alarms and magical devices designed to alert Givens to any intruders. All in all, the situation had worked rather well for Thomas Gabriel and the others, although they were never going to admit it to the imps.

'I won't tell on you this time . . .' he announced and all the imps breathed a sigh of relief. But he made sure all of them returned to their jars and the lids were screwed on tight. As a punishment, he made a small group of them take him round the house and show him all the magical devices and alarms that had been disabled as well as how to turn them on again when he left.

While Thomas Gabriel sorted out the imps, Jones and Ruby had time to study the picture on the wall. She pulled Jones back when he started walking towards it.

'The gun said it'll come to life if someone gets close enough,' she warned him.

Jones nodded and sucked in his lips. 'Tell me what you saw again, how Givens made it work.'

'He went right up to the picture and the Trolls came alive. They let him open a door with the key he had, just like this one.' Ruby took out the key she'd made. It looked more ugly and misshapen than she remembered. She ran her fingers over the disfigured end and then inspected the toothy shape of the bit, wondering if it would work. 'Well, sort of like this one.'

Jones examined the key, turning it through his fingers.

'Will it work, Jones?'

'It ain't the key I'm worried about. It's them Trolls.'

Jones looked up at the picture again and Ruby realized what he must be thinking.

'They'll only let Givens open the door, won't they? So that means we're not getting in.'

'Maybe we can if we can make a good enough *fæcce* of Givens to fool them.'

108

'Don't we need magic for that?'

'There's other ways to make a *fæcce*.'

'Oh, I thought—'

'When I cast the spell to catch the Vampire the other night, the magic was louder than ever after I got home. I couldn't sleep.'

'But if we find the Cutter and he solves your magic problem and mine, it'll be worth it, won't it?'

'Maybe, but I'm an ordinary boy and ordinary boys don't use magic.'

'Come on, Jones.'

'No. We'll make a *fæcce* without magic. Everything we need is bound to be here.'

It didn't take long to find things they could use to make the *fæcce*. Ruby pulled out black strands of hair from a brush lying on the dressing table in Givens's bedroom. There were some nail clippings in the bin too. Meanwhile, Jones shook out some unwashed shirts over a sheet and collected white flakes of skin and more strands of hair.

As they worked to collect what little pieces they could of Givens, Thomas Gabriel looked through the various potions and mixtures on the shelves in the cellar. When he found what he was looking for, a jar of yellow crystals and one full of a red powder, he took them upstairs and began to run a bath.

As he swirled the crystals into the water, turning it bright yellow, he tried not to think about the magic inside him dissolving into nothing too. He whispered a little prayer asking for the *wyrd* to be kind to him and grant what he wanted most in the world: to find this man called the Cutter who could help him right his Commencement.

'I'll be a good Badlander,' he said as the water stilled and he saw a hazy reflection of himself in the yellow surface. 'I just need the chance to prove it.' There was no time to say anything else as Ruby and Jones arrived with the parts of Givens they'd managed to find, and he gave the water a swirl again, making his face vanish.

After everything had been dropped into the bath, Thomas Gabriel held the jar of red powder over the water.

'I hope this works,' he said. 'Making a *fæcce* like this isn't the best way.'

'Told you we should've used magic,' said Ruby, punching Jones playfully on the arm.

'Pour all the powder in. It's bound to work then,' said Jones rather curtly and he glared at Ruby.

The water turned red instantly. It bubbled and foamed, giving off small plumes of steam. Suddenly, a light flashed so brightly it left red splotches inside their eyelids each time they blinked. When the water turned black, Jones leant forward eagerly.

'Here we go,' he said.

He pointed at a set of fingers as they reached up out of the water, dripping as they flexed and clawed at the air, pale and weak at first. But the more they wiggled, the stronger they became.

It took a couple of minutes for the head and torso of the *fæcce* to emerge. It sat up in the bath, panting from the effort, its black hair plastered across its head. It was a sickly-looking version of Givens. So pale, in fact, that its skin was grey, the colour of soggy cardboard.

'It doesn't look great,' whispered Thomas Gabriel. 'It might not last very long.'

'Let's get it moving then,' said Jones.

He gave the *fæcce* a towel and beckoned to it to stand up. Its movements were jerky, similar to the way a puppet might move if it had come to life, but it soon got the hang of moving more naturally.

The boys dressed the *fæcce* in clothes from Givens's wardrobe as quickly as they could. Once dressed, the creature seemed to have a more human air about it.

'You're a man,' Jones told it.

'You're Randall Givens,' said Thomas Gabriel. 'A very important person.'

'How have I become so important?' asked the *fæcce* in a rather croaky voice.

'You've done lots of important things.'

'I don't remember them.'

'That doesn't mean they didn't happen.'

The *fæcce* opened its mouth and then shut it. Ruby saw something drip from its scalp. One of its ears slipped a little.

'Come on,' said Jones, leading it quickly out of the bedroom. 'We need you to do something for us.'

Negotiating the stairs wasn't easy, but eventually they made their way to the door of Givens's study and Ruby gave the creature the key she'd made and told it what to do before pushing open the door.

The *fæcce* walked towards the picture and the Trolls on either side came to life and lunged forward out of the canvas to sniff the air. Ruby, Jones and Thomas Gabriel watched through the doorway, hoping the Trolls would be fooled. And then the two creatures in the painting nodded at each other and slipped back into the picture, their arms folded. Their murky green eyes watched with some contempt as the children dared to come closer, but the Trolls didn't say anything or try to grab them.

The *fæcce* reached out with the key towards the picture. Everything on the canvas started moving and the small house in the background shot forward until it filled the frame. Then the *fæcce* pushed the key into the lock of the door that now loomed in front of them.

With a click, the door unlocked and swung open. Ruby and the others peered down a corridor, hewn out of rock, lit by candles flickering at intervals in brackets fixed to the walls. The smell of damp stone was in the air and they could hear the sound of water *drip-dripping* somewhere in the darkness. The bobbly stone walls ran all the way down to a left turn just visible about a hundred metres away.

'After you,' said Jones, holding out his hand to the *fæcce* and urging it forward. It smiled, causing its lips to wobble.

Jones worried they might fall off, but they held firm and then the *fæcce* led them down the corridor, creeping through the shadows, and past the wimpling walls as the candles flickered.

The *fæcce*'s head had already begun to look slightly lumpy on one side, and the dim light made it appear even worse, more potato-shaped than human-like.

'We need to be as quick as we can,' whispered Thomas Gabriel to the others. 'Once that *fæcce* falls apart, it won't fool the Trolls any more and we could have a problem as soon as we come back into the study.'

Jones nodded in agreement and started walking faster. Ruby quickened up too and grabbed the *fæcce* by the hand and hurried it on, wary of pulling too hard and causing any damage.

They turned left at the end of the corridor and walked towards a large room, which looked like it could have been a crypt or a tomb. More candles flickered, throwing shadows round the walls, which glistened with damp, and highlighting patches of emerald green slime. Water was dripping somewhere.

In the middle of the room was a white marble pedestal and on it sat a head with its eyes closed. It was perfectly preserved, not shrunken or sallow. Although the face was old and lined, there was a healthy colour in the cheeks and the lips were red and plump. The nose and the ears were large, out of proportion, reminding Ruby how old people's faces always seemed to grow bigger in certain places but not in others. Hair sprouted out of the ears like white wire.

Water kept dripping. *Plip-plop*. It was cold.

Ruby, Jones and Thomas Gabriel looked at each other, unsure what to do. And then the head opened its eyes.

# ELEVEN

The head blinked like a bird, confused at first. And then it glanced at the *fæcce* and sighed wearily under its breath.

'Whatever torture you've got planned for me this time, Givens, I'm not telling you what you want to know. What makes you think I'll change my tune after two hundred years of being here?'

'I ... we ...'

Ruby stepped forward as the *fæcce* continued to stutter over its words, unsure what to say, and cleared her throat. 'This isn't Givens. It's a *fæcce*.'

The head frowned.

'We're not here to hurt you.'

The head gave a chuckle, which grew into a great, guttural laugh.

'Oh, very good, Givens. This is good! You've conjured up a girl to help twist my mind around. Now that is novel.'

'She ain't made up, she's real,' said Jones, stepping forward. 'And she's telling the truth.' But the head didn't seem to notice the boy as it whispered excitedly to itself. So he stepped even closer. 'We're here to ask for your help,' he said, raising his voice. 'We've heard you're skilled in sorting out magic.'

The head blinked at him, suddenly serious and frowning in concentration. Its tongue darted out between the lips as if trying to get a better sense of Jones by tasting the air around him. 'Hmm,' it said. 'Got a problem with magic, have you?' Jones nodded. The eyes in the head flickered as they looked him up and down and then the head pouted as if in admiration of the boy. 'Interesting to see a Commencement go wrong like that. Very rare. Very rare,' it repeated, as if in conversation with itself. 'What happened to the rest of the magic? Where did it go? Got lost, did it?'

Ruby raised her hand. 'I got it.'

The head looked genuinely surprised for a moment and then it grinned. 'Now I wasn't expecting that! Never in all my days. First, a *fæcce* and now a girl claiming to have magic.' It laughed and tutted to itself. 'What a day!'

Then the head looked at Thomas Gabriel. 'What about you? Have you brought me something too, some rare occurrence for me to ponder whilst I pass the time imprisoned here? Step closer, boy! Stop hanging back there in the shadows of this wretched light.'

Thomas Gabriel took a few stuttering steps forward only for the head to sniff the air before screwing up its face and sighing. 'No, nothing new at all. I've met your like before, ones who wanted magic when they weren't supposed to have it. You stole your magic, didn't you? Ripped the key from your Master's neck no doubt and forced your Commencement. So now the magic's rotting inside you.'

Thomas Gabriel bristled. He stood up as straight as he could. 'I *was* supposed to have it because I'm meant to be a great Badlander. And I'll do anything you want if you can help me keep my magic so I can prove it.'

The head laughed. 'That's the spirit! I was like you once. Young and full of ambition.'

'Who are you?' asked Jones.

'I am Augustus Drewman. Or at least what's left of me is.'

Thomas Gabriel took a few steps back, clasping his hand to his chest like some bad actor on the stage.

'Sir, I didn't mean to insult you. I didn't—'

'Augustus Drewman's supposed to be dead,' said Jones.

'And I might prefer it if I was,' said the head.

'Sorry, but who exactly are you?' asked Ruby.

'Augustus Drewman was one of the greatest Badlanders ever,' Thomas Gabriel told her in a hushed voice. 'He's killed more creatures than anyone else in the Badlands.'

'Go on,' said Drewman. 'What else do they say about me?'

There was a moment of uncomfortable silence as Jones and Thomas Gabriel looked at one another, then Jones cleared his throat.

'Augustus Drewman turned bad with magic. It changed his brain to mush and sent him mad,' he said. 'He died over two hundred years ago.'

The head laughed. 'If only! At least then I'd be spared this miserable existence. That's just the story the Order created to keep apprentices in line, to give Masters bedtime stories to tell their boys and strike fear into their hearts.' The head licked its lips. The rickety teeth in its mouth were stained the colour of tea. 'Do you want to know what really happened?'

Jones nodded. So did the others.

'I became so powerful that the higher members of the Order grew jealous. So they set upon me and brought me to this place to make me tell them how I was able to manipulate magic so successfully.'

'What *was* your secret?' piped up the gun in Ruby's hand.

'The Black Amulet,' said Drewman, smiling as if picturing the object in front of his eyes.

'Never heard of it,' said the gun. 'This old fool's gone crazy. Who knows how long he's been in here. He's wasting our time.' The others looked at each other and Jones shook his head.

'I've never heard of the Black Amulet either.'

'Nor me,' said Thomas Gabriel.

'Very few have,' continued Drewman. 'I found it in the ruins of an old hill fort overrun with Wraiths. How it came to be there I don't know, but I've always suspected it was made by the Wraiths I killed. The amulet enhanced my magic, but it's dangerous. It works using *áglæccræft*. Even though I resisted the power of the amulet using bitter potions, it started tearing my heart and mind apart eventually, encouraging me to do things no man should

118

do. When I saw how dangerous it really was, I hid it away where no one would ever find it before it destroyed me or anyone else.'

'So that's what the Order wanted?' asked Jones.

'Yes, but when I wouldn't tell them where it was they combined their magic into one powerful spell and split my body apart. My arms and legs and torso were taken away and hidden, leaving only my head imprisoned here. But I'll never give up the amulet to the Order. It's not for men like Givens. It's not meant for any man.'

'Can you really cut magic out of people?' asked Jones. 'Sort out Commencements that have gone wrong?'

'Yes, I have that skill, but not without the rest of me. I need my body to perform such a rite.' It grinned. 'So that's why you're here?'

Jones nodded.

'I need the magic he's got to be a proper Badlander and cast spells,' said Ruby.

'You tell 'im, girl,' said the gun.

'I'm here to get my magic fixed too,' blurted out Thomas Gabriel. 'Or else I'll lose everything. We'll get you out of here and find the rest of you so you can help all of us.'

'Impossible,' said the head. 'There's a powerful hex keeping me here that I can't undo, let alone any of you. Pluck a hair from my head. Go on! Take a couple.'

Jones marched up to the pedestal and plucked two white hairs from the top of the head and held them between his finger and thumb.

'Good, now take them into the corridor. Go on.'

Jones did as instructed and walked towards the opening that led out of the room. As he moved closer to the door, the hairs begin to glow, each one sending up a winding trail of grey smoke. He stopped and looked back at Drewman.

'Keep going!' shouted the head. 'Any bit of me that leaves this chamber burns to ash. Let them burn down, but don't drop anything. You'll see why in a moment.'

So Jones carried on, the hairs between his thumb and finger held above his other cupped hand to catch anything that fell. When he stepped out of the room into the corridor, both hairs set alight like fuses and burnt down to a crisp in seconds, the black ash falling into the palm of his other hand.

'Now come back!' shouted Drewman. When Jones walked back into the chamber, the ash reconstituted itself into two white hairs lying across his hand. He stared at them, amazed.

'The Order keeps the rest of my body as ash somewhere outside this chamber. When they first put me here, they'd bring the other parts of me back in three golden boxes to make me whole again. Only then could I be tortured into telling the Order everything they wanted to know about the amulet. They said they'd release me if I did. But I kept saying no and eventually they stopped bringing the rest of my body and resorted to other means of breaking me over the years. Now, the most recent men to have risen up the Order prop my eyelids open for weeks sometimes so I have to look at myself in a large mirror to contemplate what I am. Recently, they've started using potions to break my mind. Givens is a master at mixing them. He makes me inhale them and sends my brain spinning off in all sorts of directions.'

'But not telling them means you'll be stuck here forever,' said Ruby.

The head sighed. 'Yes, it does.' Its voice sounded a little cracked and broken. 'But that's an idea I've had some time to get used to. Perhaps it's the price I've paid for all the power I once had.'

The head paused. Smiled. Started to laugh so hard it took an effort for Drewman to find enough breath to be able to speak again. 'But now I have an opportunity to get my own back.'

'I told you the old guy's lost it,' muttered the gun.

'How?' asked Jones, waving his hand to shut up the gun.

Drewman grinned, his eyes fixed on Ruby. 'Her! Did you know that before the Order was founded girls and women did magic too?' Ruby's eyes opened wide as she shook her head. 'But men took it away from them and made it their own when the Order was created. It's been kept a secret for centuries. Anyone who dares to mention it is expelled. Or worse. The Order's rotten. Always has been. Full of selfish men who think they're better than the ordinary people they've sworn to protect. I knew that even before they imprisoned me here. That's why I couldn't let them have the Black Amulet. And you, girl, you're the one who can shake them up. If I can give you what you want, you can change everything.'

'Someone else told me the same thing,' said Ruby, nodding. 'That I can make a difference.'

'Yes, you can and that's why I'll help you,' said Drewman. 'Find the three golden boxes containing the other parts of my body and bring them here to make me whole again. Do that and I'll correct your Commencement, make you an ordinary boy,' he said to Jones, 'and you an extraordinary girl.'

'You've got to help me too!' shouted Thomas Gabriel.

Drewman grinned. 'Yes, why not. Anything to annoy the Order. But you'll need to prove you're worthy of having magic.'

Suddenly, the *fæcce* let out a yelp. Everyone turned to see a little piece of its forehead fall away and splash to the floor. 'I'm melting!' it cried in a terrified voice, its fingers searching across its face to check what else was coming loose.

'We have to go,' said Thomas Gabriel. 'We have to leave now otherwise the Trolls will know it's not Givens.'

Ruby stepped in front of the head and stared in its eyes. Her insides felt twisted and tight after hearing what Drewman had said about women and magic. 'How do we find the rest of you?' she asked.

'The Black Amulet,' said Drewman. 'The Order have always taken great pleasure in assuring me that the boxes are so well hidden with magic they can never be found. But the amulet will fire up what magic there is inside each of you, and allow you to cast the spells you'll need, far better than any other Badlanders can. Use the amulet with caution, only when you must. Share it among you to prevent it taking hold of your hearts and minds. As long as you keep using it, take bitter potions to keep your heads clear and stop the amulet taking possession of your thoughts. And, most importantly of all, once you've found the rest of my body, you must hide the amulet somewhere it can never be found.'

'Where is it now?' asked Ruby as the *fæcce* yelped again. It was looking at its hand. The thumb was gathering into a great pink drop that was getting ready to fall off.

'You'll need a Moon Globe,' said Drewman. 'Then go to St Anselm's Abbey and look for the hidden door. Open it and you'll find the amulet.'

'Givens said he was going to an abbey,' said Ruby. 'Tonight.'

Drewman cursed under his breath. 'Are you sure, girl?'

Ruby nodded. 'St Anselm's Abbey. A place known for *Wihta*, he said.'

'Then there's no time to lose. If Givens is heading there, he may have finally worked out where the amulet is. He uses potions on me, confuses me. I can't remember half of what I've told him and perhaps he's been piecing it together one bit at a time. You must find the amulet before he does if you want me to correct your Commencements.'

Ruby nodded and then Jones was grabbing her and pulling her away. Thomas Gabriel was already ahead of them, helping the *fæcce* down the corridor, an arm looped round its waist.

When they arrived at the door back into Givens's study, they rushed through as fast as they could. The top half of the

123

fæcce's body was starting to sag, particularly the shoulders, which were becoming more and more rounded. The neck was starting to gather in little rolls.

But, with Thomas Gabriel keeping it upright and Jones shutting the door, the *fæcce* leant forward and pushed the key into the lock.

One of the Trolls poked its snout out of the picture and took a sniff, then, seemingly unconvinced, it sniffed the *fæcce* again and leant further out of the picture. The other Troll appeared too. They scrutinized the man that looked like Givens and for a moment no one said anything.

And then both Trolls slipped back into the picture and the image of the door began to recede.

Thomas Gabriel and Jones ushered the poor shaking *fæcce* out of the study as fast as they could. Ruby followed, avoiding the damp patches left on the carpet by the creature.

The boys managed to push the *fæcce* up the stairs, telling it everything would be okay once it returned to the bath it had come from. It kept nodding and seemed driven by some instinct towards the water, slipping into the cold bath without a thought.

As it ducked under, the last thing they saw was its smiling face as it broke apart, the grey-looking skin and the blue of its eyes dissolving. And then it was gone.

Jones grabbed the chain and yanked out the plug and the water started to gurgle away.

'There's only one place I know where we can find a Moon Globe fast,' he said.

'St Crosse College,' agreed Thomas Gabriel. 'Pindlebury's got one.'

'We need to go now,' said Ruby, 'if we're going to get the Moon Globe *and* still reach the abbey before Givens.' She went up to the bathroom mirror and stared at it, conjuring up a picture of Givens driving with his apprentice riding shotgun.

'Looks like they're still on their way.'

Jones checked his smart watch, which seemed so out of place in the Badlands because Badlanders didn't use anything like them.

'It's not even eight o'clock yet. However far away they are, they'll rest up in the van first until much later,' said Jones. 'They'll wanna make sure no one's about at the abbey. And they'll need to be as prepared as they can if there's *Wihta* there. That's what Maitland and I would have done.'

'Me and Simeon too,' agreed Thomas Gabriel. 'Meeting one *Wiht* would be bad enough, let alone lots of them.'

Ruby peered out of the bathroom window. It was a dark spring night now. The trees looked bare and bony in the moonlight. 'It's dark enough to use Slap Dust. Let's go!' As they took out their vials, Jones paused.

'What is it?' asked Thomas Gabriel. Jones looked at them.

'It's family movie night.'

'What on earth is that?' spluttered Thomas Gabriel.

'Jones, we need you,' said Ruby. 'Your parents will understand.'

'That ain't the point though, is it?' Jones bit the inside of his cheek as Ruby and Thomas Gabriel stared at him.

'Jones, this is your chance to get that magic out of you if we can find the amulet,' said Ruby.

And the boy didn't need long to think about that. 'Let's go then,' he said, nodding.

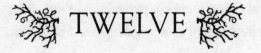

TWELVE

S t Crosse College looked the same as the last time Jones and the others had been there. In fact, thought Jones, as he stood, peering through the small side gate with Ruby and Thomas Gabriel, it had probably not changed at all over the last few hundred years. He could see why a Badlander might like it, safe and secure in the stone buildings and in rooms behind leaded windows, insulated from most of what went on outside in the world of regular people.

'It's all clear,' whispered Thomas Gabriel and they slapped their hands together and vanished, reappearing on the other side of the gate.

The quadrangle was bordered on all sides by an uneven path of cobbles worn smooth by the feet of students and academics over centuries. In the middle was a square of grass, pale green in the moonlight. Jones and the others crept quickly round the quadrangle, stopping at the bottom of each staircase to read the list of professors who had rooms in that area and a board showing who was 'in' or 'out' at that moment.

Ruby was the first one to see the name they were looking

for. 'Elgin Pindlebury' had the title 'Research Fellow' painted next to it and, according to the board, Pindlebury was currently 'in' his rooms. All three looked at each other with relief. They hadn't dared imagine Pindlebury not being there – they didn't know where else to find a Moon Globe – but it seemed their luck was in.

'So what's the plan?' whispered Ruby.

'Leave it to me,' said Thomas Gabriel, picking two glass vials out of his limitless pockets. He drank down the contents of the first vial. The second one he showed to Jones, who nodded after reading the label: Hurdy Gurdy.

'Stay here and keep a lookout.' Thomas Gabriel swept his herringbone coat around him and disappeared up the curling staircase. Ruby and Jones crept a little way up the stairs after him and sat down to wait.

'Jones, perhaps you should start wearing your overcoat again when you're with us.'

'Why?'

'Well.' Ruby shuffled her bottom on the cold steps. 'It might be useful. You'd have all your Badlander stuff you kept in the pockets.'

'Ruby, I'm not a Badlander.'

'I know, but it might make things easier. How about if you had your catapult? You're good with that.'

'I'm fine without it.'

'Yes, but—'

Jones put his finger to his lips, silencing Ruby. 'Yes, nothing. I don't need my overcoat or any of the things in it.

This is just temporary. I'm not a Badlander and I don't wanna talk about it no more.'.

When Thomas Gabriel arrived at the top floor, he saw the door he was after, with Pindlebury's name on it, and knocked briskly. A few moments later, a studious-looking man, round glasses perched on his nose, opened the door. He was dressed in a baggy green cardigan, a shirt and tie, and wore corduroy trousers the colour of gold.

'Yes?' said the man.

'Elgin Pindlebury?' asked Thomas Gabriel.

The man looked at him over the top of his glasses. 'And you are?'

'Thomas Gabriel, previously apprentice to Simeon Rowell. I wish to speak with you. It's important Badlander business. I don't have time to waste.'

'I'm afraid I don't know what you're talking about.'

'You don't need to pretend, Pindlebury. I know who you are. You're the Badlander Research Fellow here at St Crosse College. You spend your time researching creatures. Doing bookwork. Not exactly the type of dangerous life most Badlanders are used to.'

Thomas Gabriel peered in through the doorway and saw an old, comfortable sofa. Shelves of books. A desk in front of the window. A radio was turned down low, a piece of piano music burbling like running water. He tapped his foot because he was in a hurry to get this over with and return to the others.

Pindlebury pushed his glasses up his nose and stood up straighter, wrapping his cardigan round him. 'What do you want exactly, *boy*?'

'I might be young, but I've already Commenced. I'm working my way up the Order now.'

'Good for you.'

'I'm here at the behest of Randall Givens. He's my mentor.'

Pindlebury raised his eyebrows. 'Givens? What does he want?'

'If you'll let me in, I'll tell you. It's not the most private place here.'

Pindlebury studied the boy. 'Have we met before?' he asked. 'I feel like we have, but I can't quite place it.'

Thomas Gabriel shook his head. 'No, sir, I don't think so. I'd remember.' He tried not to smirk as he lied. He remembered perfectly the last time they'd met, of course. It had been a few months ago in the college chapel. The only reason Pindlebury didn't remember was because the boy had removed all memory of it.

'Yes, of course.' Pindlebury frowned as if still trying to place the boy. 'Very well, if Givens has sent you then I suppose you'd better come in.'

Thomas Gabriel sat on the sofa and started to give a very plausible explanation as to why Randall Givens had sent him. At least, Pindlebury seemed to accept it as he listened intently to the boy's description of a strange hybrid *Ent* that Givens had encountered on one of his hunting trips.

'It had three eyes, four arms, as well as a coat of red fur on its back.'

'Really?' Pindlebury seemed genuinely intrigued by the mystery creature as he asked the boy to describe it in more detail.

'Umm, there were scales on its arms. And it had a tail. Forked, I believe.'

Pindlebury stared at the boy and narrowed his eyes. 'You're having me on,' he said. 'Why are you really here?'

But by then it was too late.

Thomas Gabriel had already opened the vial of Hurdy Gurdy and released some of the clear vapour into the air, controlling the amount by opening and closing his thumb over the top like a valve. It was distilled from a variety of herbs and plants and Thomas Gabriel's former Master, Simeon Rowell, had been an expert at making it. He had passed his secret recipe onto his apprentice who always kept some in his pocket for emergencies, along with the antidote too, which he'd taken outside at the bottom of the stairs.

The Hurdy Gurdy made the air glisten gold in places, one of the clues that gave it away. But Pindlebury didn't seem to notice this. In fact, he didn't seem to notice much at all. The vapour had confused and befuddled him, and he sat blinking in his chair.

Thomas Gabriel checked the man's eyes and saw them dulled, with the telltale red dots in the pupils. Grabbing Pindlebury by the shoulders, Thomas Gabriel gave him a shake. Just enough to bring him to his senses.

'So, Pindlebury, tell me where you keep that Moon Globe of yours.'

The man grinned and raised his eyebrows.

'The Moon Globe is a special thing.'

'Yes, I know. That's why you have it.'

'Precisely.'

'So where is it?'

Pindlebury pointed to a small brown box on his desk. When Thomas Gabriel picked it up, he discovered it was locked.

'Where's the key?'

Pindlebury pointed to his mouth and tried to purse his lips, taking a moment to produce a short, rubbery-sounding note. 'It's a Whistle Lock. Only I can open it with a special tune. I'm very important, you know.'

Thomas Gabriel held up the box with the keyhole in front of the man's mouth. 'Open it.'

Pindlebury's tongue flapped like the tail of a dying fish as it poked through his lips and he tried to whistle. Thomas Gabriel started to worry that the Hurdy Gurdy was going to affect Pindlebury's whistling ability too much, but, after a couple of attempts, the lock clicked and the box opened. Inside was another locked box. Thomas Gabriel took it out and held it up to the man's mouth again, but this time Pindlebury shook his head and plucked a brown hair from his head. He pushed the hair into the lock and there was a click, the lid popping open.

Inside was the Moon Globe, a small orb illuminated from within by a pale light, sitting on a red velvet inlay. Thomas Gabriel smiled as he picked it up. He felt a coolness on his fingers that made them tingle.

'Careful with that,' said Pindlebury. 'It's special. Like me.'

Thomas Gabriel popped the Moon Globe into one pocket. He held up the vial of Hurdy Gurdy and let what was left in it out into the room.

'What's that?' asked Pindlebury.

'Hurdy Gurdy.'

'Hurdeeee . . . Gurdeeeee—'

Thomas Gabriel watched Pindlebury's eyelids flicker and close. As the man's chin came to rest on his chest, he started snoring.

When Jones and Ruby saw Thomas Gabriel come running down the stairs, they thought the worst at first. But, when he saw their worried faces, he held up the Moon Globe and its ghostly glow lit up the dark doorway to the quadrangle.

'We've got a few hours till he wakes up,' said Thomas Gabriel. 'Let's get to St Anselm's Abbey now!'

Ruby went across to a small framed notice – something to do with fire regulations. With a crease of her brow, she managed to scry on Givens by conjuring an image of him in the glass. He was sitting in his van, eating, with Wilfried. She blinked and the image disappeared. She nodded at the others. 'You were right,' she said. 'They've stopped to prepare. We can still get to the abbey before them.'

THIRTEEN

St Anselm's Abbey was just the bare bones of a place with only the ends of the building still standing. Each end framed huge archways with window shapes that must have been filled with glass once. Now the wind and the rain hurtled through them at will, making the ivy stuck to them hiss and flap. Blocks of weathered stone lay scattered over the grass. There were still walls rising out of the ground in various places, some of them leaning at precarious angles. The scattered ruins of the abbey could have been the remains of some vast prehistoric creature that had once roamed the earth.

Ruby was starting to feel not only cold but exhausted. It had been a long few hours after going to Givens's house first, then St Crosse College and now finally the abbey. But she still had a job to do, keeping watch for Givens who hadn't turned up yet. She'd been sniffing the air for *Wihta* too, because Jones had told her a Badlander would always smell a *Wiht* before seeing it and that would be her warning if there were any about.

It was dark now the moon had gone, which didn't help, and she had already stubbed her toes on the various stones embedded in the earth because it was difficult to see them. There were molehills that leapt out at her as well, trying to trip her up.

She'd tucked the gun back in her waistband after it had kept talking about a great adventure it had gone on in an old ruined abbey with Maitland and how this place wasn't a patch on that. Not only was the gun's constant chatter annoying, Ruby wanted some silence to think.

She glanced back at Jones and Thomas Gabriel moving about with the Moon Globe. They were holding it up, casting a dim glow across the broken pieces of wall that were still standing as they searched for the hidden door. When Ruby had tried to use the Moon Globe, it had made a funny buzzing sound and then all the light had drained away from it. The object had also become so hot suddenly that she'd thrown it up in the air with a great cry. Thomas Gabriel had cursed out loud as he'd caught it safely and cradled it in his hands, so she'd left the boys to it.

Ruby picked her way over the grass, pondering the fact that she'd found something else in the Badlands that didn't work for her. She'd brushed it off at first, striding away, not wanting to feel embarrassed in front of the other two. But, with each step, she started thinking more and more about her encounter with the Vampire and the Jump 'em Juice that hadn't worked either. She still didn't know how the creature had followed her to the cottage, but that didn't matter. It was her fault it had. And it was because of her that Victor Brynn was no longer alive. There was still a raw red patch in her heart because of that, however much she was supposed to accept the *wyrd*.

She missed Victor Brynn terribly. He might have been strict, but he'd been kind too, happy to listen to whatever was on her mind. She wished she could speak to him now about the Moon Globe and Jump 'em Juice, and how scared she was about never being accepted as a Badlander, because what would she do then? There seemed to be so many things to learn on her own and suddenly it all felt too much.

Frustrated, Ruby kicked the top off a molehill with as much force as she could, sending up a spray of earth. It made her feel a little better, so she kicked at more. She found herself walking out of the stone ruins of the abbey towards the small museum that had been set up for visitors. It was a sleek-looking building made of glass and steel. Peering inside, she could see various relics in cases and large stone pieces displayed behind red ropes.

When she heard a noise, she ducked down instinctively and listened, unsure what it was. She heard it again. And now it was the unmistakable sound of an engine in the distance. Two headlights appeared, sweeping over the brow of the hill and fanning light across the road leading up to the abbey. Ruby watched the vehicle coming closer, lighting up the tarmac on its way towards the empty car park.

And then she ran as fast as she could back to the boys.

*

Randall Givens shut the driver's door and breathed in the cold air, stamping his feet to get the blood moving.

'It's cold, Wilfried.'

'Yes, sir.'

'Well, let's get started then.' Givens produced a Moon Globe and started walking towards the ruined abbey, lighting a dim path. 'What we're looking for is a hidden door and this Moon Globe will help us find it if it's here.'

'What's behind the door, sir?'

'I believe it's an object of great value that the High Council of the Order wants found. They've been looking for it for many years. The Badlander who owned the object hid it very carefully because it was so valuable.'

'Who was the Badlander, sir?'

'Augustus Drewman. You've heard of him, of course. What can you tell me about him?'

'Augustus Drewman was born over four hundred years ago and Commenced in an unusual way. He was given the gift of magic by drinking from a Badlander's dirty bath water.'

'Yes, a most unusual form of Commencement so the history books tell us. And what of him as a man?'

'He was the best Badlander there's ever been.'

'*One* of the best,' Givens corrected him.

'You can find his *mearcunga* everywhere, marking his kills. More than five thousand have been counted, but it's said there are others that have never been found.'

'And what happened to him?'

'He loved magic too much. It turned him rotten.'

137

Givens shone the Moon Globe at Wilfried and the boy put his hands up to shield his eyes. '*That* is the most important thing to remember.' Givens covered the Moon Globe and the dark returned. 'Remember, Wilfried, magic can pull you into the dark, and turn you into the person you never thought you could be. What's the Anglo-Saxon for rotten?'

'*Fúl*, sir.'

'Remember that word, Wilfried, whenever you dream about magic.' Givens turned and started walking again, the light from the Moon Globe illuminating his way.

He didn't notice three pairs of eyes watching him as he led Wilfried towards the abbey remains.

'He won't find anything,' whispered Thomas Gabriel as Givens and Wilfried disappeared into the dark. 'We've looked everywhere.'

'Are you sure?' asked Ruby.

'Yes.'

Ruby watched Givens flashing the Moon Globe up and down the stone walls. 'What about in there?' she asked, pointing towards the museum.

Thomas Gabriel tutted. 'Ruby, that wasn't built when Drewman was alive.'

'It's a museum. There might be things in there.'

'Like what?' asked Jones.

'Old things,' muttered Ruby. 'You know? Bits of wall. Doors. Books.'

The two boys looked at her as if they'd never met her before.

'Have either of you got a better idea?'

No one said anything.

Jones scanned the ground between them and the museum, and pointed at a large molehill, much bigger than the ones Ruby had been kicking at.

'I know,' she whispered. 'Must be a very big mole. There's loads of molehills everywhere.'

'That's not a molehill, Ruby.' She peered closer at the mound and it dawned on her that Jones was right.

'That's been made by a Burrowing Troll,' continued the boy. 'Fresh, by the look of it.'

Ruby pulled back as if expecting something to pop up out of the turf. 'So we should probably leave then?' she asked.

'No. You're right – we should investigate the museum. We just have to go quietly. We'll be all right if we don't make too much noise. Nothing's happened yet, has it? The Burrowing Troll might have gone.'

The three of them scurried across the ground. Ruby tried stepping as daintily as she could, wary of alerting what might be hiding beneath her.

She pulled the gun out of her waistband as she went. 'Burrowing Troll,' she whispered to it.

'Or *Trolls*, you mean,' it whispered back. 'They move in packs unless it's a rogue. And they're usually the really nasty ones. Burrowing Trolls react to movement. They leap through the earth and drag down their prey.'

'Right. Anything else I should know?' asked Ruby, trying to skim as lightly as possible over the grass.

'They've got poison breath. Really noxious stuff. Roar it right in your face if they can.'

Suddenly, Ruby felt a tremor near her in the soil. The sensation was slight, like a stick tapping the soles of her shoes. She stopped immediately. When something slithered through the earth underneath her, she held her breath until it had passed.

The three of them stopped close to the museum and ducked down behind a large, black, industrial-sized bin on wheels, the lid open because it was so full of black bin bags and rubbish. Looking back over the expanse of grass, they could see the light from Givens's Moon Globe skirting the ruins of the abbey.

'We'll be safer inside,' said Jones. 'But we still need to keep as quiet as we can.'

They were all about to move when Ruby stopped and pulled the boys back down. She pointed to the grass ahead of them.

Two pointed ears, shaped like trowels and tufty with grey hair, had emerged just above ground. They were so well camouflaged with mud and grass that, if she hadn't been watching, Ruby would never have noticed them in the dark. They flicked like a cow's ears being teased by flies, and rotated in a semicircle, stopping and then returning to their starting point.

Distant voices rang out. Givens was berating Wilfried about something. A bristly head popped up out of the grass. The Troll had a large, ugly face with a snout and a crop of jagged teeth that showed as it sniffed the air.

140

'Keep very still,' whispered Jones. 'Their eyesight's poor.'

The Troll peered through the dark and then it started swaying from side to side as it tried to catch the scent of something. It seemed to like the smell of whatever it was and raised the tip of its nose and inhaled deeply. Out came the arms through the soil and it levered its body out of the ground, as slippery as an eel. As it stood up, earth fell from its body. It was about eight feet tall.

Givens's voice rang out again, but the Troll didn't seem interested at all. It started lumbering towards the bin and Ruby raised the gun very slowly.

'Easy,' said the gun. 'Wait for me to say when.'

Ruby watched the creature coming towards her, sniffing the air as it went. She caught a whiff of it, peppery and rotten, like the smell of a dead fish, and tried not to gag.

'Okay, take aim,' whispered the gun.

Ruby's finger flickered on the trigger. Out of the corner of her eye, she could see the light from the Moon Globe bouncing round the ruins. *They'll hear a shot*, she thought, *and they'll come running*.

'I told you your catapult would be useful, Jones,' she whispered.

Jones smiled. 'Don't worry, it's not after us.'

Ruby frowned. Jones pointed to the bin. 'Just stay very still. Trust me.'

Ruby's trigger finger hovered as the Troll clambered up into the bin and started rustling through the rubbish, digging down into the bags. Jones motioned for them to move and they all walked quickly and quietly to the door of the museum and lay against the wall. A Door Wurm was already wriggling between Thomas Gabriel's fingers as he looked for the lock.

FOURTEEN

The museum was quiet, the glass glazed thick enough to keep out the sound of the Troll. It meant Ruby and the others couldn't be heard by it either.

They inspected every artefact on display, scanning the Moon Globe over pieces of old stone, wooden doors and even old books, turning the pages and making them crackle. But they found no secret door. Eventually, they had explored everything they could see.

Jones pointed out of the far window. 'Givens ain't found nothing yet either.' The Moon Globe's light was still dancing round the ruined walls of the abbey.

'How about in there?' Ruby pointed to a door marked PRIVATE. Jones nodded and crept to the door, and opened it.

Inside the room were more pieces of stone and other objects that were clearly being prepared for display. Jones flashed the Moon Globe this way and that and then his arm jolted and stopped as if someone had grabbed him by the wrist. His arm pointed at something shrouded in plastic

143

sheeting. Jones could feel the Moon Globe straining in his hand, wanting to break free.

'Let it go, Jones,' said Thomas Gabriel. 'It's found something.'

Jones allowed the Moon Globe to float out of his hand and it bobbed in front of the sheeting.

Thomas Gabriel and Jones ripped off the plastic to reveal a small piece of stone held between two clamps with an inscription written in Latin. The stone was obviously in the process of being cleaned. One half was bright and fresh-looking, but the rest was still grubby. The Moon Globe floated closer to it, casting its light over the carving of a small door, roughly hewn into the stone above the inscription. There was a rasping sound and the tiny door broke free of the stone and floated clear.

It grew in size until the door was standing, full-size, on the floor. It was made of wood and stood rather like a stage prop as Ruby walked all the way round it. The Moon Globe floated down and settled on the door like a bee on a flower and then it lost its glow and became just a round door handle.

Thomas Gabriel grabbed hold of the handle and turned it. There was a click. But, as he pulled, nothing happened. The door seemed to be stuck.

'I don't think it's been opened in a very long time,' said Thomas Gabriel as the door juddered. Then, with a squealing sound and a blast of hot, dusty air, he pulled it open. Inside was a shelf, at about chest-height.

Jones and Thomas Gabriel peered in at a small metal box, both of them wondering whether to touch it.

'It might be charmed,' whispered Jones.

'Drewman didn't say it was.'

'That doesn't mean it's not.'

Thomas Gabriel reached out an arm and wiggled his fingers and then withdrew them. 'Maybe you're right,' he muttered.

A loud **CRASH!** outside surprised them all and Ruby and the boys ran to the window and peered out to see what had caused the noise.

The big black bin was lying on its side and the Troll was rearing up and growling. Advancing towards the creature were Givens and his apprentice, who was whirling a golden rope round his head. The burly Troll picked up the bin and hurled it at them, sending them scurrying for cover. The Troll then bounded towards the boy, who was momentarily distracted, and caught him with a fist as big as a brick in the ribs, sending him spinning to the ground.

The Troll roared as it reared up over the boy who cried out and put up his arms in a feeble defence.

A white bolt came streaking out of the dark and hit the creature full in the chest. The force was enough to hurl the Troll backwards through one of the glass windows of the museum with a huge crash.

Givens crouched beside the boy. As far as Ruby and the others could tell, he was in great pain and Givens was doing his best to try and reassure him. Suddenly, Givens looked round as if he'd heard something and shot a bolt of light from a fist into the sky, illuminating the grass and the ruins.

The ground was moving. Juddering. The grass bristled before jets of earth started spraying like geysers, metres into the sky. Stones fell to the ground. Some of them crashed against the windows of the museum.

Burrowing Trolls were popping up out of the ground everywhere.

A whole pack of them.

The upper halves of their bodies swayed as they breathed in great gulps of air and then began pushing themselves out of the ground.

'We have to go!' cried Jones.

Before anyone had time to say anything else, the door leading to the room they were in flew off its hinges, revealing the Troll that Givens had hit with the magical bolt. A large red mark on its chest was still smoking and it was clearly very angry.

'Keep still!' hissed Jones.

The Troll sniffed the air and then roared, letting out a cloud of yellow, noxious breath as it did so.

'Take a shot, girl!' the gun shouted at Ruby. She did as she was told, but the Troll's pongy breath seemed to have got into her thinking, clouding her mind. The room started to spin and Ruby stumbled backwards. She saw another yellow cloud come gushing from the Troll's mouth, little holes in its jaw opening and closing like vents.

'Poison!' shouted the gun.

Ruby tried to say something, but couldn't find the words. She saw Jones sinking to the floor, waving his hands about as if he was drowning. When Ruby felt the wall slide up her spine, she knew she was falling and plonked bottom-first onto the floor so hard, her teeth clicked.

The gun's voice was melting in her ears and she raised the weapon again and pulled the trigger. But only then did she realize she wasn't holding the gun at all: it had dropped from her grasp as she fell.

Thomas Gabriel had seen the door go flying off its hinges and had known instantly what was coming. He'd ducked down behind a desk and watched the Troll roar, its poisonous breath seeping out from the tiny gills in its jaw. The cloudy yellow gas clogged the room, licking itself into the corners. Ruby and Jones had had no chance given they were so close to the door and Thomas Gabriel knew it was up to him if they were all going to survive.

He wrapped his red silk scarf about his nose and mouth to buy himself some time. It was a temporary fix, because he knew what he really needed was a special mask. But, as he spoke the spell, he could only produce pale white sparks that sputtered and faded as the magic failed him.

He glanced through the door, opened by the Moon Globe, at the little metal box on the shelf. The yellow breath of the Troll was making him giddy now. So he ran to the box and opened it. Inside was the amulet, a black bracelet in the shape of a 'C'. There was no time to study it in detail, but Thomas Gabriel sensed how cool and smooth it was as he picked it up.

He clipped the amulet round his wrist and felt something click inside him, like a button had been pressed. Despite feeling dizzier and dizzier, he tried the spell again. The sparks that came from his fingers were white and pure this time and Thomas Gabriel felt the magic surge out of him. The sheer force and power took him by surprise and he tried not to gasp and take another deep breath of poisonous yellow air.

The sparks wove themselves together, creating a white, oval-shaped mask in his hand. Thomas Gabriel tore off the scarf and clamped the mask over his mouth and nose. When he felt it tighten to his face he let go and breathed more deeply, enjoying the clean air coming into his lungs, the dizziness quickly beginning to clear.

Thomas Gabriel spotted the Troll standing over Ruby, who was slumped against the wall, her head resting on her shoulder. As it opened its mouth to take a bite, Thomas Gabriel fired a white bolt from his fist that tapered to a sharp point, and skewered the Troll's chest, piercing the rough grey skin. The creature collapsed dead to the floor and no more foul-smelling gas came leaking out of its mouth.

Thomas Gabriel crouched beside Ruby and conjured a mask for her and then did the same for Jones who was lying on the floor. The fumes were receding now that the Troll was dead, but there was still a lot of toxic gas in the room.

Above his own breathing, Thomas Gabriel could hear

shouts and roars outside. Peering out of the window, he saw Givens surrounded by a ring of Trolls. He was wearing a white mask too, the air around him thick with yellow poison drifting like fog. On the ground in front of him was Wilfried, masked, and crouched with one arm cradled tight to his body, clearly hurt.

A cough made him look round. Jones was waking up as he breathed clean air. He rubbed his face, his hand feeling the mask, and then he gave a thumbs up to Thomas Gabriel.

'You need to leave,' Thomas Gabriel told Jones. His voice was raspy through the mask.

'What about you?'

Thomas Gabriel pointed a finger outside. 'I'm going to help Givens.'

'But—'

'Don't worry, I'll make something up.'

Jones was staring at the black bracelet on his friend's wrist. 'The amulet works, Jones, just like Drewman said. The magic inside me feels stronger than it ever has before.' As he stood up, Jones grabbed hold of his arm.

'You can't let Givens see the amulet. He'll take it away.'

'Go,' said Thomas Gabriel, pulling his arm free. 'Take Ruby with you.' He marched away and felt a surge in his blood as he thought about the power he wielded now.

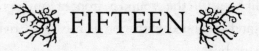

FIFTEEN

When Thomas Gabriel raised an arm, and fired a bolt of magic at the Troll nearest to Givens, the creature screamed as a sharp blade pierced its chest, and felled it where it stood.

Thomas Gabriel was aware that Givens was looking at him. And not just looking, but staring. His heart swelled in his chest and he stood a little taller. Before striding out into the open air, he'd made sure the amulet was tucked under his shirtsleeve in order to conceal it from Givens. He raised his hand and gave a friendly wave.

Givens frowned. But there was no time for any explanations because the large group of Trolls demanded their full concentration. The two Badlanders worked on the creatures, cutting them down, firing magic at will. Thomas Gabriel was smiling beneath his mask. He had never felt such power in him. Out of the corner of his eye, he could see Givens glancing at him, wary of a young Badlander outshining him in front of his apprentice who was cowering on the ground as the cries of dying Trolls rang around them. Thomas

Gabriel was careful to make some mistakes, though, wary of appearing too good and making Givens wonder why. So he made sure he hit the ground with some of his magical bolts and sent others fizzing uncontrollably up into the night sky.

It didn't take long for the group of Trolls to be culled to a manageable size and then Thomas Gabriel and Givens were working together, chasing down the remaining creatures as they dived back into the earth, burrowing down in a flurry of soil and stones.

Finally, the two Badlanders were left panting as silence returned to the ruins. The yellow fumes were still thick in the air so they kept their masks on as they went about disposing of the bodies, showering them with brown dust that melted them to nothing. Thomas Gabriel was careful to keep the amulet hidden beneath his shirtsleeve until he sensed an opportunity to take it off, with Givens busy dissolving the body of a particularly large Troll.

But removing it was harder than he'd expected.

Something in Thomas Gabriel's heart was telling him not to do it. His fingers fumbled at his wrist and he remembered Drewman's warning about the amulet and how dangerous it was.

Realizing Givens had almost finished disposing of the Troll, Thomas Gabriel plucked the amulet from his wrist and put it in his pocket. It felt like a cold spike had been thrust into his heart and the sensation stayed with him for a few moments afterwards.

The two Badlanders continued to work in silence and

then, when all the bodies were gone and the air had cleared, they removed their masks, which dissolved to nothing.

Givens stared at Thomas Gabriel, then nodded and held out his hand.

'Thank you.' They shook but Givens didn't let go. 'Now tell me why you're here.'

Thomas Gabriel looked straight back at him. 'I wanted another chance to prove I'm good with magic,' he said. 'Last time we met, things didn't go as I'd hoped. So I've been using Glassyscopes to watch you, hoping for another opportunity.' He took out a small pair of wire-rimmed spectacles from his pocket.

'You mean you've been spying on me and Wilfried?'

'No.' Thomas Gabriel looked down at the ground. 'At least I didn't think of it that way.'

'Well, that's how it seems to us. Doesn't it, Wilfried?' The small apprentice nodded.

'You've got to remember I have no one, sir. There's been a hole in my life ever since my Master died. I need someone I can look up to and learn from, like I did with Simeon. When I found out I was going to be mentored by you, sir, I was so excited. So, when things went wrong the other night with the Gobblings, I was upset, worried I'd made such a bad impression that you might pass me onto someone else and not want to be bothered with me any more.'

'So you decided to try and prove yourself tonight?'

Thomas Gabriel nodded. He could see Givens weighing up everything he'd said.

'Was it wrong, sir, to do what I did?'

Givens scowled. 'Try and convince me it wasn't.'

Thomas Gabriel thought about that. 'Well, there's always two ways of looking at things.'

'Go on.'

'As you see it, I'm nothing but a boy who's been spying on you. But the way I see it, I only want to learn so I can be as good as I can be and pass the test from the High Council. And that means I need to learn from the best around, like you, sir.'

Thomas Gabriel waved a hand at the open grass where they'd fought off the Trolls. 'Simeon Rowell might have been my Master, but I could never have done anything like that with him. I was watching you all the time, learning from you, following your lead.' Thomas Gabriel threw his arms this way and that, re-enacting the magic he'd cast. 'I could never have done anything like that on my own. You gave me a lot of confidence, sir.'

Thomas Gabriel could see Givens beginning to enjoy the praise in front of Wilfried.

'If I ever go on to be a great Badlander then I'll make sure everyone knows it was because of you, sir. I'll help add to your legacy. Simeon may have got me started, and I'll always be grateful for that, but I can see I've still got a lot to learn.'

Givens nodded, his ego flattered enough. 'That's very kind of you, Thomas Gabriel.' He tapped a finger on his chin. 'But using those Glassyscopes to keep an eye on me and my apprentice is still a reckless thing to have done. Our business is not your business. It's a black mark against you.'

Thomas Gabriel nodded and looked down at the ground.

'And turning up here, out of the blue, could have got you killed. Your aim was quite off on occasion. You were meant to be hitting the Trolls not the ground.'

'Yes, sir. Sorry, sir.'

'But,' and Givens raised his finger, 'given that Wilfried and I have benefited from your presence, making our job easier than it perhaps would have been to deal with the Burrowing Trolls, then I will say no more about it. Does that sound fair?'

'Yes, sir. Thank you. As you say, sir, I'm sure you would have had no problem with the Trolls. I'm just happy to have helped.'

Givens gave Thomas Gabriel a somewhat sour glare and then took the Glassyscopes from him and dropped them on the ground and stood on them, breaking the lenses.

'I think we're done here. I would suggest you go home and study some more on the Burrowing Troll and also on the spell for your mask. From what I could see, it looked a little underdeveloped and that could have been fatal. Clearly, from what I have seen tonight and of course the other day, you are definitely a work in progress when it comes to using magic. Don't underestimate how rigorous the test of your magical skills in a few weeks' time by the High Council will be.'

'I won't, sir. Thank you.' Thomas Gabriel took his vial of Slap Dust out of his pocket, eager to leave.

'And two more things. Keep an eye on that invitation of

154

yours. One of the High Council members wants the meeting brought forward.'

'Really?' Thomas Gabriel felt like a Gobbling had raked a talon across his heart.

'Don't worry. It's highly unlikely given everyone on the High Council has to agree, but as your mentor I'm obliged to let you know, given your upcoming magical test.'

'Right,' said Thomas Gabriel, the blood in him cooling a little. 'And the other thing?'

'I think it's best we keep this episode tonight to ourselves, don't you? We don't want the Order finding out you were spying on me. They wouldn't approve of that.' Givens glared at him.

'No, sir. Of course. No one will know.'

When he appeared in the hallway of his home, Thomas Gabriel was still grinning, long after the fizz of Slap Dust had faded from his hands. He knew Givens had been grateful for his help, but hadn't wanted to say so in front of his apprentice and appear weak.

Even though it was almost daybreak, Thomas Gabriel didn't want to go to bed. He took the Black Amulet out of his pocket. He hadn't had time to study it properly earlier, but now he saw that at either end of the C-shape was carved a small head in the shape of a serpent. Each one had its mouth open, showing tiny serrated rows of black teeth. The eyes were green, a tiny gemstone in each socket. He wondered what the amulet was made of exactly because, although it

155

looked so dark and heavy, it was light to hold, like a small bone. He fought the urge to put it on again, thinking about Drewman's warning about its power.

'So that's the amulet?'

Thomas Gabriel jumped. He looked up to see Ruby standing there and caught the faint whiff of Slap Dust. He smiled but only on the outside. His grip tightened round the amulet instinctively, like his hand was thinking ahead of his brain.

'Where's Jones?' he asked, looking about as if wary of having the amulet snatched from him.

'At home. Figured he had some explaining to do to his parents.'

'Yes, I suppose he must do, being out most of the night. So, you're both all right after inhaling so much of the Troll's breath, then?'

'Fine,' said Ruby. 'Thank you. We watched you with the Trolls.'

'In your scrying mirror?'

Ruby nodded. 'Once we'd escaped, we wanted to check you were okay. Seems like there was no need, though.' She pointed at the amulet. 'You were almost as good as Givens, wearing that.'

Thomas Gabriel couldn't hold back a smile. 'It works like Drewman said. The magic inside me was stronger than I've ever felt it.'

'Lucky you.'

As Ruby stared at the amulet, Thomas Gabriel took a step

back. He didn't want her to touch it and opened his mouth to tell her so, but his jealousy vanished as quickly as it had come, leaving him unsure what to say for a moment.

When Ruby frowned, Thomas Gabriel realized his mouth was still open.

'Givens didn't see me wearing it,' he said quickly. 'I made sure.'

Ruby unhooked the knapsack slung round her shoulder. 'I thought you should know we took care of this,' she said, unzipping the small front pocket and picking out the Moon Globe, holding it up for the boy to see, then placing it down on the floor before there was another reaction like the one she'd had at the abbey. 'The door vanished when Jones removed the Moon Globe from it. And we brought this back too.' After unzipping the main body of the knapsack, she folded it down to reveal the half-cleaned piece of stone with the Latin inscription on it. The tiny carving of the door was above it exactly as it had been when they'd first seen it in the museum. 'Givens won't find the hidden door now.'

'Thanks. I didn't think about that.'

Ruby pointed at the amulet. 'We thought we should hide that too.'

Thomas Gabriel felt his fingers tighten round the object. 'That's okay, I can hide it here.'

'Don't you think it would be safer somewhere else? No one would think to look in Jones's house,' continued Ruby.

Thomas Gabriel didn't want to give up the amulet now, not when it had made him feel so powerful. The idea of someone else having it or even touching it made his stomach clench, like a fist ready to throw a punch.

'*Hell-oo?*' Ruby was looking at him, waving a hand in front of his face. 'I said are you all right with hiding it at Jones's house?'

Thomas Gabriel blinked. He seemed to have lost a moment of time thinking about the amulet, as if he'd dropped out of the world for a second or so. Ruby raised her eyebrows. Then she held out her hand.

The anxiety Thomas Gabriel felt about giving the amulet to her grew sharper. His heart bumped against his chest. The outstretched palm of Ruby's hand seemed to widen.

'I still need it,' he said quickly.

'Why?' asked Ruby, raising her eyebrows. 'Drewman said to use it sparingly, remember? It's dangerous.'

'I've got to take the Moon Globe back to Pindlebury before he wakes up. What if I get in a fix and need to use magic? I can take it back right now, before it gets light.'

Ruby shook her head. 'I'll take the Moon Globe back,' and she picked it up off the floor.

'You can't, it's too dangerous. Anyway, you don't know how to use the—'

He froze as Ruby tossed him the Moon Globe. He caught it, just, in his outstretched hand, juggling it between his fingers.

'What did you do that for?' he shouted, glaring at her. 'It could have broken if I'd dropped it.' And then he realized exactly why she'd done it.

Ruby had plucked the amulet from his other hand without him realizing. He watched as she slipped it onto her wrist. His heart turned dark. Not only was he embarrassed at being tricked, but he was angry at Ruby for taking the amulet. He was about to tell her to give it back to him when she tutted and shook her head.

'What are you supposed to feel when you wear it?'

'Powerful, of course,' snapped the boy. 'Like you can do anything you want with the magic inside you. Now give it back.'

'Hmm. I don't feel anything.'

'You must do!' But Ruby shook her head. She raised her hand and spoke a spell. But nothing happened. Not even a single white spark on her fingers.

Ruby tutted. She held up her forearm and studied the amulet, staring at the serpents with their little green eyes. And then she tutted again.

'What is it?' asked Thomas Gabriel, already feeling calmer because it was obvious Ruby couldn't use the amulet.

'Drewman said we could all use it, but I can't. And I know exactly why not.'

Ruby pointed at the Moon Globe that Thomas Gabriel was holding.

'Remember how I couldn't use that at the abbey either?' Thomas Gabriel nodded. 'Well, some things in the Badlands don't work for girls. I don't know why. Scrying's easy-peasy for me, but other things ... well ...' She bit her lip. 'I wish Victor Brynn was here,' she sighed.

She took the amulet off and handed it back to Thomas Gabriel. His heart rose like a balloon as he snatched it back.

'Looks like I'm the only one who'll be using it then,' he said, trying not to sound too smug about it.

'What about Jones?'

'He hates using magic. Doesn't want to be a Badlander, remember?'

'Well, that's what he says. I think he's secretly regretting giving up being one.'

Thomas Gabriel snorted a laugh. 'Don't be ridiculous.'

'No, really,' continued Ruby. 'He didn't have to help us yesterday, but he came as soon as I sent the message in the jar. *And* he decided to stay with us instead of going back home for family movie night.'

'So?'

'So staying up all night with us instead of going home means he wanted to be here with us in the Badlands. I was an ordinary kid once. I know what it's like. You don't get to do anything important. Not like Badlanders do. What if Jones has realized that and is regretting the choice he's made?'

Thomas Gabriel shook his head. 'I don't think so, Ruby. Jones stayed and helped because he's desperate for Drewman to fix your Commencement. He needs the magic out of him to get on with being an ordinary boy. There's no way he'd want to use the amulet. And do you really think he'd want to give up his parents after everything he went through to get them?' He shrugged. 'Sorry, but I think you're just imagining that Jones wants to be a Badlander.'

Ruby puffed out her cheeks as she thought about that. She shook her head. 'There's definitely something going on with him,' she said. 'I know him better than anyone.'

'He's got a lot on his mind. At the moment, he's not an ordinary boy with the magic inside him and he's not a Badlander either. He's nothing. Just like you're nothing too.'

Ruby raised her eyebrows. 'So are you without that amulet,' she snapped and then instantly regretted it because, deep down, she knew Thomas Gabriel was right and that none of them were the person they wanted to be. It was why they were working together.

Ruby sighed. 'Do you really think the amulet can help us find all the bits of Drewman we need?'

'I think it can help us do anything,' said Thomas Gabriel, admiring the amulet.

'He did say the golden boxes containing the rest of him are well hidden with magic.'

'Spells for finding things can be hard,' agreed Thomas Gabriel, 'depending on how well they've been hidden.'

He put the Moon Globe in his pocket, and then took out his copy of *The Black Book of Magical Instruction*. He rifled through the pages until he found the section entitled '*Infandan þing*' with the English translation 'Finding things' written underneath.

'There's a lot to learn about using spells for finding something that's been hidden on purpose,' said Thomas Gabriel, skimming the pages. 'If Drewman's right about the golden boxes being hidden with strong magic, well ...' He

161

paused as he raised his eyebrows. 'I'll need to practise. A lot. Even with the amulet.'

And then his eyes fixed on a particular paragraph. 'There's an even bigger problem too.'

'Of course there is,' sighed Ruby. 'We're in the Badlands.'

Thomas Gabriel cleared his throat and read from the page. 'To attempt any spell to locate someone's body, a corpse for example, or any remains, you must already have in your possession some physical piece of that body. This will act as a guide for any spell you need to use.'

Thomas Gabriel ran his finger further down the page. 'It has to be a bit of them. Blood. Hair. Fingernails—'

'How are we supposed to get that when any part of Drewman turns to ash outside the room he's kept in?'

Thomas Gabriel snapped the book shut.

'I'll take the Moon Globe back to Pindlebury now and ask if he knows a way round the problem. Or has a book about it at least.'

It was almost dawn as Thomas Gabriel returned to Pindlebury's rooms in St Crosse College, creeping across the quad and then walking up the winding staircase. Although he was tired, he felt a bounce in his steps that hadn't been there for a long time. He was happy. The amulet had given him hope. Not only could he do magic, but there was a glow inside him. It was the same sensation he'd had after his Commencement. He played with the amulet as he walked, rubbing the smooth surface, and the heads of the serpents at either end. Their green eyes flashed as they caught the lights mounted on the staircase and made them look alive.

When he opened the door, Pindlebury was still asleep, having had the full dose of Hurdy Gurdy, and snoring gently. Thomas Gabriel replaced the Moon Globe into the two boxes that sat one inside the other, clicking them shut, and then glanced about to check that nothing looked odd or out of place. Satisfied, he took a Memory Leech out of his pocket and whispered gently to it.

He held the tip of the small, wriggly creature up to Pindlebury's ear and watched the creature squirm closer. He allowed it to get a grip and then he fed the Leech into the man's ear. It stretched itself thinner than a pencil to slide in and then it was gone with a *schlurp*, the tail disappearing in a circular flicking motion.

As Thomas Gabriel waited for the Memory Leech to take away any memories Pindlebury had of their earlier meeting, he looked at the collection of rare books on the shelves. One book piqued his interest. In gold embossed lettering was the title *Some Great Badlanders and their Stories* by Geoffrey Phillips. Thomas Gabriel flicked through the dense pages of prose, imagining how he might be listed in such a book in the future, if he passed his test in front of the High Council. But what struck him the most was that Geoffrey Phillips had used an intriguing way of gathering the research about the Badlanders discussed in his book. Phillips hadn't just read other people's accounts: he had gathered his research by going back to the past, and observing the various Badlanders first-hand.

According to the foreword in the book, Philips had been such a gifted scryer that he had used the skill to go back in time to watch his subjects.

Thomas Gabriel heard a slipping and sucking sound and saw the Memory Leech presenting itself from Pindlebury's ear. It fell onto the sleeping man's shoulder, noticeably fatter than before.

The boy slapped the book shut, stashing it quickly in his pocket, then moved the others on the shelf across to make the gap seem less obvious.

 SIXTEEN

Ruby had barely slept an hour or two after the previous night's exertions when Thomas Gabriel appeared in her bedroom, his palms fizzing from Slap Dust, and shook her awake.

'What? When? Who?' Ruby blinked in the daylight coming through the gap in the curtains and yawned and rubbed her eyes. Gradually, Thomas Gabriel came into focus. 'What are you doing here? Aren't you tired?'

'No, I took an extra strong tonic. I've brought one for you too.' He held out a bottle full of a sickly yellow mixture and unscrewed the top. The smell made Ruby want to gag.

'No thanks.' Her head hit the pillow and she closed her eyes. 'I'm tired, Thomas Gabriel. Come back later.'

'No. I've got something to show you.' He drew back the curtains and made Ruby groan.

'Can't it wait?'

'The clock's still ticking, remember?' Thomas Gabriel pulled out his invitation to the High Council meeting and held it to her ear, making her curse.

'Thomas Gabriel, your test is not for weeks yet.'

'So you've already worked out how to find all the bits of Drewman's body, even though we don't have what I need to cast the spell, have you?'

'No.'

Thomas Gabriel pulled back her covers. 'Well, I have.'

'Hey!'

'Ruby, drink this tonic because you've got work to do. You need to practise going back in time.'

She looked at him. 'Going back in time? Okay, now you've got my attention.'

As she sat in the kitchen, drinking some very strong coffee and eating a piece of toast, she flipped through the pages of the book. She slapped it shut and ran her thumbs up and down the spine, and rubbed the cover.

'Well, the book's real enough,' she said. 'But as for what's inside it . . .' She sucked on her teeth. 'Did this person, Phillips, really go back in time? Is that even possible?'

'You're the expert scryer. I thought you'd know.'

'I haven't seen time travel mentioned in any of the books I've read in Maitland's collection. And I've never felt it's possible when I've looked into a mirror. There must be a secret way of doing it. I'd need some instruction.'

'Well, we could try looking in my house; maybe Simeon had some books on advanced techniques?'

Thomas Gabriel stood up, ready to leave.

'Er, I'm not going anywhere till I'm out of my jim-jams and washed and dressed properly.'

'Fine, I'll go and start looking now.'

By the time Ruby appeared in the library at Thomas Gabriel's house in Hampstead, wearing her usual old army camouflage jacket and feeling more awake, Thomas Gabriel had searched through a number of bookshelves. But, after another hour or so, it seemed the hunt was hopeless.

'Let's try the cellar,' suggested Thomas Gabriel. 'Simeon kept books down there too, ones he didn't use. There might be something.'

The cellar was cold and smelt of the sea. They found tea chests full of books packed in plastic bags and insulated with shredded newspaper to protect them from the damp. But not from spiders, though. Ruby leapt back each time she found one even as they scuttled away from the light.

Right at the bottom of the last tea chest, Ruby pulled out a book entitled *Scrying Time*. It was small. Old. The leather cover was wizened and mottled like the skin of an old apple. Ruby slid the book out of its plastic cover and then looked down the list of chapters before flicking through the pages.

Most of the book talked about the history of scrying through time and the discovery of the ability to travel back to the past. It seemed to be a feat that few had ever achieved, and no one had ever managed to go forward into the future. One chapter discussed whether the future might be impossible to access because it didn't actually exist.

'Is time like a river that flows forward but only into the dark as it does so?' Ruby read out loud.

'No idea,' said Thomas Gabriel. 'And who cares? It's the past we need to be concerned with.'

'Agreed. But my brain's sore just thinking about it.' Ruby flicked on through the book to the practicalities of travelling back in time and started to read. The first thing that interested her was that, unlike normal scrying, a scryer needn't have been to a place before if they were going back to it in the past. She kept on reading, taking note of a section written in bold type:

Important!

After successfully going back in time, you must not forget to do the most important thing of all. You must pluck out a section of your entry point into the past, which will appear as a shimmering shape in the air. It will be easy to pull out a small piece from it. When you want to return to the present, this piece will guide you back to what will now be your exit point. Forgetting to take such a piece will make it much harder to find your way back to your own time.

'Well?' asked Thomas Gabriel. When Ruby looked up, she realized she'd been so immersed in the book she hadn't heard him repacking the chests of books. He was brushing dirt and dust from the sleeves of his herringbone coat. Ruby had read most of the chapter and had got the general idea.

'I can go back in time. Maybe ... Apparently, no one knows for sure until they try it. There's a ritual to go through, blah-blah-blah, and then there's the actual travelling through the glass or the mirror and arriving at the moment in time you want to. That can take practice. And even if you can do all that there might be a big problem.'

'Which is?' Thomas Gabriel plucked a twist of newspaper from his hair.

'Even if people do go back in time, they can't always get back. There are Badlanders who've gone through a scrying mirror and never been seen again.'

'That would certainly be a problem.'

'There might be a way round it, though.' She walked over to Thomas Gabriel and tested a bicep. She wasn't entirely convinced by what she found.

'The book says it's possible to pull someone back through time as long as the person doing the pulling is strong enough. Apparently, time's a bit sticky. It says on your first try you should *always* have someone there to help pull you back in case there's a problem. I'd like that person to be you if you're up for it? Having the amulet means you should have no problem conjuring up a spell to pull me back if you need to.'

Thomas Gabriel winked. 'So not Jones, then?'

Ruby thought about what he *might* be implying and raised an eyebrow as high as it would go.

'No, not Jones.'

Thomas Gabriel flexed his arm. 'Reckon I'm strong enough anyway,' he said. 'But I'm happy to use the amulet of course.' He felt something warm bubble up inside as he thought about the amulet in his pocket. Of course he'd like to use it again, after it had given him so much power last time. In fact, he was looking forward immensely to the next opportunity to use it.

Later that day, after returning to the cottage, Ruby took a bath in special oil designed to make her skin smooth for travelling through time. Thomas Gabriel had bought it for her at Deschamps & Sons, given that a girl buying such an item would have raised difficult questions.

As the water lapped round her, she lay back and imagined going into the store herself one day to order whatever she needed. Perhaps some premium polish for her scrying mirror? Or maybe a younger set of imps to help around the house? A Badlander could buy anything they wanted from the large department store in London. Jones had told her it stretched for miles deep under the city unbeknown to ordinary people. Ruby considered how wonderful it would be to walk through all the vast corridors and different departments, with regular people not having the faintest idea she was far below them.

The oil smelt of almonds and peppermint and it left Ruby's skin feeling very smooth and with a slight sheen. After bathing, she trimmed her fingernails and smoothed down her short black hair with wax that Victor Brynn had used on his own unruly hair.

As she combed the wax through her hair, she wondered if she should grow it long again. She still kept it short because she was a runaway from her foster parents and didn't want anyone recognizing her. But, despite the need to look different, she missed her long black hair. It had always been a part of who she was.

The perfume of the wax brought back memories of Victor Brynn and a lump formed in Ruby's throat as she blinked back tears, thinking about all the things they'd done in the short time they'd known each other.

Victor Brynn had loved the garden at the cottage and had taken her round it day after day, teaching her the names of plants and shrubs and trees. She'd found it boring to start with, but had come to love the garden because the man's enthusiasm had been so infectious. He would tell her stories about how certain flowers had got their names as well as exciting tales of how plants and seeds had saved his life in dangerous situations.

It made her all the more determined to prove her worth as a Badlander now by going back in time, for she knew how proud it would have made him. And achieving such a feat, she hoped, might be just the thing to shock Badlanders into sitting up and taking notice of her and make a difference to the Order as Victor had wished she might.

According to the book, the ritual bathing and cleaning were as much about being mentally ready as physically. The concentration required in preparing the body was thought to quiet the mind and focus it on the journey, giving better results. Ruby was keen to try anything that might help, given it was her first attempt at time travel.

When she was ready, Ruby went down to her scrying room where the large full-length mirror was located. Thomas Gabriel was waiting. He was practising magic, casting different spells, producing white sparks that became daggers or spears or strange, hooked scimitars at the ends of his fingers, lunging forward with them as if tackling some creature only he could see.

Ruby stood there, watching him, the amulet bobbing on his wrist. He stopped when he saw her, out of breath, his face red and his lips shining.

'Drewman said the amulet was dangerous,' Ruby reminded him. 'That you shouldn't wear it all the time.'

'I know.' Thomas Gabriel picked up an empty glass vial from the floor. 'I'm taking the bitter potions like he said.' He took off the stopper and thrust the vial under Ruby's nose, making her screw up her face at the smell. 'As long as I take them, I'll be fine.'

Ruby wanted to say something else. She wasn't sure what it was exactly that made her feel uncomfortable about it, but the Black Amulet was strange. It seemed to suck in the daylight. To have a power that was beyond any of them scared her. Thomas Gabriel had definitely changed a little, even if he was taking the bitter potions. All she could keep thinking about was Drewman's head on the pedestal.

Thomas Gabriel pointed to the large coil of stout rope beside him. Attached to one end of it was a much thinner and silkier looking material with a loop at one end, which he held up for Ruby to see.

'We'll tighten the loop at this end round your waist,' he said, slipping it over her head and sliding it down until it rested on her hips. He took a sniff. 'You smell like Victor Brynn,' he said.

'Is that a problem?'

'No.' But Ruby saw something uncomfortable in his eyes that didn't match what he was saying.

'What is it?'

'It's just . . . well, it's sad what happened to him, you know. I liked him.'

'You're right. It is sad. So let's make him proud, shall we? You never know, he might be watching from somewhere.'

'Do you think that's true?'

Thomas Gabriel looked down at the floor. Shuffled his feet. Ruby patted him on the shoulder. 'If you're worried Simeon's somewhere, watching you, and knows you took that key without his blessing then he hasn't said anything yet, has he?' The boy shook his head. 'Right, so let's focus on what we do know, shall we?'

She picked up the small tin of polish beside the mirror and flipped off the lid. She worked the polish vigorously into the mirror with a cloth, making sure all of the glass was gleaming. After admiring the shine, she tightened the loop round her waist and checked it was secure.

'Okay, let's try the test. Ready?' Thomas Gabriel nodded. 'I'll be back in a minute. Hopefully.'

She took a couple of deep breaths, then imagined where

she wanted to go. As an image appeared in the mirror, she peered closer and saw the hallway outside the room she and Thomas Gabriel were standing in now.

'If I can't get back or I'm in trouble,' she said, turning round to look at the boy, 'then I'll give three tugs on the rope. One will mean I'm fine,' and then she stepped through the mirror.

Instantly, it felt different to the experience she usually had of travelling through the mirror to a different location. Time was much thicker. Passing through it was rather like wading in mud. Ruby wondered if it might be even more difficult going a long way back in time. Did it get thicker the further you travelled?

Her hearing was muffled. There was a strange, sweet smell, rather like the buttery popcorn she used to have at the cinema. Ruby popped out into the hallway of the house and landed rather heavily, stumbling, and almost collapsing onto the floor. Her 'reappearance', as the book had called it, needed some practice, she decided. She checked every part of her had come through the glass by looking in a mirror hanging on the wall. The book had warned of lost ears and hair too, even strips of skin. Fortunately for Ruby, everything looked like it was in order, although she noticed a small rip in her jacket she would have to fix just as she had done to the holes made by the Snarl's talons and the big one the Slobbering had made after leaping on her.

The rope was still attached to her waist and she followed it back to a point at which it vanished into a rectangular void full of a very slight haze. Ruby remembered the warning she had read in the book. This faint shimmer that was barely perceptible to the eye was her entry point and would be her exit point too.

Looking into the hazy air, there was no sign of where she had come from or of Thomas Gabriel, although she could still feel him holding tightly to the rope. She went closer to the almost invisible entry point. She could just tell that it was exactly the same shape and size as the mirror she had come through. Ruby reached out and pinched out a little piece of it as the book had instructed her to do. Then she turned round and listened.

Her heart leapt with joy as she heard her own voice! It was a strange sensation to think she was on the other side of the door, but it gave her a huge thrill because it meant she had done what she'd set out to do. She had gone back in time and could hear herself in the room she had just left. She crept forward to the door and put her ear to it. Her past self was busy talking to Thomas Gabriel about Victor Brynn and Simeon. Her voice seemed different to how she imagined it sounded. More sing-songy. And bossier too.

The rope tugged gently and she knew Thomas Gabriel was checking she was all right. She tugged back once to say she was, but carefully, so as not to make a noise. The one thing she knew she couldn't do on any account was alert anybody to her presence. The book had been very clear on this rule. Badlanders who went back in time had to be *bescéawereas*, and not be observed at all, to avoid impacting on the past.

Any change risked altering the outcome of events from that moment on, creating a knock-on effect into the present and altering it forever. If such a thing happened, it meant a Badlander might return to a different present to the one they'd left.

Ruby decided it was time to leave rather than risk staying any longer and being discovered. The test had been a success and now she could return home to the present. Careful not to make any noise, Ruby held up the small piece of hazy air she'd pinched from what was now her exit point. She felt it tugging towards where it had come from. Although now she could judge where the exit point was, because the rope was coming out of what looked to be thin air, Ruby knew she couldn't wear a rope every time. Without the piece she was holding, she realized just how difficult it would be to find the exit point again under normal circumstances.

As she waded through time and popped through the mirror back to where Thomas Gabriel was waiting, Ruby breathed a sigh of relief as she looked around, realizing everything was just how she had left it. She felt elated at having travelled through time, but also scared of the dangers it posed. The thought of being stuck somewhere in the past, never to return, made her blood run cold.

SEVENTEEN

Time travelling, it seemed, made Ruby tired and hungry. As she ate and drank, she made a note of how she was feeling as well as writing down her experiences about her first journey through time.

Ruby had decided to keep a diary because she didn't want to forget anything and make a mistake, considering how much was at stake if she did. But writing everything down had another purpose too. If she recorded her experiences, it was proof of her achievement. She hoped it might lead to her being accepted by the Order, given that time travel was something only a few talented Badlanders had attempted successfully.

'That's a good idea,' said Thomas Gabriel, dumping down an armful of books on the kitchen table, and peering over her shoulder at the notes and diagrams she'd made. 'You could write a book about time travel. Badlanders love books. You could use a pen name like Adolphus Squires or something and they'd never know you're a girl.'

'I'm going to use my own name. I want the Order to

'accept me for who I am. Just like Victor Brynn wanted. And Drewman. He said the Order are rotten, remember, and that I can change it.'

Thomas Gabriel checked the pot to see if there was any tea left. It was lukewarm, just the way he liked it. 'I think you and Drewman might be expecting too much. The Order haven't changed in centuries.'

'So everyone keeps saying.' Ruby clicked her tongue on her teeth and went back to her writing. 'It doesn't mean they can't change, though, does it?'

'No, I suppose it doesn't.' Thomas Gabriel poured out some tea. 'Ruby, I believe in you. You've done things I didn't think a girl could ever do, but the Order are a different matter. It might be too risky to ever tell them. Look what they've done to Drewman. Maybe Victor Brynn was wrong about you being able to shake up the Order. Perhaps it's just not possible.'

'Which would make Drewman wrong too. And he's the greatest Badlander ever. Apparently.' Ruby closed her notebook with a **SLAP!**

'Speaking of Drewman, have you found a moment in his life for me to go back to and get what you need?' She pointed at the books Thomas Gabriel had dumped on the table. All of them were biographies of Augustus Drewman.

The boy took another sip of tea. Even though he knew Ruby quite well, having never met another girl before, Thomas Gabriel wasn't always sure how to deal with her. The best way, it seemed, was to think of her as a boy just like him. He drained his tea and put the mug down.

'It's difficult to find a moment you can go back to in Drewman's life and take a little part of him without him knowing. If he sees you, remember, it's most likely going to change history all the way up to the present. Therefore, we have to be very careful. I've only found one moment so far that might work. All the biographies mention it so I'm pretty sure it happened. It'll be dangerous, though.'

'Danger's not great.'

'No, that's why I'm still looking—'

Thomas Gabriel paused when he felt a strange buzzing sound in his coat pocket. He reached in a hand and found it closing round the invitation to the High Council meeting. The hands on the clock were spinning round and round at an alarming rate. A little message appeared at the bottom of the card:

A request by Lionel Blarb, member of the High Council, to change the annual meeting date has been formally accepted.
You are now summoned to perform in front of the Council in one week's time on 31st March.

The dials on the clock stopped spinning and returned to their gentle ticking.

'One week!' shrieked Thomas Gabriel. 'One bloomin' week!'

It took Ruby a few minutes to calm the boy down. Then they both sat in silence, digesting the fact that there were only seven days left at most to find the rest of Drewman.

'How dangerous is this moment you've found?' asked Ruby eventually.

Thomas Gabriel sniffed. Rubbed at his nose.

'Dangerous,' he said quietly.

Ruby drew in such a deep breath her toes seemed to swell. 'Right then,' she said. 'Let's give it a go, shall we?'

'And you're definitely sure about this?' asked Ruby as she stood in front of the mirror, applying more polish. The smell of it mingled with the oil on her skin, which she had reapplied as well. She had also changed her damaged army camouflage jacket to something stouter, an old waxed coat she'd found on a peg in the hallway, which, she'd discovered, had pockets that were charmed to be limitless too.

'Like I said, it's mentioned in all the books,' said Thomas Gabriel. 'Are you sure you don't want to use the rope again?'

'No, it'll only get in the way. I know what I'm doing now.'

'I'm glad one of us does,' said the gun. It was lying on the floor by the mirror. 'Are you sure you need me to go with you? Don't you need more practice at this?'

Ruby picked up the weapon. 'No time really. Not now the High Council meeting's been rearranged for next week. We haven't even started looking for the golden boxes yet. Anyway, what are you so scared about?'

'Of you mucking this up. I do not want to get stuck in the past with you if something goes wrong and we can't get back.'

'We won't get stuck. I promise.' Ruby smiled as much as she could, but all she could think about was getting stuck too.

'But—'

Ruby tucked the gun into her waistband and zipped up the waxed jacket all the way to her chin. She nodded at Thomas Gabriel one last time and then turned to look into the mirror.

'Okay, start reading,' she said, trying to sound brave.

She heard Thomas Gabriel clear his throat. Heard the creak of the spine as he opened the biography of Augustus Drewman he was using.

'It was in the year sixteen seventy-four in the month of July,' he read. 'Drewman had travelled from the county of Northamptonshire, after completing his business with officials of the Order, and crossed into the county of Rutland after reports of a sickness having afflicted a large number of people in the village of Lyddington as well as a mysterious darkness that had descended during daylight hours. Drewman stayed for a few days, listening to accounts of the village folk concerning strange weather phenomena and descriptions of their nightmares caused by a large swollen creature visiting them in their dreams. The villagers would often wake screaming and sweating, their hearts pounding in their chests. Yet, even so, after calming down, most had found a small gift from the creature on the floor beside their bed. A plant perhaps, a fistful of grass or even a mound of earth. Such afflictions were the unmistakable signs of a *Wiht*.

'Drewman tracked the creature to an old Bowl Barrow. It was the burial place of a local chieftain killed centuries before the Badlander Order had been formed in Britain.

The barrow was located in a clearing at the top of a hill overlooking the village, surrounded on all sides by conifer woods. It was here that Drewman saw the barrow lit by a green light, like foxfire, from within and he knew he must battle the foe to the death ...'

Ruby visualized the moment and her reflection disappeared from the mirror, the glass filling with night instead. Moonlight and stars broke the blackness, allowing her to see pine trees around the clearing which looked like a black wall except for the triangular tops silhouetted against the sky.

Ruby swallowed hard and wondered, just for a moment, if she could really pull this off. And then she stepped through the mirror. Thomas Gabriel's voice faded behind her and all she could hear was the sound of her breathing as she waded through sticky time.

It was much tougher than before. Clearly, travelling through centuries required more arm movement and thigh pumping. She was careful with her reappearance this time and stepped out onto the grass of the clearing as lightly as she could.

Ruby could smell the pine trees. Just. There was a foul stench in the air too. As if something was dead and rotting, and Ruby remembered what Jones had advised her at St Anselm's Abbey about smelling a *Wiht* before seeing it.

Before taking a step, she turned to face her entry point. It was easier to find by touch than sight and after pinching out a portion she put it in her pocket. Just to be sure, she kicked a large white stone into place directly in front of what now was going to be her exit point. It would be something easy to see, a marker to aim for.

Next, Ruby snuck fifty metres or so down the hill and into the edge of the pines surrounding the clearing. She suddenly felt safer, hidden away.

The barrow up on the top of the hill looked like a black moon trying to rise out of the ground. A greenish light flickered inside, drawing her eye. Ruby ducked lower when she saw a figure emerge from the treeline into the clearing and start running up the hill. It had to be Drewman going to battle the *Wiht*. Now all she had to do was wait.

She took out the gun and it sneezed almost immediately.

'Shh,' hissed Ruby.

'I can't help it! It's the pine smell – too much for me.' It sniffed as if to make its point. 'So we're here then?'

'Obviously.'

'And you've taken the piece you need, so we can find our way back?'

'Don't worry, I've got it covered. What do you know about a creature called a *Wiht*?'

'Not much. They're not very common now. I mean where we're from. They're usually male. Once a man's infected, he'll grow into something much bigger, approaching the size of a large Ogre or a small *Ent*, but the body starts rotting too. They can be ferocious and difficult to kill as far as I know.'

As if on cue, a terrible shriek rolled down the hill and rattled into the pines.

'Right. Here we go then.' Ruby ducked down behind a trunk as she saw a large figure come tramping down the hill towards the treeline. It looked ungainly and swollen in the dark and Ruby caught the terrible whiff of the creature's rotting flesh more strongly now. Further back up the hill, she could see the silhouette of Drewman. He was chasing after the *Wiht*.

The creature disappeared further along into the treeline and Ruby scampered towards it, careful not to be seen. The noise of the *Wiht* crashing through the undergrowth meant that there was little danger of her being heard. Pine needles hissed and branches shook as it tramped between the trees. She followed it carefully, slipping from tree to tree, and then stopped when she saw a man appear, breathless from his run. He quickly collected himself and conjured a large white spark in his hand that gave off a bright glow and lit up his face.

The figure in front of her was clearly Drewman. Ruby recognized him as a much younger version of the head she had seen on the pedestal.

He had an angular face, his nose and cheekbones standing proud beneath a tousled mop of milky white hair. He wore a cape stretched square over broad shoulders that swirled around him as he drew back his arm and flung the spark of magic. It fizzed like a comet, flying like a bird between the trees until it hit the ones just ahead of the *Wiht*. The trees popped out of the ground and then canted at an angle and struck the creature, batting it on various parts of its large body and sending it flailing to the ground.

The *Wiht* tried to stand up, but the uprooted trees fell onto the creature, making it squeal. It lay, pinned beneath the trunks, with its arms clawing at the air and its pointed feet stabbing at the ground as it tried to get up.

Ruby kept close to the tree she was hiding behind, careful not to be seen, but such was the power and control of Drewman as he advanced to finish the creature off it was difficult not to be impressed and want to see everything.

And then Drewman stopped.

The *Wiht* was changing. Growing fast. The trees pinning it down began to fall away. Drewman flashed his hands again and more trees toppled down, smashing the creature back to the turf. It rolled and writhed as Drewman came closer and then the *Wiht* summoned a huge surge of energy and grew again. With a brute flick of its body, it heaved off the trees, sending them flying. One of them landed close to where Ruby was hiding, but luckily her cry was lost in the noise of the tree crashing into others.

When Ruby looked again, the *Wiht* was on its feet. It was huge now, taller than some of the trees. It ripped a pine out of the ground and thrust it like a rapier at Drewman with a wild cry, the roots dripping soil. But, as a makeshift weapon, it was useless among the trees and the creature soon tossed it to the ground. Ruby understood the reason for the stench in the air now: the *Wiht* was huge, lumpy and misshapen, but clearly a rotting corpse of what had once been a man. The smell seemed to curdle the air she was breathing. It was intoxicating.

'Stay sharp, Ruby,' hissed the gun.

Drewman was clearly struggling with the stench too, holding a handkerchief to his mouth and nose. He fired up some more magic in his fingers and threw another large spark at the creature. But the creature met it with a huge fist and punched it away. It flew fizzing like a fireball into the trees, sparks flying off it.

Drewman threw another spark. A bigger one. So white and bright that Ruby had to shield her eyes as she watched it.

The *Wiht*'s fist and the spark hit, causing a huge boom that rippled through the air. Ruby was knocked off her feet by the force of it and flew violently backwards before landing on her back.

She blinked up at the trees and above the ringing in her ears she heard a voice calling her name.

It was the gun.

Ruby scrambled to sit up, pine needles falling from her hair.

'Ruby,' said the gun, sounding relieved. 'For a minute, I thought—'

'I'm okay,' she said in a wobbly voice.

The *Wiht* was lying face down on the ground, its body smouldering as a smell like barbecue wafted through the air. Badly burnt barbecue. In fact, very badly burnt.

Ruby looked around, searching among the trees, and saw Drewman lying motionless on his back.

Ruby got up and hobbled as fast as she could. When she reached Drewman, she saw that his cape had been shredded and was now covered in blood. She tore off a bloodied piece and put it inside a plastic bag that she took from her pocket, which she sealed up and hid away.

'Is he alive?' asked the gun.

'Must be,' she said. 'He can't die now otherwise he wouldn't be stuck as a head on a pedestal in the present day.'

'Well, he doesn't seem to be breathing.'

Ruby bent down and touched his throat. There was no pulse. No heartbeat.

'But that can't be right,' she said, shaking her head.

And then something caught her eye. At first, she thought it was a tattoo on the back of Drewman's hand, shaped like the feathery fronds of a fern, but the black swirly marks vanished into his skin as she took a closer look.

Ruby saw other marks flash up on Drewman's skin. On his hands, his throat and face. Intricate shapes that swirled and vanished. She bent closer to watch them and saw the Black Amulet on the man's wrist. Both sets of green eyes in the serpent heads were shining and moving in their sockets, watching her every move. Each fanged mouth opened and bit down on the man's forearm. The amulet was alive!

What it was doing, Ruby wasn't sure. But there was a power in it. She could sense it in those green eyes, full of intelligence, that stared up at her. Suddenly, Drewman jerked and she realized the amulet was working to bring him back to life.

A pulse started pumping in his neck.

Black shapes swirled and whirled with more frenzy over his skin. The mouths of each serpent released the man's arm, leaving dark puncture wounds that healed instantly. And then the serpents froze and became just ends of the amulet again.

Ruby started walking away as fast as she could without making a sound. When she was at a safe distance, she started running, pausing only to snatch a glance back to see Drewman sitting up slowly. He stumbled to his feet, lurching around like a drunk until he managed to find strength in his legs.

Ruby made it out of the pine forest and into the clearing. When she saw the white stone she'd left as a marker, she ran towards it, reaching into her pocket for the tiny piece of her exit point. She lifted it into the air and felt it pull her on.

And then she stepped through the faint shimmer in the air and left the past behind.

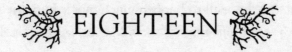# EIGHTEEN

At first, nothing happened when Thomas Gabriel attempted to cast the finding spell to try and discover the location of any of the golden boxes containing Drewman's body parts. Even the Black Amulet didn't seem to help. He sat back in his chair and looked up at the ceiling of Ruby's study and started to worry that the blood on the piece of cape he was holding wasn't enough to guide the spell and make it work, meaning Ruby's journey back in time the day before had all been in vain.

'Great,' muttered Ruby as she sat watching the boy from the other side of the desk. 'It's not working. Why's it not working?'

'I didn't sleep very well last night, worrying about the High Council meeting. Maybe my head's too fuzzy.'

'Well, de-fuzz it. Focus harder!'

'I'm trying to. It's a difficult spell.'

Ruby sat back and folded her arms and frowned. Mid-morning sunlight danced playfully over the desk as Thomas Gabriel started again.

The spell was advanced magic, beyond anything he'd tried before. Not only did the Anglo-Saxon words need careful pronunciation, but Thomas Gabriel was required to focus on *wanting* the spell to happen much more than any others he'd ever used. *The Black Book of Magical Instruction* flashed up an instruction to him as he sat back in his chair, defeated for the second time.

Think the magic into the spell to make it come alive.

Thomas Gabriel pursed his lips and sat forward again. He closed his eyes and urged the magic into the spell as he spoke it. He felt the Black Amulet straining to help him, humming with its own peculiar power.

And then something clicked inside him.

As the spell started to work, Thomas Gabriel's hand jerked to life on its own as if someone else was raising it on a string. He picked up the pencil and proceeded to draw a shape. He didn't recognize it at first. But, in a matter of minutes, he had made a detailed drawing of an island, a bird's eye view of it, far more precise than Thomas Gabriel could have drawn on his own. He wrote the name *Chiswick Eyot* beside it, before his hand became his own again and he put the pen down.

'Chis-wick Ehhh-yote?' said Ruby, who had come round to look at the name.

'You say it like the number eight,' said Thomas Gabriel, feeling rather smug. 'Chiswick Eyot's an island in London on the River Thames. There's lots of islands all along the river. They're dangerous, especially the uninhabited ones. But there's monsters hiding on the ones where people live too.'

'You're joking,' said Ruby. 'Monsters on islands? Really?'

Thomas Gabriel nodded. 'My Master, Simeon, used to tell me the islands in London are off-limits for hunting because they don't belong to anyone's *æhteland*, that they're under the control of the Order and no one's allowed on them. There's all sorts of rumours about why, though you're not supposed to talk about it. I suppose it might be because they're keeping all sorts of secrets there.'

'Do you know where this one is in London?' asked Ruby, pointing at the name.

Thomas Gabriel nodded.

'Well, the spell's obviously telling us that at least one golden box is there,' said Ruby. 'Can you use magic to find out any more? Like where it might be on the island?'

Thomas Gabriel tried the spell again, but not much more came to him. He fiddled with the Black Amulet, trying to coax some more power from it, but something was spent inside him. His head was starting to hurt. In the end, he placed a big X on the northern tip of the island.

'It's somewhere on that part of the island. I can't say where exactly. We need to take a look. Once we're there, I can try a more specific spell. We'll have to go tonight, though. We can't risk it during the day. Too many people about on the river for one thing.'

Ruby flipped open the walnut box on the desk and lifted

out the gun from the red velvet inlay as it continued to snore then splutter awake.

'We're going to a river island tonight. Could be full of monsters apparently.'

'Hoo-ya – sounds right up my street.'

'I want to get some practice in before we go.'

'Fine by me. Is Jones coming too? He and Maitland visited some river islands in their time. He'll know a thing or two.'

'Good idea.'

'If he wants to come, that is,' piped up Thomas Gabriel.

'Of course he will. I'll send him a message.'

But Thomas Gabriel just tutted and shook his head. 'You've got it all wrong about him still wanting to be a Badlander, Ruby.'

'Well, it's still worth asking him, isn't it, if these islands are as dangerous as you say?'

Thomas Gabriel just shrugged and said nothing, because at least she was right about that.

The River Thames had shrunk a lot now the tide was out.

Ruby and Thomas Gabriel stood with Jones on the shoreline where the ground was solid and pebbly, peering at the sticky-looking mud. They had snuck through someone's garden, skulking along the hedge, until they had found a ladder that let them down onto the riverbank. Behind them the city hummed as it went about its night-time business. Cars and buses droned and honked occasionally. The odd voice rang out. Somewhere, someone laughed out loud.

Beyond the narrow channel of mud in front of them, full of large stones and pools of water, was a long island covered with poplar and alder trees so densely packed they made an impenetrable green canopy with their new spring leaves. The main body of the River Thames was still flowing on the other side of the island, albeit as a narrower body of black water than usual because of the low tide.

Although he was still wearing the ordinary clothes his parents had bought him, Jones was thinking like a Badlander on the inside. He couldn't help it. Being out at night made his senses prickle far more than they had done all day at school and that excited him. But he wasn't sure how to feel about it. He hadn't told his parents he was going out with Ruby and Thomas Gabriel. As far as they knew, he was asleep in bed.

'Me and Maitland found a gang of Silver Trolls on a river island once,' he whispered to the others. 'They were hunting the cattle in the nearby fields. We picked 'em off one by one as they came out the water to feed.'

Ruby gave him a nudge. 'Sounds like you enjoyed it,' she said.

'Not really.' Jones put his hands in the pocket of his jeans. 'Well, even if I did, it was a different me then.' He shrugged as if it was no big deal. Suddenly, Jones was regretting standing on the riverbank in the middle of the night. He hadn't told his parents he was going out with Ruby and Thomas Gabriel. He had lied to them as he'd kissed them goodnight, saying he was tired and looking forward to bed. *An ordinary boy wouldn't do that*, he thought.

'Jones, I was only teasing. Is there anything else you know?'

Jones pointed at Thomas Gabriel. 'Ask him, not me. I'm not a Badlander, all right?' he told Ruby sharply. 'I wish I'd never come now. I should have stayed at home.' He dug his hands deeper in his pockets and scowled.

To Ruby he seemed as stubborn as a shell that didn't want to open. Something was definitely up with him.

'Jones, are you regretting giving up being a Badlander? You can say if you are. I know how boring ordinary life can be.'

Thomas Gabriel rolled his eyes. 'Oh, Ruby, not this again,' he muttered. 'We haven't got time,' and he pointed at the island.

Ruby ignored him. She was too busy looking at Jones, trying to figure out what was going on in his head. 'You don't have to be embarrassed,' she said.

Jones looked down at his feet. He did feel embarrassed about it because he'd always made it very clear he wanted to be an ordinary boy. But now wasn't the time to discuss it, not beside a river island, in the middle of the night.

'I don't wanna be a Badlander,' he said rather curtly to Ruby. 'I'm just here because I want the magic out of me.'

'Told you,' said Thomas Gabriel. 'Now, let's go, shall we?'

He set off across the mud towards the island without another word.

Ruby and Jones followed him in silence, wrapped up in their thoughts.

The three of them made their way across the shiny riverbed, picking a path round the rocks and the large puddles of water. The mud was sloppy and sticky and clung to their shoes. When they reached the island and started up the steep bank, they discovered large sections of it had been built up with flat stones set into concrete. They left shiny footprints as they scrambled up.

The island was boggy underfoot and it was clear the land they were walking on was submerged when the tide was up. It was choked with young willow, which made it difficult to find an easy path, so they ended up walking round the edge, which was thick with grasses and weeds and early spring flowers.

'Where do we go?' asked Ruby.

Thomas Gabriel consulted his *Black Book of Magical Instruction* and then conjured the easiest spell that could find something hidden close by. He felt the magic welling inside him and, when the Black Amulet started vibrating gently on his wrist, the magic powered up more strongly. White sparks spiralled round his hands, growing into horns like those on a snail, extending and retracting as if tasting the air. But nothing more came to Thomas Gabriel about what was hidden on the island and he tutted and shook his head.

'Keep your eyes peeled,' whispered Jones to Ruby. 'These islands can be dangerous and this one's covered in willow so that'll tell you something.'

'What?'

'*Pucan*,' he said before walking on.

Ruby's first thought was to ask Jones what he was on about. But instead she nodded, pretending she understood. She didn't want to ask him anything. If she was going to be a proper Badlander, she had to start figuring things out on her own since Jones was determined to leave her in the Badlands and be ordinary and Victor Brynn was . . .

She swallowed the lump in her throat and stopped, waiting for the boys to get a little ahead of her. When they were out of earshot, Ruby took out her Pocket Book Bestiary.

'What are *Pucan*?' she asked it in a whisper. The book vibrated in her hands before giving an answer.

Puca
(pl. Pucan)

Puca is the Anglo-Saxon name for the many
different types of Sprites, fairies and elemental beings
found in the Badlands. One such creature with the
alternative name of Will-o'-the-Wisp is known to
inhabit places where willow trees grow.

Ruby stumbled and the book went flying, landing in the mud with a loud *splat* that made Jones and Thomas Gabriel stop and look round.

The book clearly didn't like being face down in the mud. It started flapping its pages in an effort to try and get up. But the ground was too sticky. The harder it struggled, the more noise it made.

'Pick it up, will you?' hissed Jones. 'It's making too much noise.'

Ruby peeled the book out of the mud and tried her best to wipe it clean on the lush green vegetation. But the book kept flapping, trying to clean itself, making even more noise until Ruby had no option but to put it away in a pocket.

'Ask next time you don't know something,' said Jones. 'I wanna get back to my parents safe and sound tonight.'

He muttered something under his breath and walked on.

Ruby kicked at a stone. She felt so useless having to consult the book when Jones and Thomas Gabriel didn't have to. If she was going to prove herself good enough to be in the Order, she had to make sure she was at least as good as any boy, if not better.

As she walked on, she couldn't stop thinking about Jones mentioning his parents. He was lucky to have such good ones, she thought. She wished hers had been more loving and kind. She wondered whether they had been told about her running away. Perhaps they were worrying about her? They might even be out looking for her. Ruby decided it was highly unlikely. But maybe her disappearance had made them realize how much they loved her, just like Jones's parents loved him. She felt a little arrow hit her heart with a quiver. If they did really love her then they'd want her back?

When she heard her name being shouted in the distance, she looked up and saw her parents standing up in a small wooden dinghy floating on the River Thames. They were lit by an array of small lanterns suspended around them, waving at her. Quite how they'd come to be standing up in a boat on the river didn't matter to Ruby. What was important now was that they were there. They'd come looking for her, meaning they loved her after all!

Ruby veered down the bank towards the main body of the river. She ploughed into the stretch of mud by the water's edge, looking up occasionally to check her parents were still there.

As she reached the water, she felt a weight on her shoulders. Heard voices. Somebody pulled her back from the river.

'My parents,' she whispered as she tugged to get free.

Ruby felt a sharp slap on her face and she gasped with the sting of it.

'Ruby, snap out of it,' Jones said. She blinked, realizing now that he was holding her left arm and Thomas Gabriel her right. Both boys were staring at her in alarm.

Confused, she looked out across the water. Her parents weren't there. All she could see were white lights flitting low over the river.

'*Pucan*,' said Jones as he dragged Ruby back through the mud and up the bank. 'They were tricking you into the water,' he said, breathing hard. 'And now I should think they'll be angry 'bout not getting what they wanted. We need to go.'

Ruby heard a tiny shrieking sound as the lights came skimming towards them. Jones and Ruby stumbled up the bank and flopped down among the vegetation as Thomas Gabriel stood with his hands raised and fired up the magic inside him. The white sparks flicking off his fingers turned

198

into long strings lined with hooks that swirled round him as he waved his hands and cast them forward. As the hooks snagged the little white lights fizzing through the air towards them, Ruby heard high-pitched shrieks of pain. She felt her heart go out to whatever was being caught and hurt. She had to help—

'No, Ruby! You can't listen to them!' shouted Jones as he grabbed her to stop her getting up.

Ruby watched as little men swirled all round Thomas Gabriel, caught on the hooks, straining to get away. They shrieked as they clawed to try and set themselves free. But the longer they stayed snagged on the hooks, the weaker they became until they slowed, drooped and then dissolved into nothing.

Some got past Thomas Gabriel and landed beside Ruby in the grass. They peered at her with hard faces, sharp smiles and hooked noses. Some wore silver hooped earrings. Others had neckerchiefs. She pulled the gun out of her waistband, but it drooped in her hand as the *Pucan* urged to her to go into the water and she wondered dreamily if she should.

Jones flung his hands at the creatures, but they jumped out of the way like crickets. So he grabbed a branch and began swinging it around like a scythe, sending most of them spinning into the grass. The remaining *Pucan* gave up and flew away, burrowing down into the roots of the willow trees growing on the island.

Eventually, it became quiet once more.

'Are you all right?' Jones asked Ruby.

Ruby nodded. She plucked a twig from her hair.

'They were in my head,' she said.

'What were they saying?'

'That if my parents had loved me everything would be better. Ruby wrapped her arms round herself. She felt cold.

Jones looked at his muddy shoes. He wasn't quite sure what to say to Ruby to make her feel better.

'Whatever the *Pucan* told you,' he said, 'remember it's cos they wanted you drowned in that water, Ruby. They were trying to trick you.'

Ruby opened her mouth to say something else, but there was no time as Thomas Gabriel came jogging past with the snail-like horns protruding from the back of his hands again and pointing in the direction he was going.

'I'm onto something this time,' he announced. 'I can feel it.'

Ruby scrambled to her feet and ran with Jones. They caught up with Thomas Gabriel who seemed to be being pulled at a jog towards one end of the island.

'I tried a different spell,' he said breathlessly. 'One for finding things hidden by magic. As soon as I said what I was looking for, I started getting dragged along.' His legs drove him on through the boggy ground and the dense vegetation.

He stopped abruptly when the spell did, like a cord had been cut, and stood, looking round, trying to catch his breath.

He was at the very tip of the island, staring upstream at the River Thames as it flowed towards him. Lights winked on either bank. Sounds of the city rose and fell. An aeroplane's lights blinked as it cut across the sky.

Ruby and Jones were waiting expectantly when he turned round.

'The golden box is around here somewhere,' he said. 'Has to be.'

'Look,' said Ruby and pointed at a small white circle hovering in front of Thomas Gabriel at about knee-height. It looked like a tiny spotlight.

He bent down to take a closer look, careful not to put his face too near. Then he waved a hand either side of it and behind it too. Eventually, he plucked up enough courage to push a finger into the light, watching it disappear as he did so. He pulled out his finger, looking for any sign of damage, but it was fine.

'It's a hole to somewhere else,' he whispered to the others. 'The spell must have opened it and dragged me here.'

'A keyhole, do you think?' asked Jones, crouching down beside Thomas Gabriel.

'I don't know.'

Jones looked through the hole, scrunching up one eye.

'There's something in there,' he said, pressing his eye closer. 'I can see a little box.'

'Is it golden?' asked Ruby eagerly.

'Yes … I think so. Just one, though. I reckon this is a *þurhfarennesse*,' he said looking away from the hole. 'A secret compartment made with magic.'

'How do we open it?' asked Ruby.

'It says here that you can't use magic,' said Thomas Gabriel, looking in his *Black Book of Magical Instruction*. 'You have to cut it open.'

'With what?'

'It says there's a special knife, sharp enough to cut the air. We aren't getting that golden box out without something like that.'

'Maybe you can use magic to make one?' suggested Jones.

Thomas Gabriel scanned the page. 'No, I don't think—'

'Is this sharp enough?' Ruby had dug into her pocket and pulled out the Vampire's tooth. It dangled on the cord she'd strung it with.

The boys looked at the tooth and then at each other.

'Maybe,' said Jones.

'It's worth a try,' said Thomas Gabriel.

Ruby gripped the tooth by its long root and slid the sharp point into the bright hole. She started sawing upwards, tiny movements at first, trying to make an incision. The night air felt tough, like cutting through a steak with a plastic knife. But, even though progress was slow, the tooth seemed sharp enough to slice through the air.

'That's it, Ruby,' said Jones. 'Keep going.'

As the tooth made a larger cut, Ruby used her arm to start sawing backwards and forwards more efficiently.

'Stop,' said Jones. He reached forward and wiggled his fingers into the cut Ruby had made above the hole. And then he pulled. But, despite tugging as hard as he could, the dark air didn't move. 'It's like trying to fold concrete,' he said, finally removing his fingers, the skin on them red and sore.

'Look, it's healing up!' Thomas Gabriel pointed at the incision that Ruby had made. It was indeed disappearing, retreating slowly back to the bright hole from which she'd started cutting. She slid the tooth back into what was left of the slit and started cutting again. The dark felt softer this time, as if it hadn't quite healed over properly, and it was easier to cut, but, when she reached the point at which she had stopped before, Ruby noticed the texture change. She kept going, making the cut longer.

'Make sure it doesn't seal up again,' she told the boys.

Jones and Thomas Gabriel slid their hands into the space to keep it open.

When she was satisfied the incision was long enough, Ruby started cutting around the bright hole, the light from the hidden compartment shining out of it. Thomas Gabriel shuffled round, pushing his fingers into the large circle she was making, to ensure it stayed open.

After cutting almost all the way around the hole, Ruby stopped.

'Try pushing now,' she said. Jones and Thomas Gabriel pressed their hands flat on either side of the hole and pushed. The circular flap Ruby had cut started to move.

'It's heavy,' puffed Jones. Thomas Gabriel was straining too. But they managed to press the dark in further and flipped up the small circular hatch Ruby had made.

They all saw the small gold box at the same time. It seemed to be floating in the air.

'Hurry up, Ruby,' gasped Jones. 'This stuff is heavy.' Thomas Gabriel grunted in agreement. So she reached an arm in and plucked the box from the secret space.

It was cold. Like taking something out of the fridge.

Jones and Thomas Gabriel let go of the piece of night air and it flipped back into position with a clunk. The incisions Ruby had made started healing up almost immediately.

Ruby turned the golden box in her hands and opened it carefully. Inside was a small heap of fine black ash.

Jones and Thomas Gabriel peered over her shoulder.

'I wonder which bits of Drewman are here?' she said.

'It doesn't matter as long as we find the rest of him,' replied Jones. 'There's two more golden boxes hidden somewhere.'

NINETEEN

I t was easy enough for Thomas Gabriel to find the next hiding place. He didn't bother going to bed when he returned to his house in Hampstead.

The invitation was still ticking, of course, reminding him there was less than a week now until his test in front of the High Council. But that wasn't the only reason he was so keen to cast the spell. Using the Black Amulet made him feel invincible. Having used it a lot now, he seemed to be in tune with it. His body felt cold and hollow whenever he wasn't wearing it. So he had taken to keeping it on his wrist all the time. As long as he kept taking the bitter potions as Drewman had said, he knew he'd be okay.

Once more, he channelled the magic, his hand being moved to draw a picture of an island he didn't know. The image was more detailed this time, the spell seeming to work more precisely than before, and Thomas Gabriel knew it was because his mastery of the Black Amulet was growing.

The name of the island he wrote down was *Lion Island*.

Keen to use the Black Amulet once more, he cast the spell

again to find the location of the third golden box. Another island came into focus, but it was hazier this time, and his drawing was loose and basic, nothing like the detailed one for Lion Island.

He urged the amulet to give him more power and it did so, allowing him to produce a more accurate drawing. But the name eluded him. Without it, the drawing was useless.

'Give me more!' he shouted at the amulet and he felt his heart tighten as he tried to squeeze the spell harder. 'MORE!' he roared and he saw the two snake heads on the amulet come alive, wriggling and hissing.

'*More!*' he roared and he saw the two snake heads on the amulet come alive, wriggling and hissing before biting down into his arm. A surge of magic rushed through him and he knew at once the name of the island he had drawn.

He went to consult the maps in Simeon's collection, but not one of them was detailed enough to find out if the islands were on the River Thames like Chiswick Eyot as he suspected.

His mind started to drift. He knew he was tired. But he wondered if it was more than that. Ever since the two snake heads had bitten him, a slight buzzing had been ringing in his ears and he had felt drained, despite the puncture marks having disappeared, leaving no trace on his skin.

He drank down a bitter potion and decided to get a few hours' sleep. As he fell into a dream, he saw the Black Amulet spinning in front of him. It was bigger than him.

And then the snakes' mouths opened and they fell upon him with a scream as though ready to tear him apart.

When Ruby opened the curtains, Thomas Gabriel stirred. She gave him a shove and sniffed at the empty bottle by his bed. The smell of bitter potion wrinkled her nose.

'Wake up, sleepyhead,' she said as Thomas Gabriel groaned. She held the gun to his ear and it shouted loudly, giving him a shock that made him sit bolt upright, making Ruby chuckle.

'What ... what time is it?'

'The afternoon.'

Thomas Gabriel licked his lips. His mouth was dry and he was very thirsty. 'I was tired. I think using the amulet wore me out.'

He beamed as he remembered what he had done. 'I got the locations for the other two golden boxes, Ruby.'

'I know.' She held up the two drawings he had made.

'You shouldn't go through my stuff,' complained Thomas Gabriel.

'Lion Island,' said Ruby, ignoring him, 'and Appletree ...' She paused to make sure she pronounced it properly. 'Appletree Eyot. Are they on the River Thames too?'

'I'm not sure. I need to consult a detailed map to know for certain.'

'It wouldn't take a second to find out where they are on a phone or a computer.'

'I'm a Badlander, Ruby. I don't use those sorts of devices.

And neither should you if you really want to be a Badlander too.'

'Hmm, well, we all know the Order needs updating.' She clicked her fingers when something occurred to her. 'We should ask Jones to look this up for us. He's not a Badlander, or so he keeps telling us, and it'll be much quicker to find these islands on the Internet than searching through maps.'

'I don't think he'll want us turning up at his house. He's trying to keep the Badlands and the ordinary world separate. And what about us? Do we call him Jones or Ed if we go to see him? I get confused.'

'We'll call him Ed and we won't mention anything to do with the Badlands at all. It'll be fine. He needs to find the rest of Drewman as much as we do if he wants that magic out of him. And . . .' She pulled back the covers and ushered Thomas Gabriel out of bed. 'You need to make sure you pass that test of yours in front of the High Council.' She waved a hand at him. 'Come on, up! Jones should be back home from school by the time we walk there.'

They walked from Thomas Gabriel's house through his *æhteland* of Hampstead. Spring was bulging in the buds on some of the trees. In others, pink blossom had already grown like coral across the branches. Tulips and daffodils stood tall in people's gardens.

'The Order could do with a fresh start too,' said Ruby, stooping to sniff a bed of purple flowers which she thought might be pansies.

'Yes, I know, blah-blah-blah, girls in the Order, blah-blah-blah,' said Thomas Gabriel.

Ruby looked like she'd bitten into a lemon. 'Actually, I meant they should update everything. Use all the technology there is now. Like phones and the Internet and cameras.'

'We've got magic – why do we need anything else?'

'Apprentices can't use magic unless they've Commenced. And just think how much easier it would be not having to look things up in books all the time. Why not use magic and technology? It would make the Order better.'

'Books are important. They're a tradition.'

'But they're not as quick as the Internet at giving you the answer.'

'You can trust what's written in a book. Who writes this Internet thing?'

Ruby puffed out her cheeks.

'The Order will die out if it doesn't modernize, you know.'

Thomas Gabriel burst out laughing. A couple of people on the other side of the street looked up in their direction.

'It's done all right so far,' said the boy.

Ruby kicked at a stone and sent it spinning into the road. 'You're just like all the rest of them,' she muttered. 'You shouldn't be wearing that amulet all the time, by the way,' she said.

But Thomas Gabriel didn't seem to hear her.

The moment Ed opened the front door and Ruby stepped into the house, something changed gear inside her and she forgot how annoyed she was with Thomas Gabriel. For the first time since running away, she began to realize how much she was missing out on things ordinary kids her age took for granted. Like feeling safe when you shut the front door. And how little responsibility there was, meaning you only had to worry about things important to you. But above all, she realized, she missed talking to people.

Ed's parents knew all about the Badlands of course, but they chose not to mention the place at all when they realized Ruby and Thomas Gabriel were avoiding it too.

Ed beamed as the conversation developed a friendly life of its own, pulling everyone into it. Ruby could see he was happy. His mum and dad were making him feel like any ordinary boy whose friends had turned up. Ruby was happy for him too.

But then she noticed both adults glancing at the Black Amulet bobbing up and down on Thomas Gabriel's wrist.

Suddenly, the atmosphere changed. There was a strange prickle in the air and both adults began to pant. Their brows glistened. A second later, they started to shout, their anguished voices rising louder and louder.

'What's wrong?' asked Ed as he tried to calm his mother down. But she just lashed out at him and sent him lurching back, dodging her nails, which slashed through the air in front of his face.

Ruby grabbed Thomas Gabriel and dragged him as far as she could down the hallway, away from the two screaming adults. He was too shocked to say anything until they were almost in the kitchen and then he was pushing her away and straightening his coat.

'Get off me! What are you doing? I can help. I'll calm them down,' and he conjured a set of white sparks round his fingers.

'Is that so?'

'Yes! Obviously, they're having some sort of episode, something to do with the after-effects of the Witch's curse.'

'*That's* the problem,' she said, pointing to the Black Amulet. 'You'll only make it worse if they see it again.'

He extinguished the sparks around his fingers and began playing with the amulet, spinning it round and round.

'That thing's dangerous,' she continued. 'Drewman made that very clear.'

'I don't think it's that evil—'

'All Jone— I mean all Ed's parents did was see it on your wrist and look how it affected them. The power inside it must have sparked some leftover part of the Witch's curse.'

Thomas Gabriel glanced back at the adults. They were recovering, shaking their heads, and shooting looks down the hallway at him.

'You shouldn't be wearing the amulet all the time,' said Ruby. 'There's no reason to.'

'You shouldn't tell a Badlander what to do on his *æhteland* when it comes to magic.'

'Sounds like another stupid rule to me.'

Thomas Gabriel folded his arms and smiled. 'That's what's really wrong, isn't it? All those rules. All those things girls can't do or use. Or even wear.' He grinned and waggled his hand, making the amulet wobble on his wrist. 'You're jealous.'

Something hot and red welled up in Ruby at the boy's knowing smile and she took a step forward, ready to shake it off his face.

'I'm not taking it off!' hissed Thomas Gabriel, thinking Ruby was reaching for the amulet. He flashed out a hand and white sparks erupted, making her stop.

She took a quick step back, but not just because of the threat of magic being used on her. Ruby had been shocked by something else too. A ghostly version of the boy's face had leapt out at her for a split second. It was as if Thomas Gabriel had been jerked backwards, leaving a part of him behind that had been kept well hidden up to now. The face had looked vicious, with a mouth full of jagged teeth. Its hollow eyes had bored into Ruby, not seeming to recognize her or care who she was.

And then it had slipped back into the boy in the blink of an eye.

Thomas Gabriel didn't seem to be aware of what had happened. As he toyed with the sparks around his fingers, Ruby stared into his eyes, trying to see what might lie behind them, at this darker part of him that had wanted to protect the amulet. But she could see nothing.

When she blinked, she saw the ghostly black face again on the inside of her eyelids. She rubbed the goosebumps off her arms.

Thomas Gabriel snuffed out the sparks at the ends of his fingers as they vanished.

'I was only trying to give you a little fright,' he mumbled. He lowered his voice. 'It's a shame about Jone— I mean Ed's parents. But you can't know for sure it was the amulet that affected them. It could have been our fault. Maybe *we* sparked some part of the Witch's curse left in them. They haven't seen us since she was killed. No one really knows what effects a curse like that can have on people. We should be careful and considerate around them.'

Thoughts fluttered inside Ruby. Thomas Gabriel was right about her feeling angry about the Order and its rules. And, deep down, she knew she was jealous of him being able to do magic too. But she also knew that, despite all of that, she was right about the amulet being dangerous. And maybe not just for the person wearing it, but perhaps for other people too.

Ed was proud of his laptop and took great pains to show Ruby he knew exactly how to use it given she had taught him how to get on the Internet soon after they'd first met.

Thomas Gabriel was less impressed. Ruby noticed him fiddling with the amulet. It annoyed her and she grabbed his arm at one point to stop him. He shot her angry looks after that as Ed tapped on his keyboard.

'There,' said Ed, pointing at the screen. 'Lion Island is definitely on the River Thames. But it's outside London, in a place called Old Windsor. Appletree Eyot's even further up

213

the river.' He ran his finger over the touch pad, zeroing in closer on the satellite map on the screen.

'It's just green trees,' said Thomas Gabriel, peering at the pixelated canopy covering the island.

'Well, it's hardly going to show pictures of monsters, is it?' snapped Ruby.

'Well then, your stupid technology isn't as good as magic after all. If you'd scryed to find the islands then it would show any monsters too.' He smiled smugly at her.

'Wrong!' chimed Ruby. 'Any scryer knows you can't scry on a place you've never been to.'

Thomas Gabriel tutted. Rolled his eyes. 'Then how come you can go back to somewhere in the past you've never been to before then?'

'That, Thomas Gabriel, is a very good question. I'll get back to you on that. Maybe I'll write a chapter about it in my book on scrying through time that every Badlander will want to read.'

Thomas Gabriel just shook his head and grumbled something under his breath.

Ed ignored their bickering as he brought up various images of the two islands. There was nothing out of the ordinary about them that he could see.

'I think the first finding spell you used flagged up Chiswick Eyot cos it was the nearest. That's why you found out about Lion Island next, and then Appletree Eyot, the furthest one away,' said Ed. 'Whether it works by location or not, finding the other two golden boxes means going out of London.'

'That doesn't matter – we can use Slap Dust,' said Thomas Gabriel.

Ed shook his head. 'Not without knowing what might be there first.' He tapped the screen. 'Could be anything lying in wait. We'll have to go in the van.'

'A road trip?' Ruby looked at Ed with some surprise.

'Yep. Me and Maitland always kept the van stocked with things we might need on a trip, unless you've been using them?'

Ruby shook her head. 'No, everything's just how you left it,' she said. 'But what I meant was … what about your parents? And what about school? I wouldn't have thought you'd want to miss that for Badlander stuff.'

'School's finished today. It's the Easter holidays now. I'll speak to my parents. I have a feeling they'll understand.'

'But are you sure you want to come?' asked Ruby.

'Don't you want me to?' said Ed, sounding a little crestfallen.

'Of course. But …' She looked at Thomas Gabriel who just shrugged.

Ed studied the toe of his shoe for a moment. 'You were right what you said last night,' he said quietly. 'I do regret giving up being a Badlander.'

Ruby sat back in her chair and nodded. 'I knew it,' she said and threw Thomas Gabriel a triumphant stare. 'I knew there was something up.'

'But Ruby, I want to be an ordinary boy too and I can't be that with magic inside me. It's not meant to be in the regular

215

world. It needs to come out of me. And, besides, you need my share of magic if Drewman's gonna fix our Commencement, so you can cast spells and prove girls can be Badlanders. But without magic I can't be a proper Badlander either. So, however much I want to be both, I can't.' Ed sighed and shook his head. 'That's what's been bothering me.'

Ruby leant forward and took his hands in hers. 'You can still be both if you want to.' Ed looked at her, unsure what she was getting at. 'You don't have to be a regular Badlander. I won't be, even if Drewman fixes our Commencement. I'll always be a girl. I'll be different to other Badlanders. So why can't you be a different type of Badlander too?'

She waved her hands at the computer. 'One with technology and things from the ordinary world instead of magic. Who says what being normal is when it comes to anything, even being a Badlander?'

Ed stared at her. Blinking. His mouth opened and shut.

Thomas Gabriel waved his arms. '*Hell-oo?* What about the *Ordnung*—'

Ruby whirled round and looked at him. 'That's my point, Thomas Gabriel. He doesn't have to follow it. He can be something new without it. Just like being a girl Badlander.'

Ed sat there, thinking about that, and then he reached forward and gave Ruby such a big hug she thought her ribs might break.

'Thank you,' he said.

'You're welcome. Now let's go and find those two other golden boxes and get this thing done.'

Ed nodded. And then something occurred to him, and he got up and opened his wardrobe. Reaching into the back, he dragged out a plastic storage box. After flipping up the two blue clips at either end, he took off the lid and lifted out his old grey overcoat. Shook it out. And put it on.

Ed reached into his limitless pockets with both hands and rummaged around, remembering what was in them. He brought out his catapult in one hand and a silver ball bearing from the other and rolled it in his fingers. And then he looked up and grinned.

 TWENTY

When Jones pulled off the tarp from the VW camper van in the outhouse, his heart lifted. It was like meeting an old trusted friend again. All sorts of memories came flooding back as he opened the door, not only with the familiar *click* of the handle but with the smell of the van's interior too.

The cupboards were still as well stocked as when he and Maitland had been using the vehicle. He whipped off the dust sheets from the table and seats as well as the cooker and the worktops. Everything was spick and span underneath.

When he tried the key in the ignition, the engine turned over and over and he was wary of flooding it, so he stopped and waited and tried again. It started the next time and the van spluttered into life. The petrol gauge was low, but there was still a full jerrycan left from the last trip. He checked the others and was pleased to find one of the other cans was about half full as he knocked the side of it.

He poured in everything he could find and the petrol gauge went up to about halfway, which he figured would be enough. He wasn't too concerned because he knew he could get away with filling up jerrycans at the petrol station with nobody asking questions. Not only did he have his own debit card now because he had been old enough to open a bank account, just, but he knew how to use a card at the pump by typing in the number. Only a couple of weeks ago, his father had sent him to get fuel for the lawnmower at the local garage after it had coughed and died with their garden only half mown.

After Jones had checked the oil, as well as the tyre pressure and the lights and indicators, he was satisfied the trip could start. He sat with Ruby in the kitchen, drinking tea and talking, as the last of the daylight dwindled, waiting for Thomas Gabriel to arrive after the boy had gone home to collect his things for the trip. Jones had suggested driving to Old Windsor that night because, with less traffic on the roads, the journey would be quicker than during the day. If all went well, they would be able to explore Lion Island before daybreak and hopefully find the next golden box.

Thomas Gabriel was ready to leave his house in Hampstead to meet the others, a bottle of Slap Dust in his hand and a duffel bag over his shoulder, when the air in front of him started to fizz.

A moment later, an official-looking white envelope was hovering in front of him, his name written on the front in black ink. Thomas Gabriel knew, of course, that it was a charmed message designed to appear to the recipient wherever they might be. But he had no idea who such a message might be from. Intrigued, Thomas Gabriel opened the envelope. Inside was a card bearing a short message in neat black handwriting:

I request a meeting immediately
R. Givens

Thomas Gabriel read it again. And again. His heart started to thump in his ears. Now the envelope had been opened, Givens would have had a receipt of delivery, telling him the message had been received. An official request for a meeting from one's mentor was not supposed to be refused, especially when it was with someone as important as Randall Givens. Thomas Gabriel knew that doing so would be another black mark against his name and he had a few of those already.

The boy found a pen in his pocket and scribbled the word 'Accepted' and tapped the card three times. It vanished.

He set down his duffel bag and his mind turned to the amulet. Under no circumstances could he allow Givens to see that. He would have to take it off.

But knowing he had to was very different to actually doing it. His fingers hovered nervously over the amulet. It felt like a part of him now. He stood for a few moments, trying to sum up the courage to remove it. Finally, he took a deep breath. But, at his touch, the amulet tightened round his wrist as if knowing what he was about to do and not wanting to be parted from him. The little snakes' heads bared their teeth as he pulled harder and a place somewhere inside his chest started to hurt. One of the heads bit down on his hand, making him gasp, and not letting go.

'It won't be for long,' he whispered. The green eyes of the serpents stared at him and he looked as deep as he could into them. 'I will never give you up,' he promised. 'Never.'

The snake's mouth released him and the amulet loosened. As the puncture wounds vanished, Thomas Gabriel took off the amulet and put it in his pocket. His wrist looked bare without it. A piece of his heart seemed to be missing too. And then he set about wiping the sweat from his brow and smoothing down his hair, trying to make himself presentable for Givens, waiting for another message telling him where to go.

It didn't take long to arrive.

Good.
According to delivery receipt of previous message, you're at home.
Arriving in a jiffy.
I take Earl Grey tea. Wilfried does too.

Thomas Gabriel's heart sagged. A mentor could expect to be entertained by his student if he so wished, according to the *Ordnung*.

Givens and Wilfried arrived a few moments later with a flourish.

Givens beamed. 'Thought we'd come to you as we're still

221

on the road. A few bits of admin have come up that we need to attend to. But, first of all, Wilfried wanted to say thank you. Didn't you?'

When he slapped a hand on Wilfried's shoulder, his apprentice sparked into life and smiled too.

'You were really great the other night, helping us out.'

Thomas Gabriel shook Wilfried's little hand and smiled back as best he could, resisting the urge to squeeze as hard as possible. The anger and resentment inside him at being forced to take off the amulet were spinning round and round and it felt like they needed somewhere to go. But he did his best not to make a scene, although his smile was so pained it came out more like a grimace.

'So,' said Thomas Gabriel. 'What was it that needed attending to, sir?'

Givens smiled. 'Let's have that tea while we talk, shall we?'

Thomas Gabriel gave them tea in the kitchen rather the drawing room, which would have been more fitting for someone of Givens's importance. But, rather than waste time getting out the best china and setting up places around the table, he poured the tea into mugs and put out a plate of biscuits. He wanted Givens and Wilfried gone quickly because he knew Jones and Ruby were waiting for him to join them for their night drive to Old Windsor. It was already early evening and getting dark outside.

He could not stop thinking about the amulet either. He wanted it back on his wrist. His mind felt cloudy and tired without it.

When he splashed the milk everywhere, he cursed.

'All right?' asked Givens.

'Just tired.'

'Must be hard work running an *æhteland* like this one on your own, and at your age too. I'm sure old Simeon would be very proud.'

As Thomas Gabriel poured the tea and sat down, Givens smiled and took a big slurp. He picked up a biscuit and took a bite. And then he suddenly stopped chewing and burped. It smelt like rotten apples.

'Sorry,' said Givens. 'Still suffering after those Burrowing Trolls the other night.'

'The after-effects of being exposed to the breath of Burrowing Trolls can last up to a week,' agreed Wilfried.

'Quite right, Wilfried. How about you, Thomas Gabriel, no problems?'

'Everything seems okay,' replied the boy, the words barely slipping out between his clenched teeth.

'And what about your magic?'

'What do you mean, sir?'

'Well, I'll let you into a secret. We were looking for an important object at the abbey, a magical item that I suspected to have been hidden there a long time ago. I was convinced it was there, but we didn't find it, worst luck.' Givens tapped a finger on his lips. 'However, I've been thinking. I was so struck by the improvement in your use of magic that perhaps the object is there and we just didn't look hard enough for it.'

He leant forward. 'Are you sure you felt the same as usual the other night? Did you have the sense of being able to do anything? That your magical power was enhanced?'

Thomas Gabriel could see an excited spark in the man's eyes.

'Do you remember touching anything? Picking anything up? Try and think back, boy – it could be very important.'

Thomas Gabriel shook his head. 'Not that I remember, sir. Nothing felt out of the ordinary,' he said. 'I think it's just that I've been practising hard at using my magic.'

Givens sat back in his chair. Folded his arms. 'Of course.' He looked at the boy and frowned.

'Sorry I can't help.'

Givens nodded. 'Then, as head of the High Council, I have no option but to bring its annual meeting forward to the day after tomorrow in fact.'

Thomas Gabriel grabbed at his chair to stop himself falling off it. 'Wh-aa ... What?' he stammered.

Givens took a small diary out of his pocket and started leafing through it. 'The Order has been looking for this magical object for decades. It seems we are destined never to find it,' he sighed. 'The High Council must be informed of the results of my most recent search as soon as possible, once I've completed all the necessary paperwork and written up my findings and recommendations about what to do next. There are some extremely pressing decisions to be made now about what to do with the person who hid this object.'

Givens brightened. 'But that's no concern of yours, of

course. What is your concern, though, is that your magical test is now going to be the day after tomorrow.'

Thomas Gabriel's heart started beating harder and harder. 'But—'

Givens raised his hand. 'If you'll just let me adjust the meeting date, please.' He fired a white spark at the diary page he had found and smiled. 'There. Done. As head of the Council, I can change the date of the meeting if it's deemed necessary for any very important reason.' He flashed a big smile, apparently extremely pleased about this fact.

Thomas Gabriel felt a buzz in his coat pocket and he knew his invitation was readjusting to the new date.

'But I can—'

'Now, now,' said Givens. 'It's nothing to worry about. You seem to have the measure of magic, judging by the other night. But there is still room for improvement. So I think we should have a final practice. Get you ready for the big day. Other members of the Order might want you to fail, but I don't. As your mentor, any failure would reflect badly on me. Wilfried can watch and learn a few things as we go.'

Thomas Gabriel wiped his sweaty brow. Givens's smile was like a bright light getting in his eyes.

'We'll do it under exam conditions, just as you'll be examined at the meeting.' Givens reached into a pocket and brought out a glass jar. He popped off the lid and a One Eye came fluttering out. Thomas Gabriel's heart sank down into his stomach as he watched the tiny creature land on Givens's shoulder. It was a bit bigger than the one he'd owned. This creature had a red stripe across its face, running below its eyes and over the bridge of its nose.

'At your official examination, there'll be a One Eye present to ensure you're not using unfair magical means. And so it should be for our dress rehearsal too. So rather than use your One Eye we'll use mine. Where is yours, by the way?' asked Givens, looking around.

Thomas Gabriel swallowed hard. His brain was so full of thinking it was ready to burst like an overripe fruit.

'I . . . I lost it,' replied Thomas Gabriel.

'Oops.' Givens tutted. Shook his head. 'Well, mine just needs to check you over, before we can proceed.'

He clicked his fingers and the One Eye took off, fluttering towards Thomas Gabriel. For a couple of seconds, all the boy could hear was the drumming of his heart. And then the One Eye was hovering in front of his face, staring him in the eyes.

'Come on!' said Givens. 'We don't have all night,' he said, gesturing to the fact it was getting dark outside the kitchen window.

The One Eye darted down into a limitless pocket of Thomas Gabriel's coat. He could feel it rummaging around. When it fluttered out and flew to the other pocket where the Black Amulet was hidden, Thomas Gabriel's heart hammered louder and louder in his chest. It felt like the whole kitchen was pounding around him. As the One Eye grabbed hold of the pocket with its tiny fingers, and peered inside, it gave a squeak of surprise and looked up at Thomas Gabriel.

'What is it?' asked Givens.

Something snapped inside Thomas Gabriel. He flashed out a hand and flicked at the One Eye, sending it somersaulting through the air. It stopped short of hitting the wall as its wings fizzed and slowed it down. And then it growled and flew towards the boy again, baring its set of big teeth.

'Stop!' shouted Givens, putting up his hand, and the One Eye braked in mid-air.

Thomas Gabriel couldn't stand it any longer. He reached into his pocket for the amulet and slipped it on. He seemed to breathe more deeply, right into the pit of his diaphragm. His thinking became sharper. Energy surged through his body.

Givens gasped and leant forward when he saw what the boy was wearing. Words seemed to have escaped him.

'You're not having it,' hissed Thomas Gabriel. 'It's mine.'

Givens stood up from his chair with a quick movement, sending it toppling backwards. He flashed a fistful of white sparks at the boy that stretched into a pointed bolt of light. But Thomas Gabriel was just as quick and spoke a spell that sent a shower of white sparks billowing round him like a tiny galaxy of stars. They formed a protective shield that absorbed the bolt from Givens, blunting and dissolving it. Thomas Gabriel fired his own magic back, a blue wave of sparks that flew from his hands, through the glittering shield and crashed into the man. Caught by surprise, Givens was sent reeling backwards with enough force to hit the wall. He collapsed in a heap of arms and legs, and didn't move.

The One Eye hurtled into the protective screen around Thomas Gabriel, its teeth bared, but was pinged away with such force that it hit the wall with a nasty crack that meant something was broken inside and dropped to the floor.

The end of a golden rope licked itself round Thomas Gabriel's chest and he felt it tighten, pulling his arms close to his body. He looked across at Wilfried, who was holding the other end of the rope with both hands. But Thomas Gabriel was stronger than the other boy and yanked the rope, pulling him to the floor. As he raised a hand and conjured more white sparks, the younger boy raised his hands, like a criminal giving himself up, his eyes darting towards Givens who was still out cold.

Thomas Gabriel's anger was all gone. Now the amulet was back on his wrist, he was feeling a lot calmer.

'I'm not going to hurt you,' he told Wilfried. 'But you have to promise to help me. I'm not a bad person.'

'Then why did you do that?'

'Because even though he wants this,' said Thomas Gabriel, pointing to the amulet, 'I can't give it to him. I need it.'

'He told me that amulet was dangerous. That it can't be trusted.'

'Only if you don't take precautions. The person who owned it before me told me how to handle it. I'm safe.'

'No one's safe,' said Wilfried. 'It's evil. It uses *áglæccræft*.'

Thomas Gabriel ignored him. There were other more important things to worry about. A big egg-shaped bump had appeared on Givens's forehead. But the man was breathing and clearly alive.

'I won't help you,' said Wilfried.

Thomas Gabriel chewed the inside of his mouth as he stared at the boy. Thoughts flashed through his head and he nodded.

'Yes, you will.'

When Givens came round, he touched his head immediately and groaned. The chair creaked as he leant back and looked up at the ceiling to get his bearings.

'What happened?' he asked in a weak voice, his pale face all shiny.

Wilfried looked down at the floor for a split second and Thomas Gabriel watched him, in case the other boy lost his nerve and blurted out the truth. Although the amulet was hidden beneath Thomas Gabriel's shirtsleeve, Wilfried knew it was there and what Thomas Gabriel could do with it.

'It was the One Eye, sir,' said Wilfried. 'Don't you remember?'

Givens shook his head, which was clearly a painful thing to do. He took a moment to gather his thoughts. 'What do you mean? What happened?'

'Your apprentice is right, I'm afraid, sir. Your One Eye was sick. It turned on you.'

'Impossible.'

'I'm afraid not. We both witnessed it.' Thomas Gabriel looked over at Wilfried, who nodded.

'He's right, sir.'

Givens looked at his apprentice and frowned as he tried to recall what they were saying.

'Your apprentice saved you, sir. He was remarkable, keeping cool under pressure like that. He's got great skill with that golden rope of his. You've taught him very well.'

'When you fell off the chair,' continued Wilfried, 'and bumped your head, sir, you knocked yourself out. I just had time to lasso the One Eye before it took a bite out of you, and Thomas Gabriel despatched it.'

Wilfried pointed to the One Eye lying dead on the kitchen table. The red stripe across its face had faded now and its folded wings had stiffened. It was about the size of a dead sparrow. 'It could have taken half your face off with one bite,' he said.

Thomas Gabriel had relaxed now Wilfried was playing along. He could sense the boy was warming to the story. A lie was easier to get used to if you believed it, that's what he'd told him. And perhaps Wilfried was realizing now how easy it might be to curry favour for saving his Master. Thomas Gabriel had told him it would be. He pointed to the book on the table beside the dead One Eye. It was a copy of the Pocket Book Bestiary.

'We think it was down to the Burrowing Trolls the other night. The fumes can linger in the threads of clothes and cause madness. It's recommended you burn them to be absolutely safe and I'm afraid I did not. When you sent the One Eye over to me and it climbed into my pocket, all its digging around must have roused the fumes in the threads of my coat. It flew out, disoriented, and attacked the first thing it saw. You.'

Givens opened his mouth. His tongue flapped, but he coughed instead.

'It's rare, sir,' Wilfried said. 'But it can happen, according to what the book says.'

Givens stared at the dead One Eye on the table and the Pocket Book Bestiary. His eyes moved from one to the other and back again, trying to piece everything together. And then the man looked up at Wilfried and Thomas Gabriel. There was a bright look of frustration in his eyes.

'I'm sorry this happened, sir,' said Thomas Gabriel. 'Perhaps it would be best to forget any dress rehearsal for my assessment by the High Council now? The evening's getting on.'

Givens nodded. 'Yes … I think …' He coughed and croaked. 'I think you have proved yourself more than worthy of taking the test the day after tomorrow.'

When Givens and his apprentice had left, Thomas Gabriel slid the Black Amulet down his arm. It felt good to be wearing it properly again.

He knew that Ruby and Jones would be wondering where on earth he was since it was so late and it reminded him that they would nag him about taking the bitter potion too. He went to his study to look for the bottle.

But the liquid made his mouth and tongue burn and he

spat it out onto the floor, fanning his mouth to try and cool it down. He wondered if the bottle had been left open too long, making the potion go off.

He poured the contents down the kitchen sink. As it glugged down the plughole, he thought of Wilfried being unable to keep down the lie he had told to his Master. Although Thomas Gabriel had used his Memory Leech on Givens, replacing the truth of what had really happened with a new version of events, the new memory would only ever be a vague one for Givens to make it feel like he had genuinely been attacked and then knocked out, giving him only a hazy feel for what was supposed to have happened. It meant Wilfried's lie was important in backing it up.

Thomas Gabriel took out a small silver pillbox from his pocket and flipped open the lid to reassure himself that Wilfried would never tell the truth.

Lying on a red velvet inlay was a glass vial about half the length of a finger. There was a yellow mist trapped inside it, contained by a cork pushed deep into the neck of the vial. Holding it up to the kitchen light, Thomas Gabriel watched the *wælmist* shimmer as it twisted and turned. He had made it very clear to Wilfried what would happen to Givens if he ever did tell the truth to his Master.

Thomas Gabriel put the vial back in its pillbox and snapped the lid shut. Jones and Ruby would definitely be wondering where he was. It was time to find the rest of Drewman as soon as possible now the High Council meeting had been moved forward even earlier. Thomas Gabriel smiled as he imagined passing the test with flying colours once Drewman had fixed his Commencement.

He strode into the hallway and picked up his duffel bag and heard the clink of a couple of unopened bottles of bitter potion. He'd take some later, he decided.

 # TWENTY-ONE

T he journey to the village of Old Windsor took longer than Jones expected, even though they were driving at night. An accident had blocked the dual carriageway and they stood idling in traffic for some time. Thomas Gabriel became more and more agitated, given that his assessment in front of the High Council was less than two days away. But there was no magic they could do to clear the road.

As Jones sat with cars to his right in the outer lane, he was glad for the charm that Maitland had put on the van meaning that whenever the boy was driving it looked like his old Master was at the wheel.

By the time the accident was cleared, they had lost some time and the satnav on the mobile phone Jones had brought with him said their new arrival time was three o'clock in the morning. He had decided to bring the phone after Ruby's suggestion about using technology instead of magic. Thomas Gabriel did not approve, but even he had eventually agreed it was 'quite' useful when the satnav suddenly announced a different route that would save time.

When they reached Old Windsor, Ruby turned off the satnav and used one of the maps to direct Jones towards Lion Island, which lay upstream of the village. They took a turning off the main road and pottered down a lane until they found a farm track where they parked. Jones turned off the headlights and the sharp-looking sickle moon bathed the hedge next to them in silver. The track leading to the river looked icy in the light. It was three thirty in the morning.

Jones took some salt and rosemary vials from a cupboard and put them in his pockets.

'We don't know what might be on the island,' he said as he looked through the rest of the cupboards and plucked a few more things from the shelves.

Meanwhile, Ruby checked the gun was clean and ready. She also made sure she had a full vial of Slap Dust and consulted her Pocket Book Bestiary to see what sort of creatures might be found on a river island at night. The book spluttered for a minute and grew larger in her hands and the pages started filling up. And filling up. And filling up.

When it was done, Ruby had to put the Bestiary down on the table because it was so heavy.

As she flicked through the pages, there were sections about creatures that only lived in the water, as well as ones about amphibious monsters, land dwellers and those in the air too.

'Don't worry,' said Thomas Gabriel, peering over her shoulder. 'We'll be safe with the amulet.' His breath was warm and garlicky from the bitter potion he'd been sipping on the journey. Ruby offered him a white pellet of chewing gum.

'What's that?' he asked, looking at it suspiciously.

'Ask Jones,' she said, putting the gum in his hand. 'Protects against something really important.' She leant in close. 'Bad breath.'

Thomas Gabriel shot her a look and then sniffed the gum. He popped it in his mouth and started chewing. Ruby watched him take a crafty sniff of his breath, cupping his hand and breathing into it.

They had to cross two fields to get to the riverbank. The island was separated from the bank by a thin strip of water that was too wide for jumping across. Downstream of the island was a lock and a large weir over which the water tumbled noisily, foaming white before becoming black again.

'We can use Slap Dust to get across,' said Ruby as she uncorked the vial. But Jones waved her idea away. He pointed to an old dinghy tied to the bank downstream of them near the lock.

'We'll use that. It's best to approach any island cautiously and get a good look at it first. See if there are clues about what might be there before we set foot on it.'

But, when Ruby started walking towards the dinghy, Jones pulled her back.

'Let's just sit here for a little while,' he said, taking a seat on an old stump by the bank and wrapping his overcoat round him. Thomas Gabriel leant against a tree. Both boys said nothing as they scanned the river's surface.

'Can't we just go?' asked Ruby. 'We haven't got time to sit about.'

'Five minutes,' said Jones.

Thomas Gabriel didn't even look at her as he concentrated on peeling off the bark from a fresh green stick, the wood like a bone in the grainy light.

Ruby was about to ask what all the waiting was about when Jones waved at her to crouch down. He pointed to the ripples in the middle of the slow-moving water. Something had entered the river from the bank of the island and was swimming towards them.

'It's got our scent,' said Jones.

'What has?' whispered Ruby.

'I think I know . . .' Jones said and motioned for them to retreat among the trees where they crouched behind the nearest trunks. Ruby watched the dark shape slither out of the water up the muddy bank and lie flat in the grass. It could have been a long stick lying there. And then it moved and snaked fast towards them, a forked tongue darting out between fangs.

'It's a *sláwyrm*,' hissed Jones. 'A small one.' He pointed up with a finger and quickly the three children clambered up into the nearest tree. Ruby was the highest, with Thomas Gabriel just below her and then Jones, who stood on a low branch a few metres off the ground. He aimed his catapult at the *sláwyrm*, watching it move like an S across the grass, and trying to get a clean shot at it. When it stopped suddenly, its tongue flicking in and out, Jones pulled back his arm a little further. But, as he did so, the world darkened as a large cloud passed over the moon, shutting off the bright light and making the creature disappear in the sudden darkness.

Jones listened. He thought he could hear the *sláwyrm* winding through the grass again. And then he heard something below him.

Thomas Gabriel shouted out a spell and a small white light appeared in the air above the tree, lighting up the ground below. Jones looked down to see the *sláwyrm* spiralling round and round the trunk of the tree, climbing towards him.

Jones tried to take a clean shot at the creature's head, but the *sláwyrm* was too fast. In a matter of seconds, its head popped out onto the branch he was standing on. It opened its mouth and bit down on his boot. Luckily, the teeth only caught the big rubber sole. As it clung on, Jones aimed his catapult again, but, before he could fire, there was a little *phut* from above and a dart pierced the side of the *sláwyrm* and the creature fell to the ground and lay motionless.

Ruby was grinning above him.

'That's her kill, Jones!' shouted down the gun in her hand.

Jones and Thomas Gabriel clambered to the ground quickly and kicked the creature to make sure it was dead. Ruby followed. She was smiling at her successful kill. But, before she could say anything, the others were dragging her away.

'It's just a hatchling. There'll be more,' Jones told her. 'We need to back off and come back in an hour or two after sunrise, when they'll be sleeping.'

Ruby pulled away. 'But I should make a *mearcunge*,' she said.

Thomas Gabriel sniggered. 'For that little thing? No Badlander is going to take you seriously for that. Jones is right. We'll come back in the daylight.'

'If there's more, why don't we take them on now?' she argued, cross that they were both ganging up on her. She was just as much a Badlander as either of them: hadn't she been the one to stop the creature?

But Jones just dragged her on. 'Trust me, it's better if we wait until it's light. You can check the Bestiary when we get back to the van and then you'll see why.'

Jones warmed up a big Tupperware pot of soup made with chicken and pearl barley that his mother had cooked. It tasted good.

Ruby flipped through the Bestiary with one hand as she spooned up her soup.

Sláwyrm
(pl. Sláwyrmas)

The *sláwyrm* is an amphibious nocturnal creature that relies heavily on scent and sound to find its prey. It is recommended that Badlanders take great care to avoid an area with a suspected burrow at night since the *sláwyrm* sleeps during the day.

Openings to burrows are difficult to spot as they are

usually made below the waterline on riverbanks. The female *sláwyrm* will dig through the bank and tunnel up to create a dry burrow above the waterline but beneath the ground where she can lay a brood of young. This hidden burrow makes it largely secure from predators with an entrance that is underwater. The burrows are reinforced with mud and the roots of plants woven together, but the hollowing out of the ground can still make the surface above it unstable and liable to collapse.

A female *sláwyrm* can grow to between seven and ten metres long. The female will lay a brood of up to a hundred hatchlings at one time. The young will remain in the burrow for a period of months after their birth. The egg casings provide sustenance and the creatures will eat their siblings, but it is hunger that will eventually drive them out of the burrow to survive on their own in the world . . .

Ruby gave a start when Jones tapped her on the shoulder.

'Sorry, I didn't mean to give you a fright,' he said. 'Understand now?' he asked, pointing at the book.

Ruby nodded. 'It's too risky to go onto the island at night because there's a *sláwyrm* burrow there. You used our scent to check for one, didn't you?'

Jones grinned. 'Young ones are usually hungry enough to want to investigate any potential meal.'

'There's so much to learn, Jones,' she sighed. 'I wouldn't have known to wait and see if there was a burrow there.'

'Don't be hard on yourself for not knowing that. You've

only been learning for a few months. Me and Thomas Gabriel started when we were tiny.'

'I know, but you had Maitland and Thomas Gabriel had Simeon. I've got no one to teach me anything, now Victor Brynn's gone.'

'You've got the gun,' he said. 'And you've got me now.' He smiled. 'I'll teach you everything I know if you want.' He squeezed her shoulder. 'It'll be my way of paying you back for helping me realize I can be a different type of Badlander.'

Ruby smiled. 'Yes please,' she said. 'Thanks. She tapped her head. '*Sláwyrm* logged away.'

Jones yawned. He checked his smart watch, another piece of technology that normally belonged in the ordinary world, just like the satnav. 'It says sunrise is in two hours. We can go back to the island then when any *sláwyrmas* should be asleep. Let's grab a couple of hours' sleep.'

The three of them walked across the fields in the early morning light. The grass was wet and it hissed as they moved across it. Jones led them down to the lock where they unhooked the small dinghy. There were no oars in the boat, but they found some small planks of wood in a skip, offcuts from the building work being done on a house nearby.

They worked their way up the river towards the island, the water lapping and the planks dripping each time they came out of the water. Jones and Thomas Gabriel rowed on either side, working together so as not to rock the boat. It was difficult working against the current. As the sun rose higher, the riverbanks steamed and the odd piece of mist floating on the water glowed orange.

As they approached the island, Ruby got ready to jump out. She stepped onto the bank and tied the rope round the slender, stripy trunk of a young silver birch tree.

They stood on the bank, listening. Nothing but birdcalls and the distant rumble of the water over the weir. Thomas Gabriel cast the same spell for finding things hidden with magic as he had done on Chiswick Eyot, the first island. The amulet seemed to make it easier this time and Thomas Gabriel was so glad to have it. He smiled as the magic rose in white sparks from his hands and became like the horns of a snail as before. They swivelled and then all started to point in the same direction, showing him the way. Then he felt a tug and he was off, walking fast through the grass.

'Come on,' he said. The others followed him, weaving between the densely packed trees. The undergrowth was wet and left dark stripes on their trousers. They had to push back branches, setting off showers of raindrops as they grabbed hold of them.

When the horns on Thomas Gabriel's hands died away, they all stopped. It was difficult to tell exactly where they were on the island because the trees were so densely packed and the vegetation so thick. It was like being in a jungle. Through the canopy of trees above, Ruby could see patches of early morning blue sky.

'So?' she asked.

'The *þurhfarennesse* is here somewhere,' replied Thomas

Gabriel as he looked about. 'The spell should have unlocked it like last time.'

Ruby peered about too, but the sunlight coming down through the treetops made it difficult to look for a bright little hole like the one they had found before.

'The hole's called an *éghþyrl*,' said Thomas Gabriel. 'I did some reading on it in the van. It's much easier to see at night because of the light coming through it from the other side so I brought some *ascan* along, burnt rye. There's a load of it in one of the cupboards in the van. Throw it up and it'll show you where the *éghþyrl* is.'

Thomas Gabriel drew out a bottle of black powder from the pocket of his coat and uncorked it. He scattered the powder into the air, making a dark cloud that drifted a little and fizzled as it dissolved. But no one saw the hole they were looking for.

'How much of that stuff did you bring?' asked Jones.

'Only one bottle,' said Thomas Gabriel.

'But what if it's not enough? We haven't got time to go back—'

'It's more than enough,' grinned Thomas Gabriel. 'At least it is if you've got the Black Amulet.' He uttered a spell and fired some white sparks at the bottle of *ascan*. Duplicate bottles appeared in the air and fell to the grass. Thomas Gabriel gave a little laugh.

'Pick them up then – the dust will stick to the *éghþyrl* and make a black hole instead of the bright one we saw last time so it'll show up in the daylight.'

The three of them made their way cautiously, throwing up the dust in little handfuls, and waiting to see if it coalesced round the hole they were looking for.

For a few moments, there was nothing but the sound of their boots hissing through the wet undergrowth and the fizzle of the *ascan*.

'Stop!' shouted Ruby suddenly, pulling Jones back from a thin channel of water that split the island into two. The boy had been so busy looking for the *éghþyrl* he hadn't noticed it and had almost fallen in. He nodded a thank you as Thomas Gabriel took a decent run-up and was the first to jump across. The boy threw up a cloud of dust as he leapt through the air, landing hard on the other side with both feet clumping into the turf, making the ground judder.

The dust didn't fizzle this time, but twitched and moved through the air, attracted to something on the other side of the channel. It clustered together to mark a small black circle about waist-height close to where Thomas Gabriel had landed.

'It's the *éghþyrl*!' he shouted. 'It's on this side.'

Ruby and Jones took a few steps back and then ran together, jumping over the channel, landing heavily on the other side beside Thomas Gabriel. As they stood up slowly, they felt a rumble beneath their feet. The ground in front of them collapsed and all three of them fell forward as the earth gave way.

## TWENTY-TWO

Jones realized the burrow had been built close to the surface even before he landed on the black *sláwyrmas* below.

Their bodies were hard and slippery, making it difficult to stand up. The pit that had formed from the collapsing earth was so wide and deep he had nothing to cling onto. His hands and face were coated in a thick slime that covered the creatures. Standing up was impossible.

He tried looking around desperately for Ruby and Thomas Gabriel, but he couldn't see them among the mass of black slippery bodies as the sleepy creatures started to move.

A pair of jaws snapped at him, just missing the tip of his nose, and he slipped his hands inside the pockets of his overcoat, wary of losing a finger or a thumb.

It took him a few panicked moments to realize it was the sunlight that was making the *sláwyrmas* move. They were barely interested in him at all as they started sliding out of the burrow and down the network of dark tunnels that led out of it to escape the light. But some of the creatures still snapped at him as they slithered past, clearly angry at being woken, and Jones covered up as well as he could.

Bodies slithered past his face and ears. Some of the creatures were large enough, and moved so fast, that Jones was carried along until he slid off their bodies. It was in this way that he reached the far side of the pit and managed to grab hold of a tree root to stop himself slip-sliding down one of the dark tunnels.

His hands were slimy and it was hard work levering himself up. He wiped them on the soil, coating them in brown earth, and then climbed quickly, hand over hand, his fingers digging into the soil wall. The pit was about five metres deep and, when his hands felt cold, wet grass, he heaved himself out. He scrambled to his feet. The channel of water he and Ruby had jumped across was just beyond the far wall of the burrow as he looked back at it now.

In the pit below, he saw Ruby and Thomas Gabriel. They were sitting inside a white protective sphere, watching black bodies slither round them as the creatures retreated from the sunlight.

Jones could see now that many of the *sláwyrmas* were fairly small, most of them no bigger than his arm. The occasional one was a lot longer and thicker, although they seemed to be more sleepy and moved slowly, without the wriggly panic of the smaller ones.

But, as the mass of squirming bodies disappeared, it became obvious there was one very big *sláwyrm*, the female, lying underneath them all. Its body was thicker than a tree trunk and was gathered into large coils, one resting on top of the other. As the smaller creatures vanished into the tunnels leading off the burrow, Ruby and Thomas Gabriel were left sitting on the huge *sláwyrm*.

It didn't seem entirely happy about this. Its large forked tongue flicked out between two large fangs and stuck to the protective sphere. And then the creature uncoiled itself in one slippery movement which sent Ruby and Thomas Gabriel rolling across the burrow inside the ball. Before they hit the far side, the creature came after them, sliding fast. It opened its mouth wider. And wider. And then Jones heard a loud click as its jaw unhinged, allowing the *sláwyrm* to grab the whole sphere in its mouth. The fangs at the front were curved like thorns so there was no chance of it losing its grip. It bit down hard and the skin of the bubble trembled. Then it started to swallow the ball.

Thomas Gabriel was conjuring white sparks round his fingers, but with every jolt, as the *sláwyrm* swallowed, he lost his balance and went crashing against the wall of the bubble. It was the same for Ruby as she tried to aim the gun.

Jones already had his catapult raised and he fired a silver ball bearing at the creature's head, but it pinged off the skull with little effect. He took aim and fired again, aiming for a green eye this time, with its black pupil the target. He hit the eye right in the centre and the ball bearing disappeared through it. The *sláwyrm* began to writhe, its tail thrashing and taking great chunks out of the burrow wall. The far side of the burrow nearest the channel of water bisecting the island broke apart, allowing water to rush in.

The bubble was still snagged on the tips of the creature's fangs and, as the *sláwyrm* tensed and shuddered one last time, the ball began to flex from the amount of pressure being applied. And then it popped.

Ruby saw the bubble burst before she heard it. The force sent her flying out of the mouth of the *sláwyrm*. Its jaws snapped shut behind her and she felt a blast of hot breath on the back of her neck as she landed in the river water filling the burrow. The water level rose quickly and she splashed her way to the side where Jones was ready with a hand to pull her up. She stood there, shivering, and looked back to see where Thomas Gabriel was.

The other boy had been less fortunate. His coat had snagged on one of the fangs and, although the *sláwyrm* was dead and floating, Thomas Gabriel was stuck with it as long as the jaws remained shut. The creature kept rolling from side to side like a log, submerging the boy and then popping him back up out of the water.

'Take your coat off!' shouted Jones.

But Thomas Gabriel flapped a hand as if waving him away and then conjured some sparks round his fingers that turned into a sharp blade which he used to cut away at the material. He set himself loose, and swam, hauling himself onto the bank. As Jones helped him up, he noticed a rip in one of Thomas Gabriel's wet trouser legs and a cut in the skin.

'How bad is it?' he asked, pointing to the injured leg.

Thomas Gabriel pulled apart the rip to get a better look. His thigh had a narrow cut in it about the length of a finger. It was bleeding heavily.

'It's deeper than I thought,' he said.

'We need to disinfect it,' said Jones. He rummaged in his pocket and took out a small leather bag and loosened the drawstring. He shook out what looked like small black balls into the palm of his hand, which uncurled like woodlice, each one revealing an undercarriage of busy black legs and a red crown of springy antennae at the front end.

'I'm not using those,' said Thomas Gabriel. 'A city Badlander wouldn't let those *wibban* anywhere near his body.'

'There's no time to flush the poison out of you any other way.'

'I'll use the antidote I brought along, thanks.'

'Be my guest.' Jones turned to Ruby and rolled his eyes as Thomas Gabriel reached into his pocket and took out a glass vial.

'A bite from an adult *sláwyrm* is poisonous,' said Jones. 'That's why I brought these *wibban* along' he said, 'just in case. The poison's so quick-acting that, unless you use the antidote straightaway after being bitten, you're in big trouble.' He paused as Thomas Gabriel started to shake. 'As you're about to see.'

Thomas Gabriel had managed to remove the stopper from the vial, but he was struggling to drink the antidote. He kept missing his mouth. Jones bent down and guided the vial between Thomas Gabriel's lips and then tipped it up. Thomas Gabriel glugged greedily, but he didn't seem to be able to swallow and the antidote dribbled out of his mouth and down his chin. Thomas Gabriel grinned.

'Shh-ee,' he said slurring his words. 'All I nee-cched wasshh she antiii-dothe.'

Jones and Ruby raised their eyebrows at each other as Thomas Gabriel looked at them with big sleepy eyes. 'No need for liccle beetle-y like youuuuve gottt.'

'Is that right?' replied Jones. He leant in to Ruby. 'If you ever suspect you're going somewhere there might be a *sláwyrm* then take some *wibban* with you.' He pulled apart the rip in Thomas Gabriel's wet trousers and dropped the beetles into the cut. They burrowed down into the wound and disappeared.

Thomas Gabriel didn't seem to mind. He giggled and lay back on the ground, his wet clothes creaking.

'He's not gonna be much use for a bit. Let's go and see if we can find what we came for,' said Jones. But Ruby crouched down beside Thomas Gabriel. She lifted up his floppy arm and studied the Black Amulet.

'I think we should take it off,' she said.

'Why?'

'It's evil. You heard what Drewman said.'

'Thomas Gabriel's been taking his bitter potions. He was

250

doing it in the van. Anyway, it's working for him, isn't it, helping him do magic?'

Ruby bit her lip.

'Yesterday, at your parents' house, I saw something. It was . . . It was like a dark part of him came alive and jumped out at me. I think it was protecting the amulet because I wanted Thomas Gabriel to take it off.'

Ruby stretched out her hand to touch the amulet, but, when one of the snakes' heads on it came alive and hissed, her fingers crumpled like they were made of tissue paper.

'See?' she gasped. 'I don't think the bitter potions are working. The amulet's evil, Jones. I wonder what it's doing to him.'

Jones crouched down beside her and reached out to touch the amulet, but heard a noise and looked up.

The water all around the adult *sláwyrm* was rippling and starting to froth as hundreds of hatchlings began to attack the body. The water was turning red.

'It's the blood in the water. They can't resist it. They won't stop now till everything's eaten. We need to leave or they'll come for him too because of his wound.'

Jones stopped as something black slithered up the bank and made a beeline for Thomas Gabriel. It bit the boy on the hand and Thomas Gabriel yelled as Jones aimed a kick at the creature, but it dodged and reared up and bit Jones on the leg.

He heard the *phut* of a dart and the *sláwyrm* went limp and fell from his leg.

'We need to go, Jones,' said Ruby, putting the gun back

in her waistband. 'And we're not taking the boat back this time.' She poured out a ring of Slap Dust round all three of them as Jones kept an eye out for more black bodies slithering up the bank. His leg was hurting terribly and he knew the bite was deep, but at least it wasn't infected by poison because it had been a young *sláwyrm* that had bitten him.

When all three of them arrived back in the field by the van, Thomas Gabriel giggled.

'That wa-sh fun,' he said. 'Le'tsshh do it again.'

Ruby and Jones managed to get him into the van and lay him on the floor, removing most of his wet clothes and dumping them in a pile with Ruby's, before wrapping him in a towel. He stopped giggling after a while and began to moan and groan as he partly came to his senses.

'The High Council meeting's tomorrow,' he said in a panic, trying to get up, but collapsing back to the floor in a state of ever-increasing delirium. 'I'll never pass if we don't get those other two golden boxes in time. And if I'm punished by the High Council then you'll lose the cottage, Ruby, because they'll take all my things away, because I gave you that cottage, Ruby ... and ... and they'll even take my *æhteland* so Jones will be found out too ... and ... and ... punished for Commencing with a girl.'

He paused as he tried to catch his breath. 'But ... but you know what's worst of all? If the High Council finds out about me then it means we'll have failed to find those last two boxes and allowed Drewman to fix our Commencements, meaning we'll never be who we want to be.'

Thomas Gabriel raised his arms and howled. 'Oh, I won't be a Badlander then and Ruby, you won't be one either if you can't do magic and prove to the Order you're good enough to be one . . . and Jones . . . oh, Jones . . .' Thomas Gabriel licked his lips and swallowed hard. His voice was hoarse and croaky now. 'Jones, you'll always have magic in you, even though you don't want it.'

As Thomas Gabriel flung his head into his arms and sobbed, Ruby looked at Jones and shrugged. 'I'd say he's pretty much right about everything there.' She sighed. 'How's the leg? You look pale. Jones, are you—'

'The lotion I put on is healing it,' replied Jones. 'But I think . . .' He paused. 'I think that *sláwyrm* bite might have had a trace of poison in it because the creature bit Thomas Gabriel first.' His head started to sag. 'I think I might need to rest a little . . .' His head lolled forward onto his chest and he started snoring.

'Oh, great,' muttered Ruby. 'That's just great.' She looked at one boy and then the other, one sobbing inconsolably and the other fast asleep. Then she stood up and pulled out the gun. 'You and me are going to sort this out.'

'What do you mean?'

'We're going to get that second golden box.' She put on her army camouflage jacket, which was still rather damp despite being hung up outside in the sunshine, and set off.

*

She ran back across the fields towards the river, stopping every so often to pick up a stone that took her fancy. By the time she reached the riverbank, she had twenty or so in her limitless pockets.

A grain or two of Slap Dust made her vanish from the riverbank and she reappeared on the shoreline of the island near the dinghy which was still tied to the tree.

She unhooked the rope. Stepping into the boat was like standing on a seesaw, but she managed to sit down and then set off. She paddled the short distance round the island and then upstream, alongside it, until she saw the channel bisecting the island and steered the boat into that.

The pond that had formed from the collapse of the burrow was larger than she remembered and Ruby wondered if more of its muddy sides had dropped into the water. There was no sign of the dead *sláwyrm*. The hatchlings were gone too. She drifted around a little, paddling here and there according to her memory, and then she tried to stop as well as she could, using the plank of wood. As she sat there, the boat bobbing gently, she took out the bottle of *ascan* she still had in her pocket and threw clouds of it into the air. It didn't take long for her to find the small black hole she was after. Paddling towards it, she stood up and took out the vampire's tooth. When she slipped the sharp end into the hole, she held on tight to the root and managed to keep the boat fairly still. Then she started cutting.

It was even harder to open up the secret compartment than before, with the boat wanting to move all the time, and her legs braced to keep her steady. But Ruby stuck to the task, cutting a circle three quarters of the way around the hole as she had done before. This time she inserted the stones she had collected at intervals, to ensure the air she had cut through didn't heal over again.

Finally, when she had cut a circular flap, she hooked her fingers into the bottom and, with the stones falling all around her, heaved it up far enough to see the golden box shining back at her. With much huffing and puffing, she managed to slide in an arm and grab hold of the box. After pulling it out, she let go of the flap and it slapped shut. The air she had cut through started healing almost immediately.

Ruby held the box close to her chest like a secret she had sworn never to tell anyone. She could have been holding her heart such was the golden glow. She sat down in the dinghy and started paddling back out of the channel and towards the riverbank.

When she arrived back at the van, the two boys were sleeping, but they were looking much better. The bites on both their legs had healed, although she wasn't quite sure what had happened to the beetles that had been placed in Thomas Gabriel's wound.

Ruby put the golden box down on the counter and the two boys woke, blinking in the sunshine. It was almost midday and the sun was quite strong.

They could barely believe what she had done. But, however much they wanted to hear all about it, they had to get going. The High Council meeting was tomorrow and, not only did they need to find one more golden box before Thomas Gabriel was due to attend, they also needed to take all three of them back to Drewman.

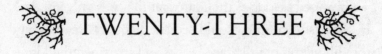

TWENTY-THREE

ppletree Eyot, the last of the islands, was upriver from Old Windsor. It was about twenty-five miles or so by road so it didn't take more than an hour to get close to it in the van. Jones drove as fast as he dared along the stretch of motorway the satnav took them on.

The eyot was on the outskirts of Reading so it meant driving through parts of the town, negotiating busy junctions and roundabouts.

When they crossed over the river, Ruby checked the map laid across her knees and pointed left, upstream.

'The eyot's a few miles up that way.'

Jones nodded.

He missed a turning a mile on from the bridge, having approached it too fast with a car tailgating him, and cursed. It took him another couple of miles to find somewhere to turn, in the sweeping gated entrance to a golf club. They came back down the road and he made sure he didn't miss the turning a second time. The road took them out of the suburbs and along a quiet lane. They seesawed down a bumpy old track and parked in a field with a rickety gate that Ruby had to open, the bottom of it scraping the ground.

They waited as long as they dared, until it was only just dark. In the distance, they could see the lights of Reading and the silhouettes of tall office blocks and apartment buildings. The night sky above them was the colour of burnt orange. As they set out towards the river, bits of the town bobbed up over the hedges. The office blocks and buildings grew taller and Ruby started wondering how frightening it was that monsters could live so close to people, right under their noses, without ever being seen. And then her mind turned to more practical matters and what sort of creatures might be on Appletree Eyot, as well as something else.

'Jones,' she hissed. 'How are we going to get across the river? This eyot's right in the middle of the water according to the map.'

'I don't know,' he replied and for the first time Ruby saw that he was stumped. He looked tired and drained. And a little worried.

Thomas Gabriel coughed. '"Be prepared" – that's the Badlander motto, isn't it?' He wiggled his wrist, jiggling the amulet, and the green eyes of the snakes' heads caught a little bit of moonlight. 'We will be.'

With a flourish, he cleared his throat and ran a hand through his hair.

'Jones, that phone thing of yours – can it find a picture of a dinghy with oars on the Internet?'

'Yes,' said Jones.

'What good is that going to do?' asked Ruby. 'We can't row across the water using a picture.'

'You'll see.'

As they walked the rest of the way, Jones scrolled through his phone and found a suitable image. Standing on the riverbank, Thomas Gabriel studied the picture and nodded and conjured white sparks over his hands. He cast the spell and there appeared on the water, with the river lapping gently at its sides, an exact physical duplicate of the boat on the phone screen.

'Easy enough,' he said to Ruby. 'I created those duplicate bottles of *ascan* on the last island and this is just an advanced version of the spell. I've been learning all its variations on the journey.'

'Oh, yeah?'

'Be prepared,' said Thomas Gabriel and smirked.

He nodded approvingly at the phone. 'I think I might be onto something here, using technology and magic too. I'm surprised no one has thought of bringing more technology into the Order.' He grinned and went to inspect the boat.

'That amulet is definitely coming off,' Ruby whispered to Jones. 'And not just because it's dangerous … It's turning him into a right—'

An owl hooted as it took off from a nearby tree and sailed out over the field.

Thomas Gabriel turned to look at her. 'Did you say something?'

Ruby pursed her lips and nodded. 'I was just saying to Jones, I wonder where we should hide the amulet when we're done. Drewman told us to put it somewhere no one'll ever find it. I think I'd throw it in the river.'

Thomas Gabriel's smile turned sour at the edges. His fingers toyed with the amulet. He shot her a dirty look before turning back to the boat.

There were two eyots in the middle of the river, end to end, both of them covered with dense trees, the canopy of spring leaves hiding the ground.

'It's the first one,' said Ruby, consulting the map she'd brought from the van. They stood on the riverbank, watching out for anything suspicious, the newly created dinghy bobbing on the black surface of the water. A goods train rumbled past on the opposite bank, the long line of yellow wagons visible under the lights that hung their heads over the track.

'Okay then, let's go' said Jones. 'But keep your eyes open. It's important to keep looking out for anything suspicious.'

They paddled across to Appletree Eyot. It was a wider stretch of water than they had encountered before and the flow of the river was tougher to paddle against this time, trying to push them downstream.

Ruby kept watch as the boys rowed. She sat in the prow, scanning the bank of the eyot for any movement and watching the surface of the water too. The moonlight was bright, but there were dark patches between the trees too deep to fathom. The gun in her hand was also looking. Ruby could feel how tense it was, ready to fire if she saw anything.

They tied up the boat as before, stepped onto the eyot and picked their way through the trees. Thomas Gabriel cast the required spell for finding things hidden with magic and the horns appeared on his hands again, wiggling in the air. Suddenly, they stiffened and all pointed in the same direction, towards the dense undergrowth.

The vegetation was thick and wet. Thomas Gabriel trampled it down with his boots, taking great strides and stamping down hard to force a path through. The others followed behind him. No one said a word. Their hearing prickled as they tried to listen for anything out of the ordinary.

'There,' said Thomas Gabriel, stopping at a point he decided must be about halfway up the eyot. He pointed at the bright hole ahead, easy enough to spot in the dark, and suspended in the air at roughly chest-height. The others saw it too and no one said anything as they listened before going on. Nothing but the sounds of distant traffic. A siren wailed right on the edge of their hearing and then was gone.

Jones studied the ground and the trees around them. No marks. No suspicious bumps or humps in the earth. Thomas Gabriel moved forward and Jones didn't stop him. He watched to see if the boy's movement might alert any creatures. But nothing came bounding out at them. There were no bright eyes blinking in the dark. Not even an odd smell, except for the damp earth. So he walked on too. But he was wound tight inside, ready for anything.

The *éghþyrl* was the same size as the others, but, as Ruby looked closer before cutting into it, she realized it looked different.

She bent in to look more closely and saw the hole was slightly misshapen. Instead of being a clean circle, it was bobbly around the edges as if something had nibbled it. She ran a finger round it and felt little nicks and dints on the inside. Confused, she bent down and looked through the hole like it was a telescope, shutting her other eye for a better view.

'Oh,' she said.

Jones had felt the little strings in his heart tighten as soon as he'd seen the hole was a little bit misshapen. The unexpected was not usually a good sign. As Ruby peered through the hole, he'd heard a rustling sound and looked frantically about. But nothing had appeared. He guessed it might have been the leaves on the trees or a small animal scuttling through the undergrowth. And then he thought he heard a faint sound, like air coming out of a tyre.

'Jones!' said Ruby. 'You should see this.' She was dragging his arm, pulling him down to have a look through the hole, but he wouldn't bend. He was listening out for the hissing noise. His fists clenched tighter when he heard it again, but a little louder this time. He shrugged off Ruby's hand and heard her say something. Judging by the tone of her voice, it wasn't a compliment. But he was too alert to the other sound to care about that.

The hiss came again. Jones was sure he'd heard the same noise before when he'd been hunting the Badlands with Maitland. But what was it?

Something caught the corner of his eye, a movement among the trees. He thought it was mist at first, but it moved like it was alive. With an intelligence. The blue tinge to it was mesmerizing.

A lock clicked in his head. The answer came to him.

'Wraith!' he shouted. But it only came out as a whisper as he tottered backwards, fearful of the creature.

Thomas Gabriel was dimly aware of Jones saying something. He was busy crouching down to look through the *éghþyrl* to find out what Ruby had seen. When he peered through, he saw not a small compartment, as he had expected, but a whole chamber, as deep as a cave. It was full of items, packed out like the storeroom he'd once stood in at Deschamps & Sons while his Master had argued with one of the store's clerks about the order of Slap Dust he'd been expecting to collect that day.

Thomas Gabriel whirled his eye round the hole, looking this way and that for the last golden box. But he couldn't see it.

'Wraith!' Jones's voice pierced his thinking. Even before he whirled round, Thomas Gabriel had realized a few important facts at the same time. The *þurhfarennesse* had become home to a Wraith. Such creatures were attracted to magical items and no doubt the *þurhfarennesse* had proved too appealing for it to resist. Somehow it had got in and made the place its own.

By the time Thomas Gabriel had removed his eye from the hole, and stood up, Jones and Ruby were already backing away. It distracted him for a moment and then he looked beyond them as something else flickered at the edge of his field of vision. A long finger of mist, unfurling into a point like the tip of a spear, was only about half a metre away from him. It caught him on the shoulder before he could twist to dodge it and the tip disappeared through the fabric of his coat and his clothes. He felt it puncture his skin. It was like being speared by an icicle.

The dull pain rang like a low-sounding bell for a brief moment and then Thomas Gabriel felt nothing, his shoulder numbed by whatever had impaled him. The cold seemed to be in his head too. For, as he raised his hands and tried to conjure up a spell, there was no spark in his brain. It seemed that all the words that he needed were being sucked out of him before he could say anything.

The Wraith materialized out of the block of mist in front of him and he saw its hand plunged into his shoulder. He wanted to move but he couldn't. The Wraith reached for the amulet with its other hand, the misty fingers like tendrils wrapping round it. The creature's head was dipped in concentration. Even though its face was a blur of mist, the dark red eyes the only defining feature, Thomas Gabriel could tell it was fascinated by the amulet and anger surged through him as it touched the object. The red eyes seemed to shine brighter. The mist that made up the Wraith's body became darker for some reason.

Thomas Gabriel shouted to tell it to stop, but all that came out was a low grunt. The Wraith picked at the amulet, lifting it part way off his wrist, and Thomas Gabriel heard an angry drumming in his ears. It blotted out everything, all the fear and pain. He was jealous of the Wraith wanting the amulet as much as him. Unless he stopped it, he knew the creature would take it and keep it with all the other magical items it had hoarded in its home, inside the *þurhfarennesse*.

The amulet seemed to be interested in the Wraith too. The two snakes' heads looked at the creature. Thomas Gabriel dimly remembered what Drewman had said, that he had found the amulet among Wraiths and had presumed they had made it.

Before the amulet was removed from his wrist, Thomas Gabriel's anger sharpened his brain enough for him to cast a spell which was full of rage. He didn't want to lose the amulet to anyone or anything. From his hand flew a great barrage of white sparks that hit the Wraith so hard the creature was knocked backwards with a scream. Thomas Gabriel was hurled the other way and, although his eyes closed instinctively and he curled into a ball to protect himself, he knew the amulet had been taken from him, dragged from his wrist by the Wraith. He knew it from the stab of pain in his heart.

And then he hit something hard behind him and crumpled to the ground.

# TWENTY-FOUR

Ruby opened her eyes. The dark sky above her swirled until she focused on a bright star and everything slowed to a stop. Blinking seemed to make her brain spark and the first thought she had was that she was alive.

She began to shiver because she realized she was cold too, lying in the wet undergrowth. Her hands crept about like spiders, testing out the ground. She had no idea where the gun was.

When she heard a train rattling past on the tracks on the other side of the river, she remembered where she was and why. More importantly, she remembered the Wraith. Sitting up quickly made her head hurt and she thought she was going to be sick. But she wasn't. Her jaw was throbbing. She remembered landing hard. When she realized there was no sign of the Wraith, a big screw inside her loosened and she began thinking through what had happened.

She had seen Thomas Gabriel cast a spell. Something so big, and so booming, it would only have been possible with the Black Amulet. He'd flown backwards into her with such force that her legs had been chopped away, and they'd both taken out Jones who had been standing beside her. All three of them had gone crashing to the ground like skittles, Thomas Gabriel tumbling on into the dark with the force of the spell.

Jones was lying cradled in the undergrowth.

'Jones?' she whispered. But there was no reply. 'Jones!' The boy groaned. His hands moved to his head and rubbed it and Ruby's heart lifted.

She had no idea how long they'd been out. Seconds maybe? Perhaps minutes? Trying to work it out was impossible, like trying to lick your elbow.

There was no sign of Thomas Gabriel. Ruby stood up to look around.

'Thomas Gabriel?'

Nothing. Not even a groan. She shuffled through the undergrowth towards the place she'd last seen the Wraith, looking about for any sign of the boy.

When she saw what was left of the Wraith lying in the grass, she knew it must be dead. The misty body that Ruby had seen attack Thomas Gabriel was split into lumpy parts like snowmelt. The dark face had been sheared into two pieces, each half containing a red eye.

As Ruby stepped forward to see more, she saw the glint of a green gemstone. The amulet was lying among the remains of the Wraith. She remembered now that the creature had been trying to remove it from Thomas Gabriel's wrist and then the boy had unleashed his spell and sent them all flying.

Ruby crouched down, wary of picking the amulet up at first. But the longer it lay there, the more confident she became and finally she reached out a hand. She still held it away from her, though, as if expecting it to bite.

A thought came to mind and then Ruby was walking, stumbling through the thick undergrowth, before picking up pace until she was going as fast as she could. When she reached the bank, she hurled the amulet as far as she could into the river. It landed with a small splash and vanished, the current smoothing out the ripples on the surface of the water in a matter of moments.

'Hey!' came a distant voice. 'Where are you? What's going on? Why am I up here?'

Ruby followed the voice and found the gun in a large, thick bush where it was lodged in the prickly branches.

'What happened?' it asked. 'What's been going on?' And Ruby told it everything as she went back to find the others.

By the time she returned, Jones was bent over Thomas Gabriel, who was lying virtually hidden in a patch of long grass, trying to rouse him. The unconscious boy choked and spluttered and opened his eyes. He sat up quickly and Ruby noticed that one nostril was heavily clotted with blood as if a berry had been squashed into it. He wiped his nose on his coat sleeve and left a long red smear, then took a few juddering breaths.

He caught sight of the dead Wraith and grinned up at them. And then Ruby saw him look down at his wrist – bare and pale without the amulet. Ruby swallowed hard and shuffled her feet, flattening down the grass with the soles of her boots. She had no idea what she was going to say, or even if she was going to say anything at all.

Thomas Gabriel scrambled to his feet and hobbled to where the Wraith was lying in lumps. He kicked through them, breaking them up into smaller pieces, and they rose and fell like tiny clouds of fog.

'It's gone, Thomas Gabriel,' said Ruby. The boy looked at her, eyes popping at first before he frowned and screwed them deep down into his head.

'What do you mean, gone?'

'It's not there.' Ruby cleared her throat. 'I mean, it was, and then I threw it into the river after I found it.'

Thomas Gabriel stared for a moment, opening and closing his mouth silently like a fish, and then he strode towards her. He was shouting something, but she wasn't listening. At least she was trying not to. She could see his tongue waggling at her like some strange pink flower.

'I hate you!' he shouted. 'Hate you!'

And then he collapsed to his knees and began to cry, clutching at his stomach as if in pain. Ruby crouched down, a hand squeezing his shoulder.

'It's for the best, Thomas Gabriel. The amulet was evil. It was hurting you, turning you into someone else, wasn't it, Jones?' As Jones nodded, Thomas Gabriel looked up at them.

'I suppose . . . I suppose I should be thanking you,' he managed to warble through the snorts and the tears. 'Not shouting at you. The amulet wasn't doing me any good

270

at all, was it?' He took a big sniff. 'I can see everything differently now it's gone. The amulet was always whispering to me, telling me to do things. It was in my head, all the time. I couldn't say no to it. I would never have let you take it. I would've kept it. But I can only say that now it's gone.'

He wiped his nose and sniffed again. 'I think you might have saved my life, Ruby. But it still hurts in my bones not to have the amulet now.' He curled himself into a ball and sobbed.

'It was evil,' whispered Ruby, trying to console him.

'You're better off without it,' agreed Jones. 'It might not feel like it but you are.'

'Thomas Gabriel, you can still be a Badlander and go on to do great things,' said Ruby. She pointed at the *éghþyrl* which was still shining. 'Let's get that last golden box and go back to Drewman, shall we? We're going to do it: we're going to get our Commencements fixed and start being who we want to be.'

They worked quickly on the *éghþyrl* with Ruby cutting open the air around the hole as before with the Vampire's tooth. She created a much bigger opening this time, a hatch big enough for someone to crawl through.

Jones and Thomas Gabriel snuck into the extended *þurhfarennesse* to look for the golden box among all the other objects the Wraith had brought there. Ruby kept urging them to hurry up, as she held open the hatch, wary that the night was starting to dwindle now and it would soon be dawn.

Thomas Gabriel found the golden box hidden behind a collection of urns, stacked one inside the other. After holding it up for Jones to see, they clambered back out through the hole and Ruby let down the hatch. It took the boys a moment to readjust to the dark after the bright white interior of the *þurhfarennesse*. The cool air on their hands and faces gave them goosebumps. Ruby was already very cold, and she kept her hands stuck in her armpits as they walked smartly back to the dinghy, saying she was ready to get back to the van.

As the daylight started to strengthen, Ruby put the last golden box down on the table in the van beside the others. She allowed herself a little smile. They'd done it.

'There's no time to drive to Givens's house,' said Thomas Gabriel. He pulled out the invitation to the High Council meeting and put it next to the boxes. It was still ticking.

'Today's the day,' he said. 'The meeting's at two. I need Drewman to fix my commencement before then. Anyway, do you know where Givens's house actually is? I don't. That satnav of yours can't tell us, can it, Jones?'

'No,' said Jones.

'Okay, we use Slap Dust, then, to get there,' said Ruby, but she felt her insides sag. 'How are we going to get in to see Drewman?' she asked. 'We've got the key I made. But do we make another *fæcce*? Is there even time for that?'

'No, we don't need a *fæcce*,' said Thomas Gabriel. 'We'll get Givens himself to open the door this time.' The others looked at him as though he'd just told them he wanted to be an ordinary boy. 'I've got the Memory Leech. He won't remember a thing.'

'And how do we get him to open the door in the first place?' asked Jones.

'If he's even there?' piped up Ruby.

'Oh, I reckon he'll be there. It's the High Council meeting: he'll be getting ready for it. Wanting to look his best.' He looked at Jones. 'I'll show you how we'll make him open that door. Come outside.'

As they stood outside the van in the ever-growing daylight, Thomas Gabriel took out a silver pillbox and opened the lid. He held up the vial that was inside it on the red velvet inlay and tilted it. The yellowish mist inside caught the early rays of sunlight and glinted.

'Givens will do whatever we want when I show him this,' said Thomas Gabriel.

When Jones saw the mist in the vial, he could hardly believe it. 'You've cursed Givens with *wælmist*?' Jones heard the surprise in his voice and it sent Thomas Gabriel's smile arching higher at the corners.

'What is it?' asked Ruby, straining to get a better look at the substance.

'A fatal curse,' said Jones. 'The holder of the *wælmist* commands whoever's been cursed with it on pain of death. Take off the top and let the *wælmist* out and they're as good as dead. I ain't never seen it before, only drawings in books. Where did you get it?' he asked Thomas Gabriel.

'Simeon owned it. He told me it was a present from his Master after he Commenced as a boy. But he never used it.'

'There's no cure once you've cursed someone with it,' said Jones. 'Not once the *wælmist* knows the name of the person you whispered to it.'

'Givens'll know that too.' Thomas Gabriel held the vial up to the light and they all watched the mist twisting round in the bottle like a stream of water coming out of a tap.

'You're full of surprises, Thomas Gabriel,' said Jones.

'Just thinking ahead,' replied Thomas Gabriel with a grin. He pointed to the wing mirror of the van that was catching the sunlight. 'Can you use that to scry and see where Givens is? I bet he's at home, just like I said.'

As Ruby stood in front of the wing mirror, she was aware of how tired and dishevelled she looked. The two boys looking on behind her did too. Although, as her eyes looked at the reflection of Thomas Gabriel, she thought that perhaps he looked a little fresher than he should. He seemed to have a glint in his eye. She wondered if it was because he was excited about his plan.

'Come on, Ruby,' said Jones. 'Can you look or not?'

Ruby cleared her mind and asked to see Givens, wherever he was. The glass fizzed and an image of the man appeared. He was standing in front of a bathroom mirror in a bathrobe, snipping at his nose hair, tilting his head to trim a particularly troublesome tuft.

'Looks like the bathroom we made the *fæcce* in all right,' said Jones. 'I recognize the tiles. And the towels.'

'Told you,' said Thomas Gabriel. 'I think we should go and pay Givens a visit now, don't you?'

TWENTY-FIVE

When all three of them arrived in Givens's bathroom together, the Slap Dust still ringing in their ears, Givens was so surprised he almost snipped off the tip of his nose with the pair of scissors he was holding.

'What ... what are you doing here?' he asked as he looked at Thomas Gabriel. 'And you ...' he said, looking at Ruby. 'You, girl ... but you're ... you're dead! The Slobbering ate you in the—'

Givens paled as if he really was seeing a ghost. 'A girl,' he stammered. 'A girl here in the Badlands ... in my house ...' And then he stiffened and raised his hand, little sparks of magic licking the ends of his fingers. Ruby thought about going for the gun in her waistband although she knew she'd never use it.

'Stop!' said Thomas Gabriel. 'No magic.' He held up the *wælmist* in front of the window. 'It might be the last thing you do.'

Givens stared at the *wælmist*, watching it twist and turn

in the vial. He seemed to deflate a little and then shook his head and raised his hand again. 'You're just bluffing.'

Thomas Gabriel prised the cork out of the vial a little way and the *wælmist* sensed it, rushing up into the glass neck. Givens gasped. He dropped the scissors and clutched both hands to his chest.

'Can you feel it, Givens? Can you feel the *wælmist* wanting to hurt you?' Thomas Gabriel drew out the cork a little further and Givens whimpered, clearly in pain.

'Stop!' said Ruby. 'You're hurting him.'

'We just need him to open the door,' said Jones. 'You're only supposed to be frightening him.'

Thomas Gabriel pushed the cork back in and Givens took a step back and crumpled against the wall, panting hard.

'We're not here to cause anyone any harm,' said Jones.

'What's the meaning of this, Thomas Gabriel?' asked Givens in a quiet voice, the colour slowly returning to his cheeks. 'And who are these people?' His eyes flickered towards Ruby. 'You, girl. What are you doing here?'

Ruby cleared her throat and held up the string bag she was holding that she'd found in the van, the three golden boxes clinking inside. 'To show you that girls are just as good as boys at being Badlanders.' Givens gasped when he saw the golden boxes through the material of the bag, unable to believe what he was seeing.

'What Ruby means is we're here to see Drewman,' said Thomas Gabriel. Givens opened his mouth to say something and then remembered the bottle in Thomas Gabriel's hand. The boy waggled it.

'Come on, we're going downstairs.'

As they left the bathroom and walked down the landing towards the stairs, Jones could see that Givens was trying to piece everything together as he kept glancing at them and at the bag Ruby was holding, the golden boxes clearly visible through the string material.

'What do you want with Augustus Drewman?' asked Givens as they went down the stairs.

'To fix our Commencements,' said Jones. Givens frowned as he thought about that because he didn't quite understand.

'Don't I know you, boy?' he said.

Jones stepped off the last stair into the hallway and shrugged.

'You were Maitland's boy. But—'

'No time,' said Thomas Gabriel. 'Study. Now!'

Givens paused to tie his bathrobe tighter. And then something occurred to him and he smiled at Thomas Gabriel. 'So the rumours are true. You did steal the key from Simeon and Commence without his blessing and now your magic's failing and you want Drewman to fix it.' He started to laugh and a little spot in the corner of Thomas Gabriel's jaw started to pulse.

'Come on, Givens, move. I've got a test to do this afternoon in front of the High Council.'

Givens shook his head. 'I don't think so.'

'You won't remember a thing about this. I'll be standing in

front of you and the rest of the High Council this afternoon and I'll pass with flying colours.'

'I don't know how this has all come about or who some of you are,' said Givens, glancing at Ruby, 'but it won't end as you say it will, Thomas Gabriel.' And, with that, Givens sat down on the floor.

'To curse a fellow Badlander with *wælmist* is an act of treachery and dishonour. Your Master, Simeon Rowell, and your Master Maitland,' said Givens, staring at Jones, 'would never have believed such a disloyal thing could happen. But I must bow to the *wyrd*. It seems this is how my story is to play out.' He folded his arms. 'You may open the bottle of *wælmist* whenever you like because you are not going to get to see Augustus Drewman. Of that I am certain.'

Thomas Gabriel laughed. He couldn't help himself. 'Come on, Givens, there's no point bluffing.' He tweaked the cork halfway out of the vial with a rubbery-sounding squeak.

But, despite being in pain, Givens looked up at him with grey eyes, as hard and glassy-looking as marbles, and Thomas Gabriel knew this wasn't a bluff at all. The man was prepared to put his duty to the Order before his own life.

Thomas Gabriel looked at Jones and Ruby, unsure what to do.

'Get on with it, boy,' gasped Givens, his body juddering and twitching. 'Or don't you have the guts?'

Suddenly, a door slammed somewhere in the house and there was the sound of footsteps. Wilfried's voice came ringing through the house.

'Sir, I've picked some flowers to choose from for your buttonhole, just like you wanted.' When the boy came strutting into the hallway, he dropped the flowers he was holding and ran to his Master as soon as he saw what was happening.

'Stop!' he cried. 'Stop!'

As Givens tipped over in great pain towards the floor, Wilfried rushed to the man and tried to sit him up. He went round the back of Givens and pushed him back into a sitting position and crouched down behind him, trying to keep the groaning man upright.

As Thomas Gabriel wondered what to do next, he saw a flicker of gold out of the corner of his eye. Something came at him so fast, hissing through the air, that he didn't have time to react and the next thing he knew, the *wælmist* was plucked from his hand by a golden rope that lassoed round it and took it back to Wilfried who grabbed it. The apprentice pushed the cork back firmly into the vial and Givens began to breathe more easily and a fire came back to his eyes. He whispered a word and magic appeared at his fingertips. He held one hand out at Jones and Ruby, who went for the gun in her waistband and then paused, to keep them at bay. He pointed the other at Thomas Gabriel.

'He made me lie, sir,' sobbed Wilfried. 'It wasn't the One Eye that attacked you – it was him. He has the Black Amulet.'

Thomas Gabriel felt something ping inside him, like a button bursting off an ill-fitting jacket, and a red-hot anger surged through him as Wilfried clutched the *wælmist*. He fired up magic in his hands, but all that came out were tiny sparks that flickered and drooped and died away.

Givens laughed. 'The Black Amulet, eh? Well, I'd say he doesn't have it any more, Wilfried, wouldn't you?'

Givens fired a bolt of magic at Thomas Gabriel and sent him crashing into the wall. 'Your Master, Simeon, was right not to want to Commence you!' shouted Givens. 'You don't deserve magic. Because you don't deserve to be a Badlander. Now tell me, is Wilfried right? Did you have the Black Amulet? And, if so, where is it now, boy?'

Thomas Gabriel's shoulder was hurting from hitting the wall so hard. But his pride was hurting so much more. He sat up and looked at Givens as he felt something crawling down the skin of his arm, unseen, under his clothes. It tickled as it passed the crook of his elbow and it made him laugh.

'Tell me where the amulet is, boy!' said Givens.

'It's gone!' shouted Ruby. 'I threw it away!'

'No, you didn't,' said Thomas Gabriel, laughing. 'No, you didn't.'

He held up his arm and his coat sleeve drew back to reveal the Black Amulet slithering down his forearm and curling round his wrist.

'It was just a copy, Ruby. I knew you'd throw the amulet away if you had a chance. You said as much.' Thomas Gabriel sniggered. 'I lay in the grass and watched you do it.'

When Givens fired a bolt of magic, Thomas Gabriel reacted by firing an even bigger one back, vaporizing the one aimed at him.

No one in the hallway moved. No one dared. Everyone was staring at the Black Amulet.

Thomas Gabriel scrambled to his feet. 'I don't need Drewman. I don't need to fix my Commencement and pass that stupid test today.' He held out his hands, sparks dancing at the end of his fingertips, daring Givens to fire another bolt of magic. 'I'm going to be a different sort of Badlander from now on, just like you wanted to be, Ruby, and you too, Jones.'

He made them all walk into Givens's study, great licks of white magic rising out of his fingers.

'Give the key you made to Givens, Ruby,' said Thomas Gabriel. And she had no choice but to do so.

Givens didn't want to go over to the picture and pass the Trolls' inspection and then open the door to the hidden room, but Thomas Gabriel forced him, with hands raised high and the amulet bobbing on his wrist. Once the door was open, he gestured for them to go through it, one at a time. He plucked the *wælmist* from Wilfried's hand and took the string bag containing the golden boxes from Ruby.

'Why are you doing this?' she asked in a quiet voice, not letting go of the bag.

'Because it's my amulet now,' he hissed at her. 'My secret. I'm going to go down in history as a great Badlander like Drewman did. But no one can know how I did it. That's the mistake Drewman made. People found out about the amulet. But no one will know my story. It won't be rewritten like Drewman's was, because the only people to know I have the amulet will be in here. Forever. Drewman's chamber is bound to be magically secure. Isn't that right, Givens?' shouted Thomas Gabriel, but the man just grunted.

Thomas Gabriel ripped the string bag from Ruby's hands and waved her on through the doorway. When she didn't go, he pushed her hard enough to send her stumbling through and Jones caught her before she fell.

Thomas Gabriel stared at Ruby and Jones as they looked back at him, a little twitch jumping in his jaw.

'We're your friends, Thomas Gabriel,' said Ruby. 'It's the amulet that's making you do this.'

Thomas Gabriel grunted and shook his head. 'I always knew I'd be a great Badlander and now I will be. It's the *wyrd* that's going to make it happen. And now I'll let fate decide what happens to you too.'

Before he could slam the door shut, Ruby grabbed hold of it. 'Please, Thomas Gabriel, if you lock us in here, there's no way out.' Her voice was quiet and desperate. Her eyes were scared. Something quivered in her throat.

But not one bit of Thomas Gabriel cared about her. He tutted and shook his head. 'Girls and magic don't mix,' he said, before slamming the door shut.

When he took out the key and put it in his pocket, the door vanished into the background of the picture.

The two Trolls peered out at him, sniffing the air. When they wrinkled their noses and looked at each other, they shook their heads and started to clamber out of the picture towards him.

'*Forbærne!*' White sparks rippled across Thomas Gabriel's fingertips and he hurled them at the picture in the form of a fireball, causing a huge flame to sprout in the middle. It licked quickly across the canvas, consuming the picture before the Trolls had time to step out into the study and they were sucked back into the fire and burnt to a cinder along with the picture. The frame split into pieces with a great **CRACK!** before it, too, was consumed by the fire and turned to ash.

In a matter of moments, all that was left was a charred mark on the wall where the picture had been hanging.

'Goodbye!' shouted Thomas Gabriel.

After the door was shut, it vanished, leaving just a blank wall made of large sandy-coloured stones. The others had already started walking down the corridor towards the chamber where Drewman was on his pedestal, but Ruby had waited, hoping the door might reappear. The candles in their brackets on the walls flickered like the hope in her chest that, deep down, Thomas Gabriel cared and would have a change of heart. But, when she heard a loud noise from the other side, she wondered what had happened and then guessed as she heard Thomas Gabriel shout, 'Goodbye!'

She turned and walked on down the corridor after the others.

Drewman's head started chattering away, asking what was happening, when everyone appeared in the chamber, but nobody seemed to be interested in answering. Givens and Wilfried stood in one corner while Ruby and Jones stood in another. They watched each other in silence until Givens cleared this throat.

'This chamber is magically secure as Thomas Gabriel guessed. A powerful hex keeps that thing ...' he waved a hand at the head on the pedestal, '... locked in here. There is no way in or out of this chamber except through that picture. I suggest we resign ourselves to what the *wyrd* has decided for us. To die slowly in front of that,' and he glanced at Drewman again.

He looked at Ruby, studied her and smiled. 'At least perhaps the Order has been saved from the female of the species.' He began to chuckle to himself and let rip into a great guttering laugh that made the candles swoon. 'What a load of tripe,' he said. 'What rubbish! Girls are not worthy of being Badlanders.'

He ranted on, starting to curse and shout at the top of his voice, and Ruby knew that he was not angry at her, but at what had happened. But, even so, the man's anger scared her and she tried to blot it out, touching the gun in her waistband to remind her it was there, just in case.

As she looked about the chamber, trying to find something to focus on other than Givens, she spotted something standing in one of the dark corners. It was difficult to see it clearly, with the candlelight barely reaching it, and she took a few steps forward, unable to believe what she had found.

'Why is there a full-length mirror in here?' she asked, turning to face Givens. The man stopped his shouting and scowled at her, his chest heaving.

Before he could say anything, Drewman piped up from his pedestal.

'It's to torture me. I told you before: sometimes they bring a mirror and force me to look at myself for weeks on end to try and break me and find out where the Black Amulet is.'

'No need for that any more, is there?' muttered Givens, giving a long, hard stare at Jones and Ruby.

Drewman made a strange yelping sound as he laughed. 'You found it then! You found the amulet! Where is it? Where did you hide it?'

But Ruby ignored the head on the pedestal. She was already standing in front of the full-length mirror. It was difficult to see too much in the dark corner so she tried dragging the object out into the middle of the chamber. It was heavy and hard to lift.

'Jones!' Ruby looked back at the boy for help and he was already there beside her. They lifted the mirror into the centre of the chamber where the candlelight was strongest.

For the first time in what seemed like ages, Ruby smiled.

'What?' asked Givens. Ruby tapped the mirror. She touched the wood surround. It was made of oak as far as she could tell. She felt the urge to look deeper into the glass, at whatever she wanted. Her gift for scrying was alive and wanting to be used.

Givens tutted. 'You see, Wilfried. We have before us a girl and all she's interested in doing is admiring herself, in seeing how she looks. If she were a great Badlander then she'd use her exceptional gift for scrying to get out of this damned place and save us all.'

Ruby waited for Givens's words to stop echoing round the chamber and then she turned to look at him.

'That, Mr Givens, is exactly what I'm going to do. Unless you want to be the hero instead and show Wilfried here how it's done and save us all?'

Givens's mouth dropped open so wide Ruby could have stuffed her fist inside it.

'No? Okay then, so why don't you tell me what sort of a plan you had in mind?'

## TWENTY-SIX

R
uby waited for Givens to say something. But he seemed to be in a state of shock.

'Mr Givens, I'll ask you again. If I were to go through this mirror, how would I save you, Wilfried and Jones, because I'm guessing none of you are anywhere near good enough at scrying, so it's going to have to be me. A girl.' She heard Jones cough a few words under his breath and she wondered if perhaps she was enjoying all this too much. She folded her arms. Waited for Givens to speak.

'Why don't you show him what you can do, Ruby?' suggested Jones quietly. 'It might help.'

Ruby cleared her throat and stood in front of the mirror. There was a tin of polish in her pocket and she rubbed some of the soft white contents into the glass. Then she imagined Givens's study and watched it appear in the mirror. Drewman gasped. So did Wilfried.

Everyone in the chamber could see the ashen remains of the picture. They were smouldering below the black mark on the wall. Ruby pushed a hand through the glass and it disappeared.

288

Givens cursed, but Drewman chuckled. 'The Order's going to be so much better with girls in it one day, Givens, mark my words.'

When Ruby brought her hand back out, she waggled the fingers to show they were all right and then looked at Givens.

'So. What do you want me to do? How can I save you? If you want to be saved by a girl, that is?'

Givens spoke quietly. 'There is another way in and out of the chamber. A back door. In case the picture ever got damaged and I couldn't enter.'

'Where is it?'

'In the attic. There's a window at the far end. Run at it and you'll open a door that will lead to this chamber.'

'Right, so I run at the window. And I'll end up in here.'

Givens nodded. 'It'll open a door that we can all use to get out.'

'Sounds simple enough,' said Ruby.

She was about to step through the mirror when Jones grabbed her. 'What about Thomas Gabriel?'

Ruby looked in the mirror and scanned the study. But there was no sign of him. 'Either he's gone or he's making himself a congratulatory cup of tea. I'm presuming the former.' She took a large stride through the mirror and her leg disappeared. 'Won't be long.'

She gave Givens a big smile before she vanished.

The study smelt of burnt picture. Ruby sneezed and stood listening, hoping that Thomas Gabriel had indeed gone. It seemed that way after waiting a little while, but she tiptoed to the door anyway before looking out into the hallway. Not a sound except for the ticking of a clock. She pulled out the gun from her waistband and started walking and whispering, explaining what had happened since it had been tucked away.

'That Thomas Gabriel's gone too far,' it whispered back. 'Too far! You should have let me do the talking.'

'I'm not sure that would have worked,' said Ruby. 'He wasn't exactly in the mood for listening. The amulet's in control of him.'

'He would have listened to my particular kind of talking,' said the gun. 'One clean shot and . . .'

Ruby knew what it was getting at, but she said nothing else as she stood in the hallway and listened. Satisfied there was no sign of Thomas Gabriel, she walked quickly up the two flights of stairs to the top of the house to find the attic. Her thinking spiralled round too. As she went, she seemed to pump anger into herself about what Thomas Gabriel had done. Not only had he taken away the chance for her and Jones to finally sort out their Commencement, but he'd tricked her on that final eyot.

She'd been scared of him less than an hour ago, but, by the time she reached the top floor of the house, she was feeling very different.

'Okay, I'm angry now,' she said to the gun as she caught her breath. 'But angry in a calculating, let's-sort-this-out kind of a way.'

'*Riii-ght*,' said the gun. 'I'm not sure what that means, but isn't the attic maybe up there?' it asked as Ruby passed a small flight of narrow stairs and veered into a large bedroom.

'Probably,' said Ruby. She walked round the bedroom and tutted when she couldn't find what she was looking for and went into the next room. Her eyes lit up when she saw a full-length mirror screwed to the back of the door.

'Er, Ruby. What precisely is going on in that head of yours?'

Ruby touched the mirror and liked the feel of it. 'If Thomas Gabriel thinks I'm stuck in that chamber with the others, I've got an advantage.'

'Which is?'

'The element of surprise. He won't be expecting me to turn up wherever he is.'

'No, he wouldn't expect you to be so stupid. He's wearing the Black Amulet and you can't do magic.'

'I don't mean to take him on. But what if I can steal the golden boxes me and Jones need? If I can get them, Drewman can still sort out our Commencement and everything we've done will still matter. Givens doesn't think much of girls being Badlanders, but if I can do magic perhaps he'll change his mind. I've shown him a thing or two already. We need to get those boxes back.'

The gun sighed. It looked at itself in the mirror. 'You know what, Ruby?'

'What?'

'Will whatever I say make any difference?'

Ruby thought about that and shook her head.

'I didn't think so,' said the gun.

Ruby used the mirror to scry on Thomas Gabriel and find out where he was. It only took a matter of seconds. She saw that he was packing a bag in his bedroom, a limitless one, she presumed, judging by the amount of things he was putting in it.

'What about the boxes?' asked the gun.

Ruby searched the house, trying to find the string bag. When she saw it hanging off the back of the chair in the kitchen, she punched the air. 'Oh, this is going to be easy,' she said and tucked the gun into her waistband.

She asked the mirror to focus closer on the bag and, carefully, she reached through to take it off the back of the chair. It was heavier than she remembered, but she managed to unhook it. Yet, in her eagerness to have it, she pulled it towards her so quickly that one of the string holes caught on a protruding nail. The chair screeched across the floor and toppled over and gave her such a shock that she dropped the bag and it fell to the floor. Breathing hard, she heard a thunder of feet down the stairs and she knew she had to reach in now or never get the boxes. Plunging a hand back through, she grabbed the bag.

And then she felt a tug as Thomas Gabriel took hold of the other end.

He yanked so hard, and Ruby held on so tightly, her fingers

wrapped in the string of the bag, that she was pulled head first through the mirror.

Thomas Gabriel stumbled back as Ruby slipped through the glass like an eel and they both landed on the floor.

'How did you get out?' he screamed as he struggled to stand up, his lip bleeding where it had been struck by Ruby's elbow. 'How are you out of that chamber?'

Ruby didn't answer. She was too busy focusing on getting up first which she managed to do. She didn't look back at Thomas Gabriel and scampered through the doorway as a burst of white sparks shattered the door frame. She ran up the stairs and into a room and shut the door.

Ruby looked around and realized she was in a spare bedroom. There was a large rectangular mirror on the wall and it was high. But it was one way out. And then she thought about the golden boxes and how this was her only chance to try and get them.

She dragged a chair across to the mirror and then left it there, instead of leaving, and climbed into the large pine wardrobe in the corner, taking out the key. After shutting the door, she hid in the musty-smelling dark and drew out the gun in a shaking hand.

'What the hell are you doing?' it asked. 'Where are we? Why's it so dark?' and Ruby hissed at it to be quiet.

'I've got a plan,' she said.

'Oh, you mean another bad one, judging by it,' said the gun.

Ruby heard the bedroom door slam open. Thomas Gabriel

was breathing hard. She could hear the anger in him. He walked across the room and stopped.

Ruby imagined he must be looking at the mirror and the chair, and she hoped he was going to fall for the idea she'd set up for him. But he started walking again, the footsteps coming closer. She braced herself against the inside of the wardrobe door, to keep it shut. She felt the cold surface of a mirror on the inside of the door. But she didn't move. She didn't dare make a noise. Thomas Gabriel tried the wardrobe door and Ruby held it tight, making it seem as though it was locked. When he gave up trying to open it, and Ruby breathed a very quiet sigh of relief.

She listened as Thomas Gabriel stood for some time in the room. She could hear him breathing hard and shuffling his feet, tapping a knuckle on the mirror, and thinking everything through. She flinched when she heard the mirror on the wall break with a great booming noise and pieces fell to the floor in a great crash.

Thomas Gabriel slammed the bedroom door hard as he left and only then did Ruby relax, realizing he'd fallen for what she had intended.

She stayed in the dark of the wardrobe, not daring to move, conjuring up Thomas Gabriel in the mirror on the back of the door, and watching him. And what she saw next she did not like.

The boy was in the kitchen with all three golden boxes lined up in a row on the counter. One after the other, he opened the lids and tipped out the black-looking ash in them down the sink, flushing it down the plughole with the taps on full blast. And then he tossed the boxes onto the floor and left.

Ruby thought she heard her heart burst with a **POP!**

'Ruby, it's over. Drewman's gone. There's nothing left of him except for that head of his now. Thomas Gabriel has flushed the rest down the sink.'

Ruby thought about that in the dark and then she spoke again.

'Now.'

'What?'

'Now, you said the word "now". You said there's nothing left of Drewman except for that head of his now.'

'Yes, that's what I just said,' groaned the gun. 'So give it up and save yourself. We need to leave.'

'But Drewman's still all there in the past.'

'What? What are you talking about?'

Ruby took out the little tin of scrying polish in her pocket and rubbed a white nub of it onto the mirror. She stared at the glass and thought about where she wanted to go. The interior of the VW camper van appeared. She could hear distant voices outside.

Carefully, she crept through a slightly sticky patch of time, her old army camouflage jacket snagging a little, before crawling through into the van. She plucked out a little piece of her exit point back.

It was early morning. Ruby could hear Jones, Thomas Gabriel and herself, standing outside, talking about going to see Givens now they had all three golden boxes and forcing him to open the hidden door to see Drewman. Through the window, she could make out a couple of buildings in the distance and knew they were parked on the outskirts of Reading.

The three golden boxes were sitting on the table in the van next to Thomas Gabriel's ticking invitation.

'Ruby,' whispered the gun in her hand. 'You can't change anything in the past. If you do, it might change the future. If that happens then the time we've come from could be very different. We might not even *be* here, because you might not have gone back in time in the first place. Oh,' it moaned, 'this is not good for my brain.'

Ruby was surprised to hear that the gun thought it had a brain. But she wasn't too interested in whether it did or not. She had a plan for the problem it had mentioned. First she put the gun into her waistband. Then, as she listened to the voices outside, she found an empty jar in one of the cupboards as quickly as she could and carefully poured the contents of all three golden boxes into it and screwed on the lid and stuck it in her pocket. Then she poured some Slap Dust into each box and put them back on the table.

It didn't take long and she didn't hang around, but, when she heard footsteps outside and the door to the van starting to open, she held up the piece of her exit point and felt it tug her towards the way back to her own time.

Ruby dived through as the door to the van opened.

*

She landed in the wardrobe, slamming into the back of it with a loud **BANG!** that she worried Thomas Gabriel would have heard, wherever he was in the house. The mirror in the wardrobe had shattered and she had nothing to scry with.

She opened the doors and clambered out, taking the gun out of her waistband.

'What's happened?' it asked. 'Were you seen?'

'No, I don't think so.'

'How do you know?'

'The future would be different. We're back in Thomas Gabriel's house and nothing's changed.'

'So Thomas Gabriel's still here?'

'I guess so.'

She heard footsteps hammering up the stairs.

'We need to leave.'

'Looks like it'll have to be the old-fashioned way,' said Ruby, looking at the broken glass of the mirror that had been on the wall.

'You mean Slap Dust?'

'No, we're out of that.'

'So you mean the front door?'

'Yes!'

'And we're just going to walk out of it, are we?'

Thomas Gabriel thundered down the landing.

'Ruby!'

'If I'm not good enough to be a Badlander then *you* think of something,' said Ruby and hurled the gun onto the floor in frustration. It spluttered something she didn't hear because she was almost in tears as the door burst open and Thomas Gabriel ran in, his face dark with rage and his hand raised, white sparks flickering round the ends of his fingers.

Ruby saw his face turn from delight to pain in an instant as his arms went flailing and he slipped, as though he was on ice, and flew through the air and collapsed in a heap.

The gun squirted out from under his foot at the same time and thudded into Ruby's shin, making her curse.

But there was no time to rub her leg as she watched Thomas Gabriel scrabbling round in the glass, trying to stand up, and she picked up the chair that had been in front of the mirror and hit him hard on the head. He fell like his legs had been cut away. Ruby stood with the chair raised, ready to hit him again. But this time he wasn't moving. It looked like a large egg had been laid on his forehead as the bump swelled up.

She put the chair down and picked up the gun. 'Well, that worked out rather well,' she said with admiration in her voice.

A hiss made her look round. The two serpent heads of the Black Amulet were wiggling and moving and they clamped their mouths down on Thomas Gabriel's arm. Black shapes moved over his skin. He started to twitch.

'Time to go, I think,' said the gun.

'In a moment.'

Ruby reached into his coat pocket and rummaged around, then drew out the little silver pillbox and opened it, to check it contained the *wælmist*.

'Ruby, I won't say this again—'

'All right! We're leaving,' said the girl. 'I just need to find a mirror.'

She ran downstairs and saw a big square one on the wall in the hallway. She jumped through it like a dolphin through a hoop.

She landed on the floor of the landing in Givens's house, rolling over in a single somersault and lay on her back for a moment, looking up at the ceiling. And then she smiled.

She stood up and ran upstairs to the attic and looked at the window at the far end. She weighed up the blue sky through the window.

Ruby gritted her teeth and ran as fast as she could down the attic towards the window and dived through, trying not to scream as she fell, the gun yelling out loud.

Ruby appeared through a door in the wall of the chamber, in front of a very surprised Givens, and grinned as she bent over to catch her breath. The silver pillbox was clutched tight in her fist.

'Here you go,' she said and handed it to Givens. The man stared at the pillbox lying in his hand and swallowed hard as he opened it and saw the *wælmist* swirling inside the glass vial. And then he looked up at her and nodded.

'Thank you,' he said in a quiet voice.

'You're welcome.'

When Givens kept staring, Ruby wondered if she

should say something else. But Drewman piped up and hollered at them.

'She's as good as any boy, Givens, you've got to admit that.'

Givens cleared his throat and nodded.

'Yes,' he agreed. 'As good as any apprentice I've ever seen.' He turned round and ushered Wilfried towards him as he headed for the door.

Ruby grinned and felt herself turn red at the edges. And then Jones was there, grabbing her hand.

'What about the boxes?' he asked.

Ruby reached into her pocket and drew out the glass jar full of the black ash from the golden boxes.

'All in here,' she said.

At first a look of relief washed over Jones's face and then he frowned and opened his mouth, ready to ask a question.

'I'll tell you later,' said Ruby before the boy could say anything.

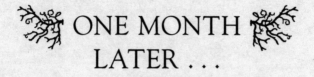

ONE MONTH
LATER . . .

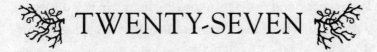

## TWENTY-SEVEN

Ruby crept down a dark street. It was late. A cat skittered away from her, its tail flicking before it jumped onto a fence and then disappeared as it leapt into the dark. Ruby stopped and tried to breathe again.

'Keep focused, girl,' said the gun.

'I will if you let me,' said Ruby. She put the gun into her waistband and carried on walking. She couldn't hear the Vampire, but she knew it was following her. She'd seen a dark shape behind her when she looked both ways to cross the road. The little hairs on her neck prickled as she strained to hear anything. But the Vampire was so quiet it gave nothing away. Ruby kept on going, telling herself that this was all happening because she'd meant it to happen. This was all part of her plan.

She turned and crossed over another road and then turned right, down an alley she'd picked out earlier because she knew it led to a dead end.

She walked slowly, her hands plugged in her pockets. Her feet rang on the cobbles.

Before she reached the end of the alley, she heard a noise. It was a little laugh.

'I think you've run out of places to go,' said a voice. Ruby looked back and saw a thin-looking man. He was dressed in a dark suit. There was a hat on his head with a deep groove down its middle. She didn't know what sort it was because she didn't really know much about hats except for what a beret was because she'd been made to wear the saucer-shaped thing once by a couple who'd tried to foster her. The Browns.

'Nice hat,' she said. The Vampire stopped and observed her, as though weighing up who exactly this person was. Clearly, it wasn't used to such confidence.

'I am a girl,' said Ruby. 'But I'm one you don't want to mess with.'

She took her hands out of her pocket and spoke the words she'd been practising all day, learning them from *The Black Book of Magical Instruction*. She opened and closed one hand four times and silver sparks came out of her fingers to make the corners of a square.

'*Cnyte*,' said Ruby and the silver *fengnett* started to knit together, stretched out taut across the alley. It only took a few seconds to form and then the threads started playing delicate musical notes.

The Vampire had already tried to turn, but it didn't seem to be capable of moving very well. Its feet stayed rooted to the spot as it tried to move its arms to turn its body. As the *fengnett* played its song, the creature stopped struggling and just watched it, entranced by what was happening. The very light music coming off it was so soft and delicate, even Ruby felt a little woozy.

When it was time, the Vampire walked towards the net, as if in a trance, and lay against it and started to smoke and melt. And then it was gone.

Ruby plucked the single white fang from the net and looked at it in the light from the street lamp. 'It's a nice one,' she said to the gun as she started folding up the net, its song tailing off abruptly.

When Ruby returned home to the cottage, the thrill of having done magic was still raw and bright. Every time she cast a spell now, something inside her became a little stronger. Partly it was to do with the magic. It told her as much, whispering that the more she used it, the more powerful it would become, allowing her in turn to cast better spells. But there was also something of her that was growing stronger too. Now she was becoming the person she'd always wanted to be, ever since she'd heard of the Badlands. She was still not a proper Badlander, though. At least not yet.

She looked at the ticking invitation on her desk. On it were written the words:

The High Council formally invites
Ruby Jenkins
to its annual meeting on
30th April

She decided she should get some sleep before her big day tomorrow. Givens had advised her the test of her magical skills would be extremely challenging, to see if she really was worthy of being called a Badlander. But before she turned in, Ruby wanted to inspect the dreaming seeds she had planted in memory of Victor Brynn. They had sprouted delicate green shoots over the last few days and, as she watered them, she whispered how much she would love to speak to Victor Brynn one day in her dreams and tell him all she had acheived. She knew it would make him so proud.

She didn't sleep well, nervous about the big day ahead. But in the morning Ruby got up and took a bath and made an effort to look as smart as she could. She tried on different clothes but in the end she settled for what she was most comfortable wearing, jeans and her old army camouflage jacket, which bore the marks of various creatures she'd encountered in the Badlands.

When she was ready, Ruby tried to clear her mind of nerves before slapping her hands together, and feeling the Slap Dust fizz on her palms.

She arrived in a long hallway and walked down it to the double doors at the end as she had been told to do at the appointed time.

As she straightened her jacket, she took out the gun from her waistband.

'How do I look?'

'You're gonna knock 'em dead.'

Ruby nodded. 'Thanks. I couldn't have got this far without you, you know.' Ruby could have sworn the gun blushed and then it spoke in a rather wobbly, emotional voice.

'And not without Jones, either, of course.'

Ruby smiled and nodded before placing the gun into her waistband. She took a deep breath and closed her eyes for a few seconds, remembering how much she had prepared for this moment over the last few weeks.

When Ruby opened the double doors, she saw Givens sitting on a dais in the middle of a large room with other men seated either side of him. She thought she saw him give her a glimmer of a smile and then he cleared his throat.

'Ruby Jenkins, are you ready?'

'Yes,' she said.

'Then let it be known that this test of your magical ability has now begun,' announced Givens. One of the other men sitting beside him released a One Eye into the air and it fluttered towards her. As the tiny creature circled around her, she saw that it looked very similar to the one that Thomas Gabriel had owned and her mind wobbled a little as she wondered where the boy was. There had not been one sighting of him since she had last seen him. Even when she had looked in her scrying mirror she had not been able to locate him.

The One Eye gave a little squeak and nodded at her and then flew back to the hands of the man who had released it.

'Ready your magic,' said Givens.

Ruby nodded and conjured some strong white sparks at the ends of her fingers, ready to do whatever the men of the Badlander High Council required.

GLOSSARY

of

BADLANDER

TERMS

Æhteland (ANGLO-SAXON)

Translates as 'territory' or 'landed property'. The term refers to a district managed by a Badlander in a city, primarily London, which is split into a number of different territories. Only a Badlander who manages his *æhteland* is allowed to hunt on it and he is responsible for the safety of all ordinary people who live within its boundaries.

Asce (-an) ANGLO-SAXON)

Translates as 'something burnt', 'dust' or 'ash'.

Augustus Drewman

Augustus Drewman is considered by many to be the greatest Badlander to have ever lived because of his renowned skill with magic and the number of creatures he despatched in the Badlands during his lifetime, reckoned to be over five thousand. However, his legacy has been tarnished due to the fact the magic inside him turned bad, leading to madness and death.

Drewman was born over four hundred years ago, unable to speak, and grew up mute, tending the pigs of the village in which he lived. He became a Badlander at a young age after drinking the dirty bath water of the man who was to become his Master. Such was the young Drewman's connection with magic the bath water allowed him to Commence on the spot. He also experienced another effect – the magic gave him the gift of speech, meaning he could cast spells. His relationship with magic went on to make him very powerful yet ultimately it distorted his mind, sending him mad, and he died a broken man after living a long life, extended many decades through spells. All the biographies written about him have attributed his death to the natural process of the *wyrd* (see separate entry). However, there are some who still question to this day what really happened to Drewman, given his body was never found. The odd theory even exists that the High Council of Badlanders imprisoned him, keen to learn about his connection with magic and how he became so powerful, but this rumour has never been substantiated.

The Badlands The Badlands is a term used to describe any location where creatures might be lurking. It normally refers to places right on the edge of normal people's lives. However, it is a name that encompasses a wide variety of places, from a distant valley to a park in the heart of a city, or even to a house in the suburbs. Wherever a creature is found then that location is considered to be a part of the Badlands.

Badlander The given name for members of the Badlander Order, a secret society of monster hunters. The Badlander Order evolved in Great Britain during the 5th century after the arrival of Anglo-Saxons from continental Europe, who brought with them their own secrets and methods of fighting monsters. Ancient Britons adopted these techniques as they gradually embraced the culture and language of Anglo-Saxons. The teachings and organised living of early monks also helped to create early Badlander practice. Initially, Badlanders were trained in the monasteries until the Order began to emerge with its own established set of rules in approximately the second half of the 7th century. The influence of monasteries may explain why the Badlander Order is exclusively male.

The Badlander Bestiary – Pocket Book Version A small, portable reference guide to all the various monsters found in the Badlands. The pages are blank until the user demands to know information about a specific creature, at which point all the relevant information will be revealed. Because of this function it is usually used as a field guide on hunts and is particularly valuable for apprentices who are learning about creatures.

'Be Prepared' An old motto used by Badlanders to ensure that they are always ready for whatever they may encounter in the Badlands. This phrase has been adopted into the larger society of ordinary people too (for example, the Scout Movement).

Bescéawere (-eas for plural) (ANGLO-SAXON) Translates as 'observer'.

The Black Book of Magical Instruction

Presented to every apprentice during the act of Commencement, *The Black Book of Magical Instruction* can only be read by those who have Commenced and been given the gift of magic. This ensures the secrets of spell-casting are reserved only for those deemed special enough to Commence. The book is vital as a teaching aid for young Badlanders, allowing them to learn how to use magic. It is interactive, leading apprentices through various lessons and answering their questions.

Charles Du Clement

(1770 – present) Born in Bordeaux in 1770, Charles Du Clement grew up as a member of the Badlander Order in France, although he was itinerant and travelled widely, researching a vast array of creatures across Europe. Eventually, he settled in England in 1820, preferring the English way of life to that of continental Europe. After being bitten and infected by a *Lich*, captured from a Bronze Age round barrow (burial site) in Dorset, Du Clement was imprisoned in the crypt of the chapel of St Crosse College, Oxford (see separate entry on St Crosse for more information) for the benefit of Badlander scholarship, because of his vast and detailed knowledge of creatures and monstrous beings. Despite being an important asset, Du Clement's imprisonment is kept a secret by high-ranking members of the Order because of his transformation into a *Lich*, a creature Badlanders are sworn to destroy.

As well as advising on creatures, Du Clement has the

final say on whether the thesis of the Badlander research fellow at St Crosse passes or fails.

Commencement

The act of advancement of an apprentice Badlander by which he is given the gift of magic. Commencement is entirely at the discretion of the apprentice's Master who will formalize the Commencement by handing over a silver key. This key is worn around a Master's neck for the duration of the apprenticeship and unlocks an oak chest that has the properties to set an apprentice's Commencement in motion.

The term Commencement was agreed upon by the Order in the early 17th century prior to which various terms had been used to describe the process and its different elements.

Cynte (ANGLO-SAXON)

Translates as 'knit', 'tie' or 'bind' and is the imperative form of the verb *cnyttan*.

Dark Magic – *áglæccræft*

(ANGLO-SAXON) A dangerous form of magic only really understood by those who use it. All Badlanders know that once they have Commenced, the magic inside them (see separate entry for Magic) needs to be controlled otherwise it may try to corrupt the minds of anyone using it and tempt them into using Dark Magic. Therefore, many Badlanders practise forms of meditation or wear various types of undershirt (see separate entry for *undersyrc*) to protect against this. However, magic can alter in other ways and force Badlanders into using Dark Magic: either through a bite from a creature (such as a Witch or Vampire) or if a Badlander uses a dangerous magical item of dubious provenance. Being bitten is by far the most common reason for magic changing inside a Badlander and usually results in transformation into a No-Thing, the term for a Badlander who practises Dark Magic and is required to drink blood in order to cast spells.

Badlanders who want to use powerful magical items can

drink bitter potions to try and guard against any ill effects.

Deschamps & Sons

Deschamps & Sons is an extremely large department store in London that sells everything a Badlander might need. It prides itself on providing the highest quality products, catering for a range of tastes. The store started as a small shop in the late 16th century. After being founded by Monsieur Deschamps, who had arrived from Paris, it grew into a much larger business over time. Almost all of the shop is concealed deep underground, beneath the city of London, with the entrance at street level, to what seems, at least to the ordinary person, to be a small tobacconists called Deschamps & Sons. There are various Deschamps & Sons stores all over the world catering for Badlanders in different countries.

Door Wurm A very useful creature employed to open locked doors, however big or small. Wurms are very easy to use and once inserted into any lock, they will change into the required key. Door Wurms were originally just ordinary garden earthworms charmed by Badlanders but over time they have been bred specifically for their current purpose.

Dreaming Seeds

Dreaming seeds cause much debate amongst Badlanders, given that some believe they allow communication with the dead in dreams, whilst others categorically deny such a thing is possible. Much discussion about the seeds arises because they only seem to work for some Badlanders and no one is entirely sure why. One reason often given is that a Badlander must wholeheartedly believe the seeds can work before planting them in the ground if they want to use them; other theories cite the need for particular growing conditions and the quality of the seeds used. Those for whom the seeds work (one drinks a tea infused with the flowers of the plant that grows from the seeds) can converse with a deceased person of their choice. This conversation can only happen when a person is dreaming and therefore it cannot be experienced by anyone else, making it a very private conversation. (For more information see *Into the Beyond* by D. P. Thompson.)

Éghþyrl (ANGLO-SAXON)

Translates as 'eye hole'.

Eyot (pronounced 'eight') A small island, usually referring to one located on a river.

Fæcce (pronounced 'fetch') (ANGLO-SAXON) Derived from the Anglo-Saxon word *fæccan* meaning 'to fetch'. A *fæcce* is very similar to a doppelganger, namely the magical 'double' of a person, and can be created either with a spell (the most effective method) or by using a combination of various powders added to water, together with some physical evidence of the person being duplicated. On the rare occasions a Badlander steals a child from a family to be his apprentice he will create a *fæcce* to replace it. Usually, a *fæcce* will not live long after its creation, but in some instances, they have been recorded as living for up to three or four years. However, they do become progressively more sickly and unwell over the time they are alive.

Fengnett (ANGLO-SAXON)

Translates as 'catching net'. A *fengnett* is a special net created with magic for the specific purpose of catching a Vampire. It is constructed from silver threads as fine as gossamer. When the spell is cast properly the net will stitch itself together in mid-air and be stretched out, ready for use. It emits a delicate and beautiful music that lures any Vampire within range towards it. The creature will not be able to resist the music and will lie against the net, which, being made from silver, is fatal to a Vampire. The net will leave to the Badlander who made it a single fang, as evidence of what they have achieved, given that killing a Vampire is a dangerous task.

Forbærne (ANGLO-SAXON) Translates as 'burn!' and is the imperative form of the verb *forbærnan* meaning 'to burn'.

Gristbatian (ANGLO-SAXON) Translates as 'gnash the teeth'.

Glassyscopes A pair of magical glasses that can be used to spy on a person wherever they are. Glassyscopes are considered to be a fairly limited item by most Badlanders because, once a particular individual has been observed through the lenses, the wearer of the glasses cannot adjust them to watch anyone else.

High Council of Badlanders A select group of high-ranking Badlanders. The High Council meet annually to discuss any important business relevant to the Order and are responsible for maintaining the *Ordnung* (see separate entry), and ruling on any changes to it. Members of the High Council are voted in for life.

Hurdy Gurdy A fast-acting sedative, in the form of a vapour, that will put someone to sleep for a number of hours if they inhale it, unless they have taken the antidote beforehand. It is created from a variety of herbs and plants. Although it cannot be seen or smelt it can make the air glisten in patches once released. Hurdy Gurdy can be given to a person in small quantities to make them drowsy and force them to lower their guard. Aside from the obvious symptoms of drowsiness and sedation, it also causes red dots to appear in a person's pupils.

Imagining Book A rare item that allows the person using it to create a real version of whatever they are imagining and drawing on a page. Usually these books are the size of a notebook, meaning that only small items can be drawn and made real. A page can only be used once so the owner of an Imagining Book should use it sparingly in order to make it last.

Jump ´em Juice A tart-tasting liquid that turns any person who drinks it invisible immediately for a certain period of time, depending on its strength. Not only will it affect the individual but anything they are holding or touching too.

Learning Book A notebook commonly kept by apprentice Badlanders. It is a simple way of way keeping notes about the things they learn that are useful and important to know.

Léasspellung (-e) (ANGLO-SAXON) Translates as 'empty talk'.

Ley Line Lines of magical energy that run deep through the land, they hold a deep significance for Badlanders (See Magic).

Limitless Pockets Any coat, jacket or pair of trousers a Badlander wears will usually be charmed to have limitless pockets, meaning that many objects can be carried around. To retrieve what a Badlander wants from a pocket all they need to do is insert their hand and imagine what they require. Bags can be charmed to be limitless too.

Magic The most important tool in a Badlander's armoury for tackling monsters, magic is fundamental to surviving the Badlands. It is also vitally important because it allows for the creation of charms that make everyday life easier for Badlanders, given the lifestyle restrictions placed on them by the *Ordnung* (see separate entry), allowing them to co-exist in the modern world alongside ordinary people. The gift of magic is granted at Commencement and becomes 'fused' with the apprentice receiving it.

Magic is a natural element that Badlanders have managed to control through ancient means, drawing it from the heart of the land and forcing it to work for them. Therefore, magic is always looking for a way to release itself from being controlled by the Badlander Order. This means magic can be fickle and unpredictable, attempting to lead Badlanders astray if they are not disciplined in how they use it. As a result, Badlanders are taught to treat magic with great respect at all times.

Mearcung (-e, -a for plural) (ANGLO-SAXON) Translates as 'marking', 'branding' or 'characteristic'. The formal name given to the mark that a Badlander makes after killing and disposing of a creature to make it clear to other Badlanders what has happened in a particular location. It is also a way for Badlanders to show others how successful they have been in the Badlands and promote their legacy.

Memory Leech Memory leeches are used to remove the memories of people, when required, by literally sucking them out of the brain. To do this they must be inserted into the head of the subject, usually through the ear canal. They are very clean and efficient removers of memories. Leeches work according to the amount of time they are instructed to remove from a person's memory so they are most commonly used to remove only very recent memories. Various rare sub species of leeches can work to remove older memories if they are given precise instructions about the date and time of the exact memories to be eliminated. After deleting memories, leeches will excrete a hallucinogenic substance that causes a false memory to be created, accounting for the missing time in a person's memory.

Moon Globe Moon Globes are very rare, with only a handful thought to be in existence. How they came to exist is mired in mystery. They are spherical as the name suggests and about the size of a small apple. The glow that a Moon Globe emits is akin to the pearlescent light of the moon, hence the name. Quite what makes them glow is not known given that the scarcity of the objects makes study almost impossible. However, various Badlanders have postulated theories about them. The most detailed studies on Moon Globes were carried out in the early 20th century by Piers van Anhelm who came to the conclusion that they are fashioned from fragments of meteors that have landed on earth. Very few Badlanders have ever used a Moon Globe and their owners tend to be very secretive about them because of their great value. The reason they are so valued is they can often be the only way to open certain concealed doors or entrances, meaning that something extremely valuable can be locked away securely.

Nædl (-e) (ANGLO-SAXON) Translates as 'needle'.

One Eye A One Eye is one of the very few creatures the *Ordnung* allows Badlanders to use to help them on their hunts, having the skill for sensing magical as well as unnatural and dangerous things. They are akin to a sprite or fairy (*ælf* or *puca* in Anglo-Saxon), having wings and a diminutive stature. However, there are two key characteristics that differentiate a One Eye from these types of creatures: the big single eye in the centre of the forehead and a set of large, sharp teeth, which only come to prominence when bared. The colour of the eye is used to define the various types of One Eye that exist. In the wild the creatures are aggressive and have to be tamed by Badlanders using a four-leaf clover. Over time, One Eyes can be trained to become obedient and willing servants to their owners.

Ordnung (German) A German word, meaning 'order', 'discipline', 'rule' or 'system', *Ordnung* is used by Badlanders to describe the strict code of rules their Order must follow. It was a term adopted by Badlanders in the early 15th century when new rules for the Order were established.

Rosemary and Salt

A common mixture of two substances that Badlanders use as an all-purpose weapon against many creatures. It can cause burns on a variety of monsters. If sprinkled on the ground around the user it can also form a protective ring that repels many different creatures.

St Crosse College, Oxford

St Crosse College, founded in 1450, is one of the colleges that make up the University of Oxford, one of the oldest universities in the world. The college admits undergraduate and graduate students. It has groomed four prime ministers as well as numerous lords, clergymen and scholars. What is not written in the guidebooks of the college (available for four pounds and fifty pence from the black wire shelves inside the main gate) is the legacy of its Badlander scholarship.

Ever since the foundation of the college a Badlander research fellowship has always existed. The Badlander holding the position of 'resident research fellow' is entrusted with the primary aim of researching rare creatures, studying the combat techniques, weapons and magic that might be most effective against them.

No questions are ever asked about the fellowship on account of a generous and anonymously run trust that funds the position. The trust also donates generously to the college, and even the university, whenever there is a need. The research fellow is resident for three years at the college and is required to be discreet at all times about Badlander affairs given that he is living amongst ordinary people. He is allowed to participate fully in normal life as required, however most keep themselves to themselves.

The position of research fellow, despite being highly regarded is considered by some to be a 'poisoned chalice' (a direct quote from *Getting Cross with St Crosse* by A.J. Heap) because adaptation back to life as a Badlander after living amongst ordinary people can prove difficult and there is a history of mental health issues associated with fellows in later life. The Badlander research fellow also has the difficult duty of looking after Charles Du Clement, a *Lich* (See Charles Du Clement).

Scrying Scrying is the act of observing a person or location. It is an ancient skill that is largely vocational, meaning those Badlanders with a natural talent for scrying are drawn to trying it, usually through feeling an urge to hold a scrying object that is nearby. However, scrying still requires a great deal of practice and years of learning to perfect it. A person may only scry on a person they have met before or on a place they have visited previously.

Undersyrc (Anglo-Saxon) Translates as 'undershirt'. An item of clothing a bit like a 'hair shirt' worn by some Badlanders to remind them of the perils of magic.

Seolfor (Anglo-Saxon) Translates as 'silver'.

Slap Dust Slap Dust is a way of travelling from one place to another instantaneously. After a small amount of dust has been placed in the palm of one hand, all the user has to do is announce where they want to go, then slap their hands together, and they will travel to their desired location. The dust originated from a combination of charms that were mixed together by early Badlanders in the late 9th century and has been used ever since. There are many different grades and strengths of Slap Dust available to purchase.

Although the dust offers a lightning-fast and efficient mode of transport it does have its problems. Common issues are judging the right amount of dust required for a particular journey; materializing in too confined a space; lack of secrecy, since the user must announce where they are going (although some rarer forms of dust only require thought) and being seen by ordinary people by accident. There is also some evidence to suggest that using the dust has an unhealthy effect on the body if used too often (A good source of information on this subject is *Why Dust Might be Bad for You* by J. Heaslip).

Þurhfarennes (pronounced th-urck-farennes) (-se) (Anglo-Saxon) Translates as 'inner chamber'.

Tonic Different types of tonic are available for Badlanders to drink, enabling them to suppress any feelings of extreme tiredness. Given that a lot of work in the Badlands is done at night, tonics can be extremely useful although overdependence on them is not considered to be very healthy.

Vamp Venom A poisonous toxin used to eliminate Vampires. To be successful the venom must be delivered directly to a creature's heart. It is not considered to be a particularly effective method of killing a Vampire because of how close a Badlander must get to use it (See separate entry for *fengnett*).

Wælmist (Anglo-Saxon) Translates as 'death mist'. *Wælmist* is a way of fatally cursing another person and to do so to another Badlander is considered a very 'low' act by the Order. To use *Wælmist* a Badlander must whisper to it the name of the person they want cursed and, then, once released from its container it will, without fail, cause death to that particular individual.

Wibba (-n plural) (ANGLO-SAXON)
Translates as 'beetle'. If bitten
by a creature with a toxic bite
some Badlanders will use a
handful of *wibban* to neutralize
the poison. The small beetles
will burrow down into the
wound and clean it before
secreting a fluid that enables fast
healing. As the wound heals,
the *wibban* will crawl out and
hide in a safe, dark space where
they will build cocoons and
eventually hatch out of these as
small brown moths.

Wyrd (pronounced like the common
English word 'weird') (ANGLO-SAXON)
Wyrd is the name in Anglo-
Saxon given to the concept of
fate or personal destiny, which
cannot be resisted. It is a noun
formed from the verb *weorþan*
(pronounced we-or-than) which
means 'to come to pass', 'to
become', or 'to happen'.

ACKNOWLEDGMENTS

Thank you to everyone who has prodded, cajoled and edited this book into existence. And special thanks to those who made the tea and coffee.

You all know who you are ...